Smudged
Mascara

Michael G. Casey

ISBN 978-1-9160264-0-7

Second edition, 2019

Published by Azimuth Publishing

Dublin, Ireland

Layout, cover design by iCulture

Please visit michaelgcasey.com

ABOUT THIS BOOK

This is a light-hearted story about two young men and their girlfriends in the rowdy, lived-in Dublin of Brendan Behan, Patrick Kavanagh and Flann O'Brien. They pit their wits against all comers in a last fling before adulthood.

Murf is a 'chronic student' who lives dangerously, savouring the roar of the crowd. He is fortunate to meet Gobnait, a kindred spirit, who could become a steadying influence. She sees through his posturing to the deeper reasons that make him a risk junkie.

Rolo is a nervous, gentlemanly sort, often scared by Murf's escapades. Will he find his feet when he meets the stunning Maura?

While the gals have steady jobs, the lads eke out a living by smuggling condoms from Northern Ireland into the South. This 'modest trade' lands them in serious trouble with their 'clients', the British Army, and eventually the IRA and the police. They lurch from one crisis to another and are repeatedly bailed out by Gobnait and Maura – and by a club of gentle transvestites.

Will their splendid women help them grow up or will the lure of shenanigans prove too strong?

"This is a wonderful immersion into the Dublin of the early seventies, a city making do on an island held together by string, bandages and impious prayer. The lead protagonists are immediately credible, their mental and emotional contortions on full display. The plot is like a colourful, writhing snake that may intend no harm."

— Peter FitzGerald

BOOKS PREVIOUSLY PUBLISHED
BY MICHAEL G. CASEY

Come Home, Robbie, a novel, published by The
O'Brien Press, 1990
> "...page-turning urgency ... spine-tingling
> compulsion ... the sheer quality of the writing
> lends the story some of the stature of heroic
> tragedy."
> —The Education Times

Treadmill, an award-winning Chapbook of short
stories, published by Tipperary Arts Centre and
Start Magazine, 2008
> "...Casey brings to life vivid characters who
> captivate, amuse and engage ... (He) has a wry
> observation and quick wit."
> —Mike McCormack

*Ireland's Malaise: The Troubled Personality of the
Irish Economy*, published by The Liffey Press, 2010
> "...(Casey) shows the same Confucian wisdom as
> his hero, T.K. Whitaker in his brilliant new book."
> —Eoghan Harris, The Sunday Independent

The Visit, a novel, published by The Anaphora
Press, 2011
> "...a small Irish town deals with a major event ...
> an interesting addition to the genre ... clear-eyed
> ... vivid description..."

—Denis Fahey, Historian

"...a lovely clear prose style ... some great characters and beautifully crafted vignettes."

—Stella Kane, Quartet Books Ltd

Broken Circle, a collection of poetry, due to be published by Salmon Press in Spring 2019

"...very powerful, intelligent poems made their presence known immediately ... (Casey) uses casuistry and persuasiveness to rival Robert Browning's dramatic Monologues..."

—Derek Selen

Michael G. Casey's most recent novels, *Maura's Dance with Uncle Sam* and *The Killing of Ros Grenham*, from Azimuth Publishing, are available in Kindle and print versions through Amazon.

DEDICATION

To innocents everywhere.

"Well it's a clean bed and soft with it, and it's great luck and company I've won me in the end of time – two fine women fighting over the likes of me – till I'm thinking this night wasn't I a foolish fellow not to kill my father in the years gone by?"
—J.M. Synge, The Playboy of the Western World

"Rolo asked me to tell this story without trying to justify or mitigate the youthful idiocies."
—The Present Writer

PROLOGUE

THOUGH THE LITTLE boat rides the swell gamely, it is almost out of control and is beginning to ship water. Against the awesome thundering of the elements the inboard motor is no louder than the hum of a stick insect.

Land recedes. The colourful houses of Dún Laoghaire and the Martello towers have disappeared from view; so too the piers of the harbour and even the isochronic flash of the lighthouse. Cloud banks obliterate the stars. Darkness closes in with grim inevitability. They are lost, more lost than ever, in the immensity of space.

A short while ago a helicopter had searched for them, its powerful searchlight raking over the waves. Now that light, too, has gone. They are given up as lost. Despite Rolo's entreaties, Murf refused to send up a flare. That fixated lunatic will kill them both.

Lying in bilge water, his bad leg aching, Rolo makes one last desperate appeal, "Turn back for God's sake! Before it's too late … We will serve, give back the money…throw ourselves on the mercy of the Special Branch… The IRA will understand… Turn back…!" Rolo's words, lost on the wind, come swirling back to him, unheeded syllables of spindrift. It makes no difference anyway. Their drowned bodies will feed the fishes soon at the bottom of this nuclear ocean. It had to end like this. He should have predicted it. There were so many straws in the wind but, for some reason, he was unable to clutch any of them.

"Put this on … and have a swig of grog." Murf passes back a life-jacket and exposure-bottle of Jameson. Rolo ignores both crutches, his one and only act of disdain. He sobs into the bruised night, adding his measure of salt to the epidemic brine. Ah, Maura, lovely, undeserved Maura, we sailed once together under cloudless skies and laughed at fishermen and submarines. You are the one for me. Such sad certainty now when it is too late. Remember me…

When did it all begin to go so badly wrong? Not that stupid prank, surely. Or the modest trade in designer prophylactics? Who can tell? The incident at the border didn't help, nor stepping on toes of the IRA and intelligence spooks.

Independent events perhaps, yet somehow linked with the thread of happenstance in an impossible weave.

No way back now … unlikely to make landfall anywhere … Remember me… Rolo lived once, never made an impression on anything, but an existence must be worth something … Maura, love of my life, remember me…

" ... A sort of glass wherein beholders do generally discover everybody's face but their own."
—Jonathan Swift, The Battle of the Books

CHAPTER 1

SET TWO ROUND objects vibrating on strings. The period of oscillation does not depend on the mass of the pendulum. The arcs the balls describe are cycloid. The property of isochronism... Oh Lord, I can't concentrate on this stuff. And that brunette opposite uncrossing her legs with a quite audible whisper of thigh. While I chafe against the turned mahogany leg of this library table, and Rosenberg's 'Mechanics' lies fallow and impenetrable.

But soft, her lashes flutter up and teal-blue orbs stare past my shoulder into the middle distance as, like a swan drinking, she ingests the point just read. Eyes down again to text to lap up more from the well of knowledge and I am ignored. Again.

And now, Murf is on the town, probably in Harto's inner snug, holding a master-class in varletry, accepting the libations of a pink-faced audience as late-April sun filters through sanctified glass. While I labour in vain in the grip of unrequited lust in this unforgiving library. What am I doing here anyway? The answer is too complicated for me … better to hand that poisoned cup to the proper narrator who knows me better than I know myself.

Rolo Sangster, fair, tall and awkward, born well into mainline Philly, bred on Catholic doctrine stiffened by Pennsylvanian puritanism (no scandals back then, at least none exposed), the three Rs, regimented games, soft pretzels and cream cheese. But a lonely enough childhood in the pastures of Cheltenham just outside the city line after his father died, trying to connect with a wraith-like Mom who blamed the world for widowhood.

He had a coming out of sorts when eighteen, hand in hand with his superego, pimples, and a maundering yen for the bizarre. The mould had settled on a long, stooped frame, weak blue eyes, sometimes watery and red-rimmed, megalithic teeth braced straight in the nick of time but still uncomfortably set in a liberal and ambivalent mouth. Fair hair fell over the drawn pale face of a mime artist, slightly zany with a lazy eye, which gave a sense of dry humour behind the bifocals. And, oh yes, his left leg was lame.

There was nothing he could do about his lameness or the pin in his femur, but he worked hard on what everyone called his gentle disposition. This was a slander he tried to live down, reading it as a soft, suety, doe-eyed trait. Growing up with mother and sister in a doll's house full of cuddly toys and porcelain knickknacks, where scented hankies flicked grit from his face, and red-nailed fingers were forever smoothing down his cow's lick or picking lint from his collar, he had to fight for what he perceived to be a manly aspect.

At school he liked languages and poetry but decided to slave over the hard sciences. Finally forcing an interest in engineering, he read about the Timoney diesel engine and came to Dublin, the hard man's Mecca, to get a B. Mech. Eng. And to find himself. He didn't study very hard and found Murf instead.

His lameness came from a spelunking accident when he was eleven. In the dark cavern dripping lime like tallow, he lay on his back exhausted from insinuating himself into the core of the earth, and it occurred to him that he didn't really like this macho sport of pot-holing at all. Megatons of rock lay two inches over his shallowly breathing chest; the tiniest detour in the planet's orbit would turn him into a fossil. His pal, Bobby, was further ahead in an opening to a shaft and called back, his excited voice echoing in the confined space. "Come on, Rolo. These strata are fantastic. They are…"

Rolo heard another sound, distant gods clearing throats, askance at slumber disrupted. He lay petrified, curled in his dark niche as the noise grew menacingly, until it became the terrifying thunder of rock-fall. Columns of grainy dust backed up the tunnel choking him as he clutched in fear, waiting for the convulsion to spend itself.

He called out to Bobby but there was no response. The way forward was blocked because of the rock-fall. Dimly aware of pain in his leg, he crawled towards the obstruction and started to dig through the debris, calling to Bobby again and again. The blockage could have been several feet thick; there was no way to tell. He had to decide whether to keep digging or to crawl back, exit the tunnel and go for help. The ominous rumbling in the background gave little time for thought. Frantically, he made his first and last real decision.

He wormed his way out and ran to the nearest village, the pain of the buckle fracture flaring in his leg, but not slowing him down. An hour later, Bobby was taken out, dead from asphyxiation, his face contorted by that final effort for air. And the blockage, after all, had only been three feet thick; he could probably have saved him if he'd stayed. He made the wrong decision. Oh Bobby, my friend.

That was why Rolo never resented being lame and didn't bother much with physical therapy. Lameness wasn't enough, however. Fear of running away *again* kept him from getting close to anyone. Hence the appeal of engineering, the safety of things and numbers, and latterly the lure of Murf who had ... Let's wait and see what he had or didn't have.

The lodgers had finished their tea of one Clover sausage and three slices of Mother's Pride apiece, and had come upstairs from the kitchen to sit awhile in the front room overlooking Northbrook Square before going their separate ways for the evening. A quiet, tooth-picking reverie reigned, grease was beginning to settle and the landlady's tirade during tea, about piss-mires forgetting to flush the toilet, was happily fading into memory. The peace was broken only by an occasional aside to which a grunt or murmur was answer enough, the flare of a match and the odd tapping-out of a dented fold in a newspaper.

The arm-chair Murf sprawled in had come from one of those used furniture shops in Aungier Street that smell of mouse droppings, and have an iron bedstead in the window and sometimes a sleeping cat or two. The stretch cover of the arm-chair was bile green in colour and, judging by the gaping holes, was the sort of fabric that melted rather than burned when touched by a cigarette. The chair was normally reserved for Crowley, senior lodger and Dean of Digs, but Murf had again beaten him to it in the mad stampede up from the kitchen. Crowley for once did not demur but accepted a straight-backed chair near the fire on which he now sat archly, airing, in spread-eagled hands, his interlock combination underwear over the modest hearth, a thin finicky bigot with the pink, bespectacled, not unpleasant face of a Nazi doctor.

Ruminating on the evening's promise of

diversion set against his own dwindling finances, Murf stared at the ceiling, hands locked behind his head almost lost in black hair so thickly overgrown it would make a bald man's demised follicles tingle with envy. Each time he puffed a Gold Flake the hand holding the cigarette completely cupped his mouth, improving the draw and trapping the flavour. His dark eyes, smudged in by his Maker's thumb, were saved from mysticism by a reckless glint deep in the core.

Rolo sat at the table covered by a threadbare diamond of tassled cretonne, a textbook propped against a bowl of plastic fruit. His good leg juddered nervously on the ball of the foot as he tried to screen out Crowley's grunts and concentrate on the kinetic friction between two bodies.

The door of the sitting room was flung open. Mrs. McCarthy, the formidable landlady, known as 'The Cart', jammed a large surgical-stockinged foot against it to stop it quivering against the rubber spud. Her russet wool cardigan resembled a fishing-net, so tightly were the stitches pulled around her massive frame. One pocket sagged with keys, the other bulged with dust-cloths and receipts.

"Who put coal on the fire?" Her voice shattered the gentle evening discourse of the lodgers, and an anguished silence fell. Crowley stealthily withdrew his Long Johns from the hearth and stuffed them under the Evening Press which lay on his lap.

"I told you never to put coal on the fire … If you knew what it cost nowadays…" The Spartan furnishings of formica, leatherette and linoleum could not muffle the shrill cadences of The Cart's rebuke. "Don't ye know I can hear everything from below in the kitchen?"

The lodgers kept their heads down, weathering the storm. Some covert glances were directed towards Murf who alone had no fear of The Cart, but he was lost in calculations of cash-flow. The bovine passivity of the lodgers provoked The Cart who set about culling them one by one, "Why aren't *you* at the library?"

Sensing that he was the chosen foil, Rolo looked up and stammered, "G-guess I'll be going soon…"

"Be sure you do. I've a reputation to keep up with the College. And as for you," she turned to one of the shrinking bank clerks. "You were late for work again yesterday."

"Toothache." He put his hand to his jaw. Diffidently, he went back to the task of parcelling up a bundle of clothes in brown paper. As was the custom in those days, young men posted their laundry home to their mothers as often as twice a year.

"Yeah. Well toothache never stopped my old man, God rest him." Odd, how in mid-nag she would sometimes risk a personal aside that featured her dear departed. Was she shining his halo to make up to him for hounding him into an early grave? The lodgers had become a little weary of this oft-cited paragon. She poked the miserable fire and threw nutty slack on it to make it last longer.

"That'll do. You don't pay much. If you were in Mrs. Whelan's you wouldn't have a fire at all. In early April. Sure, you're spoiled rotten…" Spotting a malfeasance out of the corner of her eye, she whirled around, "Get your feet off that chair. You're not at home now."

Tim, the crazy one in this happy family and the butt of all jokes, jumped as if scalded, and shot out of the room. It didn't matter if he was guilty or not; he was always afraid of being picked on by The Cart. She replaced the coal scuttle, noting that it was three-quarters full; if, on her return, it was only half full there would be hell to pay. She marked the coal scuttle as others might mark a bottle of whiskey. When she finally dusted off her hands—a welcome signal that she was about to leave—there was a faint collective sigh of relief. Murf followed her out.

"Mrs McCarthy, about the rent money…"

"You paid on time for a change." She consulted a receipt in the pocket of her cardigan.

"Prematurely, I fear. Not realizing that Horse Show Week was upon us, with relatives pouring into the city expecting treats…"

"How much?"

"Shall we say a fiver? To prime the pump until the round generates its own momentum." He followed her down to the basement kitchen. The table had been cleared, its primrose oil-cloth

showing slightly embossed swirls of dried dish-
water where the cursory swipes of a damp cloth
had not fully followed through. Flanked by bread-
bins, the TV which was never switched on for the
lodgers, but merely reflected the ceiling light in its
dumb screen, now flickered and danced
miraculously with a sudden infusion of
personality, even though it was only a newsreader
droning on about Vietnam and the cold war.

She went to the cash box wedged under the
porcelain sink amid the clutter of brooms, dust
pans and cleaning fluids, and handed him two
pounds. Her face confirmed that the figure was not
negotiable. She had a sneaking respect for a man
who liked his pint; her dear husband was known to
have slipped the leash on occasion. Anyway, she
had long since written Murf off as a 'chronic' who
would never get his degree. But he was a
character, and that excused a multitude. He would,
as Brendan Behan and others had done, "die
roarin'," and that gave him some rights denied to
the pious and the cautious.

"Much obliged," Murf said. "A candle shall be
lit for you in White Friar's Street Church. Pay you
back on Monday…"

"Mind now. No noise when you come in." She
crashed the cash box shut and dropped the keys
into the hammock of her cardigan.

In the sitting room Crowley had resumed
airing his underwear which he needed for the next
day's bird-watching outing to Wicklow. He would
have to be on site at the crack of dawn to catch the

peregrine falcons.

"For two pins I'd give that woman a piece of my mind." He frowned gravely, showing how he'd had to restrain himself out of common civility.

"Come on," Murf said, "You were scared shitless. Anyway, why not give her a piece of the other and do us all a favour. If you played your cards right you could hang your hat up here." He winked conspiratorially in Rolo's direction.

"Don't make me throw up," Crowley retorted with a shudder. He opened a jar of wintergreen to heat at the fire and, with some bravado, poked through the nutty slack until he got a modest blaze going. A prickly close man whose eyes were always watchful, though misplaced behind the bifocals, he seemed able enough and widely read, but had little to show for his sixty-odd years and was still a full-board lodger in a young man's digs with only his insurance book to his name and a fledgling reputation as an ornithologist. Treasurer of the Irish-German Society and hater of all things British, he believed that Shakespeare was Dutch because an Englishman wouldn't recognise a rhyming couplet if he fell over one. It was widely assumed that he was an IRA supporter but he never quite admitted it. He was a teetotaller too, and never forgave Murf for pouring a Baby Power down his throat one Sunday afternoon when he dozed off with his mouth open. He took offence easily and liked to compensate by scoring points, especially at Tim's expense.

Holding the flannel combinations to his face

and taking a doe-like quivering sniff, he pronounced them done and swapped them for his Evening Press which he unfurled with great deliberation.

"Good God," he intoned scanning the headlines. "Mayhew's in the news again."

"Who dat?" One of the bank clerks asked, knowing how much Murf hated it when Crowley treated them to snippets from the paper.

"You've never heard of ex-British Army Colonel 'Rap' Mayhew, M.B.E.?" There were two layers of sarcasm in his voice; one chided the bank clerk for his ignorance, the other mocked the credentials of Mayhew. "He's a gun-runner, a lovely piece of work. Started in Vietnam, now he's at it again, selling arms to the Protestants in the North, hoping the Catholics will be wiped out. A mad dog, if you ask me, and a descendant of Cromwell." His eyes went venomously back to the newspaper to confirm the worst.

"Who cares?" Murf asked indifferently but there was a glint of provocation in his eye.

"You should care!" Crowley's voice was sharp and jagged as a filleting knife. The beard rash on his crêpey neck turned the colour of raw liver. "It's our people we're talking about."

"Well, Mayhew sounds enterprising," Murf said lightly. There was no way he could have foreseen that their paths would cross sooner or later, that the levers launching them on a collision course had already been thrown by the jaded deities.

"One day you'll appreciate the need for good intelligence," Crowley said with an air of mystery.

"*Military* intelligence, I suppose? Come off it. All you do in that German society of yours is drink Schnapps and watch Blue Tits in the Sally Gap."

"You should be ashamed of yourself. Rolo there, an American, is more concerned than you."

Rolo felt obliged to make some response. He coughed and said, "I'm not really *au fait* with … the situation…" His nervous neutrality helped restore a fragile peace. Through the tall rectangular windows came the sounds of children playing in Northbrook Square where Georgian nannies once pushed bonneted babies in big-wheeled prams while their mistresses languished over tea in fussy drawing rooms. The rain had stopped and a diffident sun filled the room with steaming fecund smells of mulchy soil and vegetation.

Murf patted the two quid in his pocket. "Can't stay here chatting all evening. Must away to bookish pursuits and mind-expanding endeavour. Coming Rolo?"

"Just a second." Rolo rushed up the lino-covered stairs to the bathroom on the landing. He was washing his hands in the sink when Tim came crashing in, wild-eyed and desperate, in a flurry of farts and groans, and sat naked on the toilet.

"Hey, do you mind? I'm not finished in here."

"I won't go till you're done," Tim promised with urgent pleading in his voice.

"That's hardly the..." Rolo began, then realized that there wasn't much time to debate the matter, as he noticed through the cracked mirror Tim beginning to crouch in earnest. Curtailing his ablutions, he made for the door.

"Do you think Mrs. McCarthy blames me for putting coal on the fire?" Tim's voice rang hollow in the porcelain privy, his eyes anxious and staring.

"No. Relax. She won't throw you out. Don't worry about it." Rolo smiled despite the fact that Tim was just beginning to break his promise of continence. "Take it easy."

The door closes behind them, brass knocker lifting and clunking back, as they set off down Northbrook Square flanked by terraced houses, red-brick from eaves to street level, then granite from oriel windows to sloping basements. Each front garden, surrounded by spear-topped railings and boxwood hedges, gives the impression of ordered family life, yet most of these houses are set in digs or flats, and the street has that certain abandon of the fly-by-night. In his worn brothel-creepers, Murf stabs the ground with each foot, his movements jerky but purposeful. He cranes forward as if walking into a stiff breeze while scouting the lie of the land. Beneath the outcrop of black hair, as dense as a ledge of basalt, the face looks vaguely Latino although the swarthy imperiousness is beguiled by sprigs of nostril hair and a ruddiness that gives the mistaken impression of honest toil.

Rolo limps fast to keep up, as they cross the canal bridge which opens up a vista of tree-lined water, ruffled in chevrons by gliding fowl, a limpid blessing amid the earth tones of red and ochre brick-work. They stop at the kiosk in Leeson Street where the blue-rinsed lady, like a saint in a shrine, sells cigarettes individually to the impecunious. Checking his loose change, Murf asks for twelve Gold Flake, and Rolo, who rolls his own, buys a tin of Old Holborn and a packet of papers. He will provide the spittle himself.

They reach St. Stephen's Green where the Three Fates, in their fountain island, spin man's destiny, ignoring the lumps of organic matter that man regurgitated on their bronze drapery the night before. A blind man has crossed the street and become embroiled in a pedestrian railing, fencing the bars with his white cane, not knowing which way to turn. Some faint-hearted passers-by pretend they haven't seen his predicament.

"Hold on there!" Murf yells. "You've gone astray. Here, grab my arm." He leads the blind man around the railing and back to the pavement. "Now, you're on the right road."

"What was the nature of the impediment?" the man inquires. "Was it a stationary vehicle?"

"No. A pedestrian railing. It's new I think."

"Jasus, trust those Corporation officials. A

shower of cunts, erecting obstacles all over the kip."

"Complete and utter cunts," Murf agrees with a grin, enjoying the unexpected profanity of a blind man.

They turn left into Earlsfort Terrace and mount the limestone steps into this forcing house of facts. In the main hall Murf takes up his favourite position by his personal radiator, dividing his bottom around the hottest blade. Lighting the first of the twelve Gold Flake, he gazes through the early puffs of smoke at the girls click-clacking on their way from the Ladies' Cloakroom, where they've powdered up, across the chequered hall towards the Aula Max, skirts flapping gently against smooth calves. No jeans or slacks allowed in this old-school place, unlike the more progressive – and Protestant – Triune Poly further down the road.

"Look at 'em all queuing up for the library," Murf observes more in sorrow than anger, nodding languidly to the odd familiar face. Mindful of the two year's work he has to catch up on, Rolo feels a prong of panic tipped with guilt.

"I think perhaps … I might also join the queue…" The intention is murmured diffidently, an apology for weakness.

"Have you lost your marbles? Don't you know what night this is? The results of the Medical finals are out. Jollity will be forced on us if we but linger a while."

"I've got a lot of work to do," Rolo protests,

following Murf as he prises himself off the radiator and moves lazily, on squeaking rubber soles, across the hall towards the bulletin boards; as expected, the results of medical exams are posted.

"Stay here," Murf advises, "And we'll be swept along to hostelries with rejoicing quacks. For one last fling before they descend on the public and start burying their mistakes." Scanning the lists for familiar names, he gives intermittent grunts of satisfaction and surprise. "Ashur made it. He scraped a pass but it's a miracle. He'll definitely be buying."

"I really do have to study," Rolo demurs, trying hard not to weaken.

"You'll miss a good night," Murf warns in a bantering lilt, then suggests a tantalising compromise, "Tell you what, I'll look for you in the Annex at eight."

"No thanks," Rolo declines as firmly as he can, regret etched in his face, which bears uneasily the stigma of party-pooper. "Anyway, you'll be three sheets in the wind."

"One can but hope."

"Don't go getting into…" No need to finish the admonition. One look at Murf is enough; the die is cast. Already he is mingling with smiling Meds, offering congratulations, pounding shoulders and insisting, "Of course, we knew you could do it." He rides the joyous crest through the Doric portals in the direction of Hartos. A fabled 'chronic', he commands with all celebrating groups a sort of *droit du seigneur*, and is made more welcome than a tenor at a wedding. It is a little like European aristos being paid to attend parties in Hollywood.

At a discreet distance, a big dour fellow in a sheepskin coat follows the group out. Rolo does a double take that causes a swatch of hair to flop over his eyes. Where has he seen this guy before and why does he have an uneasy feeling that he's tailing Murf?

When the library doors open, late as usual, there is much pushing and shoving from the eager crammers, and a porter is called to regulate the flow. As usual Rolo gets shouldered aside in the crush, but a large ignoramus, keen to get him out of the way, shoe-horns him by accident into the reading room. He fills out a docket for Loney's 'Elements of Dynamics' and hands it over the counter to a balefully insouciant librarian with a nose that could rip stitches, who, without glancing at it, says, "It's out." Her jaded eyes are fixed somewhere on the vaulted ceiling where plaster cherubs cavort and copulate in cob-webbed friezes.

"But it's a standard text."

"It's out." Her voice rouses itself from torpor, edging towards displeasure. His existence is clearly an affront.

"Could you at least check ... Please."

"It's out! Next!"

"Thank you."

Rolo sits and flicks through his own worn

copy of Rosenberg's 'Mechanics', bought for fifty pence on Aran Quay, sick with frustration, cursing the tables which are spaced perfectly for distracting views of thigh. Looking up in quiet despair, he sees another troubled soul, Tim, careering around the perimeter, a fag-end stuck to his lip, peaked cap shading wild eyes, his badly shaved face speckled with bits of toilet paper. Poor Tim, for years torturing himself with a night degree, his dream of independence, when he couldn't sit still with his jingle-jangle nerves for more than the turn of a page. He shouts that he didn't put coal on the fire. Confronted now in mid-canter by hatchet-faced librarians, turned like a maverick steer, and herded out. Civility preserved, an outrage foiled, the giggles wane and cramming heads subside again in mellow stained-glass light.

Unrewarded by one evening of virtue, Rolo wrestles with thoughts of imminent exams, his deficit of work, spurts of guilt, an unknown future if any, his head in an uproar, loins running amok in bittersweet frustration, he tries to apply himself to the lamina of symmetrical bodies. And is just about settling into it when ...

"Excuse me. You are sitting in my seat."

"I beg your pardon?" Rolo looks up, the leading eye curling around the challenge of a query, to see the brave embarrassed face of a fresher peering.

"Sssssh ... Sssssh!" Struck by such desecration, a horrified librarian drops her knitting with a clack of needles, opens the counter-hatch and expels them both. Silence infraction. Rustication, one day, no appeal. She goes back to her wool, dreaming of libraries without the inconveniences of books … and readers.

Rolo confirms the worst. The fresher has been rented the seat by Murf for a fiver a year, a reasonable rental given the state of the market and the fact that James Joyce himself favoured that very seat when in residence. Rolo explains the situation as best he can and the fresher goes away, disappointed but also consoled by the thought that the perpetrator of the con was Murf, whom he has heard of in dispatches. Rolo watches him move off with a spring in his step and a story to tell. The Italians had a word for it, 'furbitzia', and he himself was also drawn to the same green fuse and crooked rose – a good clean 'stroke'.

Exclaustrated from the library, Rolo has no hope of working, and wonders what to do with the balance of the evening. He tries the Annex for a cup of coffee but it is too early. Perhaps a modest work-out and refreshing shower but the gym alas is set up for GAA training and is off limits. Everything about this angular place designed to impede and harass; the virtuous are sorely tried.

Fighting the urge to join Murf in Hartos, he goes for a stroll in Hatch Street, but inadvertently offends a lady of the evening. She had been striking a rate with a client leaning from a black Mercedes when Rolo passes idly by. The client who resembles a luminary of government is heard to remark, "A tenner? You could get chastisement for that!" Noticing Rolo's interested glance, the dignitary revs suddenly and departs on squealing tyres, leaving a wisp of exhaust floating in the crisp air. Wrapping her nylon leopard-skin coat about her person, the business lady turns her wrath on Rolo.

"You just put the kibosh on me best customer, you little bollix. Shag off out of it with your gimpy leg."

He ducks the whirling brolly though a protruding spoke parts his hair, and he does limp away as rapidly as possible while trying to maintain a semblance of dignity. He recalls the night Murf brought one of her colleagues into the library and auctioned her favours by sealed bid, earning him a life-time expulsion which didn't bother him at all since he had no intention of ever using the library.

Rolo turns into Newman House and curls up in an arm-chair; it is a relief to get in somewhere at last. This, he knows, is where poor Gerard Manley Hopkins spent a few miserable years with his depression and sprung rhythms. Rolo hasn't thought about his own vocation for several years, though there was a time when he really did want to become a priest. He decides not to ruminate any more on that. Let the dead bury the dead.

With a desultory eye on TV he learns from some jowly reporter that hoggets made seventy pence the pound and that Nojar could banish white scour and liver fluke. These facts seem to be on a par with those of the cold war, though he knows little of that either. He rolls a cigarette, nips off the loose end and lights up. Outside the stately windows a bell tolls faintly, as park attendants close up Stephen's Green. Shortly after that a porter walks through the stone corridors, announcing that Newman House is about to close. Everything closing, closed barred and bolted down or out of service in this town of wet Sundays. And he too is out of order in a maundering time warp.

On the way back to the digs he steels himself passing Hartos, imagining pints being pulled, white heads settling like doves folding wings. How hard to do the right thing where all the cards are stacked against rectitude, and character means not moral fibre but a lust for the bizarre, a firm commitment to idleness, and a profound love of strokes. Fatally attractive it might be, but there are serious risks.

Limping up Leeson Street, jaundiced by street lamps, he fantasises about meeting a girl who might teach him to relax until he could let his mind gently sneak up on the mysteries of Atwood's machine and the Parallelogram of forces. Maybe that brunette in the library? Although Murf said College women were a waste of time and effort. "Too stuck up. No imagination in the ways of the flesh. Debs from Ailesbury Park and Ballsbridge, saving themselves for solicitors and turf accountants with big practices and wallets. Better by far a good little goer from Drimnagh."

On the stairs, Tim shoots past him towards the

bathroom, a high-octane jet making one pass over the target zone. The bottoms of his pyjamas are down to knee level by the time he reaches the door. Rolo reads in bed for a while, listening to the chimes of Rathmines town-hall clock float over the roof-tops. Freezing under a thread-bare blanket, he wonders if he might risk using the one-bar electric fire Murf has hidden in the wardrobe. Better not, in case The Cart would see, in her basement den, the metered watts fly by. Instead, he puts on his socks and throws a duffle coat over the blanket.

A kerfuffle of sound rasps through his light slumber – brake screech, door slams, foot poundings, stair creaks – the sequence jumbled in the shock of such a rude awakening.

"Come on Rolo, old son. The night begins. Join the Meds and me. To the Tramp's Other Ball we hasten in the old Olympic. An event not to be missed on a night such as this." Murf whips a sheet off his own bed and drapes it toga-like around his shoulders. "A costume of Ciceronian simplicity. Let us now dress Rolo for the ball."

Rolo feels hands clawing at him and sees bedclothes flying. Porter breath and the scent of sundry expulsions fill the room. He can hear The Cart's broom doing a passionate Paso Doble on the floor beneath.

"What's going on? Stop that racket at once!"

Imperious in his toga, Murf meets her lumbering up the stairs, brush handle to the front, like a charging rhino.

"Do not distress yourself, kind landlady. Rome is safe, the rabble put down." He ducks inside the arc the broom describes. "My faithful standard-bearer, bring to me a cup of Falernian wine."

Unaware of the commotion and driven by inner turmoil, Tim shoots out of his room across the landing and hares for the bathroom, lowering his pants as he goes. Murf uses the interruption to rope in Ashur who is going through drawers to accessorize Rolo.

"Mrs. McCarthy, may I introduce Dr. Ashur McIlvenney, a brilliant young gynaecologist, specialist in polystyrene matriculations, and personal physician to the College of Loreto."

Ashur, grinning, bows from the hip. The Cart, deflated and torn between civility and the momentum of her temper, grunts, "Pleased … I'm sure. But could you keep it down? This is a respectable house."

"Just going, dear landlady." They sidle past her on the stairs, dragging the hapless, pyjama-clad Rolo cringing in his sobriety, and pass the open bathroom where Tim gives vent on his porcelain throne.

Murf lies back in Ashur's crammed Mini Minor, his feet out the passenger window.

"Onward to Mount Olympus. And don't spare the horses."

Fighting for breath, Rolo gasps, "I don't think I'm … up for this…"

"There's gratitude," Murf exclaims. "We sacrificed valuable drinking time to pick you up. I am stung, cut to the very quick."

"Ashur, he doesn't mean it at all," Ashur says in that gombeen way of his, urging the laden car forward on sunken shocks. "Get your phalanges off the gear-stick, Costello. The clutch is jumpy enough already." Leaving the tree-choked railings of Northbrook Square, they turn at the moon-washed church of St. Malachy into Camden Street.

"Don't you just love it," Murf muses, "when medical men converse? What chance do we laymen have, blinded by science and bedazzled by savoir-faire? Over there, Ashur, a parking spot."

The queue at the Olympia stretches around the corner into Synge Street, fed at the tail by tributaries meandering from The Flying Horse and Igo Inn. Such costumes as are in evidence owe more to desperation than flair – football strip, nightshirts, pyjamas and of course the ubiquitous sheet, protean in its different forms. A diminutive Rip van Winkle who wears his sheet in Gandhi style tries to jump the queue and is halted near the entrance by a stocky bouncer in a bulging tux.

"Get back in line. Hey, I know you. You're barred, you little shit. Go on, get out of it." He puts an arm-lock on him and manhandles him down the steps of the neon-lit entrance. The puny van Winkle wriggles free, lands a respectable jab on the bully's nose, and flees. The bouncer takes off after him.

"I smell a ploy," Murf says. "Let's follow them."

The chase goes around three sides of Camden

Square, then, as expected, down a narrow alley where the bouncer runs into the outstretched arms of three rugby forwards who pinion him and grin. Dancing around his captive, van Winkle pours stout down his trouser-front, rips the satin-lined tux from stem to stern and finally wipes his hands on the ruffled shirt-front.

"Now who's barred?"

"Ashur, that's poetic justice," Ashur marvels.

The bouncer staggers back to the ball-room, tatters of monkey suit flapping, foam seeping through flies, ruffled shirt bearing the imprint of grubby hands. The motley queue hoots and cheers. It's not often that fate smiles on the small man.

Inside the sweating ballroom, the mirrors weep with condensation and the yellow stucco walls under the balcony seem like melting almond paste. The pine floor heaves underfoot like the planking of some old sailing ship on a swollen sea, as the turgid masses lurch together to the deafening beat of the resident showband half hidden behind banks of amplifiers. A light show with flashing palette-daubs completes the scene.

"What we do to get laid," Murf groans as he ploughs into the serried ranks of costumed wallflowers, and takes the plunge with a quite passable Indian squaw. It is one of those rare breaks, for inside the redskin make-up and tasseled buckskins lives a girl of secretly soft embellishments. The first-presented face of tribal hauteur, wedged between black braided plaits viciously parted along the crown, bones of cheek and flanges of nose streaked with war paint, gives way as they dance, to a softer, fun-loving expression in which round blue orbs edged with sprightly lashes size up the world in a bantering way.

"Apache?" Murf asks when he gets his second wind.

"No. Choctaw."

"Shall I call you Running Water?" He inquires above the din of the showband, guiding her forcefully, for she is mettlesome and inclined to lead – probably danced the man's part at convent school.

"Hot and cold." She grins, dancing so close that her single feather tickles his nose. "Who or what are you supposed to be?" She runs her flighty eyes over his grubby toga which has a triangular tear, caused by a long sharp toe-nail.

"Isn't it a shame? My costumier let me down at the eleventh hour. I had to improvise with this silk sheet. Or is it Damask?"

"It seems as if your costumier let a lot of people down." Her sideways glance takes in the collectivity of fluttering sheets, many of them in need of laundering. An inward smile puffs the plucks of her face, giving the impression of harvest merriment, roasted apples and hot punch in Toby jugs.

"I wonder if by any chance you might move your feather around. It's tickling my nasal passages." He feels her curved back move silkily inside the suede, beaded bolero and is tempted, as her knees joust with his, to clutch her rump. She is his speed all right. What a break, first time out on this epileptic floor.

"Sitting Bull never complained." The same pool of laughter wells up behind those apple cheeks and mischievous mouth.

"He didn't have my sinuses. I'm a martyr to them."

"Oh, all right then." She takes the feather and sticks it in his hair. A nice intimate touch; he feels as if she might have staked a claim by planting her pennant on his crown. He wants to test this a little bit.

"Are we blood brothers now?"

"You need to cut your wrists for that."

"I'm game."

After dancing a complete set, he feels the time is right to suggest a lemonade, The First Move, according to ballroom mores.

Loosening his collar beneath the sheet, he says, to lend a whiff of plausibility, "It's so warm in here, don't you think? Would you care for a lemonade?"

"You're a fast worker." This girl doesn't pull her punches and has scuppered his niceties.

"You're not supposed to say that. You should simper and say, 'A lemonade would be enchanting'."

"I don't simper much and would prefer a pint of stout." Again that same dimpled control of a smile that wanted to break for the border. She could grace a bar-stool with him any time. He guesses that she has several brothers who can tell a tale of being arm-wrestled into submission by her.

With some regret he explains, "The Olympic's liquor license is no more, alas, having been revoked on foot of diversions that got out of hand."

"You weren't involved by any chance?"

"Perish the thought." Incubating her warm hand in his, he leads her through the heaving throngs, up the stairs to the balcony, a sort of poor man's mezzanine. He places his other hand on the small of her back to guide her to the chosen spot, to sit and sip and begin that tender interrogation that marks all budding friendships. On the way he has the first glimpse of her legs which are long and shapely, smoothly curved from moccasin to mandible; he didn't expect anything less. So many boxes already ticked, those remaining have got to be eminently tickable. They claim a small round table and face each other across it. Cicero and Running Water, blowing hot and cold above the jostling crowds on this observation deck.

Hypnotised by the rawhide thongs dangling over a pronounced shelf of breast, he asks where she works and is told, "St. Vincent's."

Oh joy, a nurse. Images of cool palpating hands, snug white uniforms and a general empathy with, and forgiveness of, the flesh, all spring to his happy mind which sets about the task of delicately establishing where she lives. To plot the coordinates of this hidden abode he asks obliquely, "Do you take the bus to work? Those number elevens are always breaking down, aren't they?" Ever since he was banned from driving his beloved motorbike for speeding through Stephen's Green, he has to check out the geography to minimise shank's mare and, worse still, taxi fares.

"Are they?" She gives him a curious look. "I usually hop on a seventeen A. Sometimes I even walk."

Allah be praised, triangulation has worked. The coordinates cross somewhere between Mespil Road and Burlington Avenue, not an ass's roar from Northbrook Square. The prospect of dropping by for creature comforts when The Cart's fare palls is roseate in its appeal. And no taxi fare to see her home on this night of nights. In this cosy scheme of things, multiple blessings are showering down like balloons on New Year's Eve. Must give humble thanks in Newman's kirk for favours received, for such a precious find amid this throbbing mediocrity. A definite ten in all respects.

Hobbling around the balcony, Rolo stalks a Pierrette who keeps disappearing in the strobe-lit swelling crowd beneath. Wiping steam from his glasses, he hears a familiar voice.

"Rolo, would you care to join us in a lemonade? May I introduce … Beg pardon, my civilities are adrift. Fair one, how are you called? Tiffany, Esmerelda, Solange … ?"

"Gobnait."

"I see … Rolo, Gobnait … Gobnait, Rolo."

Having shaken hands, Gobnait moves to one

side and gives Rolo half of her chair on which he sets a bony buttock. "I didn't catch *your* name," she reminds Murf.

"Eric de Willaby at your service. Would you care for another lemonade?"

It starts with a painful croak, intermittently suppressed, then the knotted plucks of her face give way; the laughter that bubbles forth is of the warbling variety, a deep-throated jumble of oboes crooning up from soft abdominal chambers. Rolo can't help grinning and even begins to bray.

"You're such a fraud," she hoots. "Eric de Willaby ... the number eleven bus ... do you think I came ... up the Shannon on a bicycle?"

"I don't understand." Murf remains deadpan, trying to maintain what remains of his image. This iconoclasm, especially in front of Rolo, simply won't do. But after a while he recovers his composure. It is after all a jolly, promising night. Nice to have shifted so early and to be safe above that writhing sea of frantic souls and ruddy faces, lush isles looming on the horizon. He has an urge to share his good fortune.

"Rolo, stop gawking down at the riff-raff with your tongue hanging out. I'm sure Gobnait has a friend for you. Don't you, Gobnait?" In generosity of spirit he repeats her name. What, after all, is in a name that usage and passion cannot put right?

"Yes. My flat-mate is here," Gobnait dries her eyes. "But she may have met someone."

"'Met' someone?" Murf queries. "'Met' someone?"

"You don't think we came here to dance? We like to shift, too."

Outmanoeuvred yet again, he takes further stock of this girl who is right up at the net smashing back his best lobs with frightening élan. "You really take the gateau," he says with not a little awe. "Is she Rolo's type? Why ask? Of course she is." The thought of two nurses in a flat near Northbrook Square is cosily compelling. His mind toys with the prospect of dropping by when at a low ebb, of graciously accepting the kind ministrations of two nurturers bearing plates of scones and barmbrack with soothing words in this misbegotten world. A home from home, and perhaps even … Steady. Best not lose the run of oneself in heady speculation. Rolo will play his part even if the 'friend' proves unexceptional. Stout lad, good to have him on the team. And girls like package deals, to compare notes, dream of double weddings or whatever – a nice synergy of bliss. Peering over the balcony, he asks for a description of the friend.

"Tall, like Rolo, and fair. She came as a Cowgirl."

"This is too good to be true. Cowgirls and Indians. It takes me back to my cloudless youth. Rolo, tighten the string on your jammies and join in the search."

Leaning over the balustrade, they peer into the swirling inferno from which a blast of sweaty heat rises like gasses from a crocodile-infested swamp.

"I can't see very much," Rolo declares, wiping

his glasses and feeling a little awkward about being pandered to. He would like to have shifted someone all by himself, but given his limitations with the fair sex, he will take all the help he can get. The Showband, just underneath them, hurtle into 'The Spanish Gypsy Dance' with crashing flamenco chords and nostril-flaring hauteur. A forest of upraised clapping hands makes the search more difficult.

Leading a retinue of Meds, Ashur prances by, leading a wild conga line; more oiled than before, it is clear that he has been slipping out to the six packs in the Mini.

"Good on you!" Ashur sends a French salute with an envious message. "See you shifted already, Murf. Ashur, you could always throw the shape." He signals to his followers and the Conga line jives on, weaving its way around the balcony.

"Who are those people?" Murf makes a *moue* and takes a delicate sip of lemonade to rid himself of the memory. "Any sign of our Cowgirl?"

"I've got a ballerina," Rolo calls back over his shoulder.

"Not quite the same thing. Look for leather boots and spurs." He looks hopefully at Gobnait to see if boots and spurs might have any associations for her.

"It's difficult to see footwear from up here," Rolo reports back faithfully, giving his glasses another wipe. "I see a witch though."

"No. You're getting cold."

"Puss in Boots."

"Colder."

Gobnait intervenes, "You two couldn't organise a dog fight. Rolo, if you would like to meet Fiona I can ask her…"

"How? It's bedlam down there." Murf points with the glowing tip of a Gold Flake. Just then Ashur, who is trying to lead the Conga line up on to the balustrade, loses his footing, clutches air and falls gracelessly into the percussion section of the showband. Dislodged high hats and amplifiers set up an ear-piercing wall of sound which attract dancers around the band-stand. Getting unsteadily to his feet, Ashur grabs the mic and sings incoherently until the bouncers cut a swathe through the rapt audience in his direction. He skips away to enthusiastic applause.

"He's too far gone," Murf observes judiciously, shaking his head. The unwritten rule of frivolity is to go to the limit as often as possible but not to cross the line. To every art its discipline. Ashur was just the once-a-year sort of dilettante to bring the whole art form into disrepute. Dismissing the incident from his mind, Murf turns to Gobnait and resumes where they had left off, "Well, how do we find Fiona?"

"Easy." Gobnait hands him her cloakroom ticket on which she has scribbled a message, and explains the logistics.

With Murf holding him by the legs, Rolo dangles over the balcony and hands the announcement to the lead vocalist of the band. It is that simple.

Fiona turns out to be Nordic-looking and pleasant. While there is no incandescent chemistry between this newly-matched pair, she is also prepared to play her part, and Rolo is comfortable with her. Doesn't have to lie about his leg – the shrapnel yarn. Murf lies back like a planter in his rattan chair, fanned by palmy fronds, the harvest gathered in, his wants spoken for – not having to live on wits anymore, for the pantry is full.

Following the showband's butchery of the National Anthem, Murf leads his little group to the main exit where they see a crowd outside cheering.

"Oh no!" Rolo is the first to witness the unstoppable Ashur climbing up a drainpipe towards the window of the ladies cloakroom. "Come on down," he shouts.

"Wanna see some tit." Ashur reveals the purpose of his assault on the south face of Mount Olympus. "Biddies wouldn't dance with a chap. Gonna see what they're so stuck up about…"

"It's embarrassing to see one of our gender let the side down like this," Murf remarks.

Ashur inches higher as the bouncers shake the rickety pipe trying to dislodge him. Fiona, grimacing, clutches Rolo's arm, "They'll hurt him."

Rolo rushes forward just as the pipe comes away from the wall and loops down to deposit Ashur safely in waiting arms. In the melee which follows, he tunnels his way out of the ruck and makes good his escape in the general direction of

Wexford Street.

The two pairs strolling towards Appian Way stop frequently by the canal to kiss and canoodle. It has been a long time since Rolo has had such fragrant softness in his arms. Fiona's long hair, diaphanous in the street lights, sends a violet bouquet into his nuzzling nostrils. It is, after all, a wonderfully easy part to play. The only mote in the moonbeam is the glimpse, in his peripheral vision, of that large individual in the sheepskin coat, leaning against the timbers of the canal lock.

Stepping into the cosy basement flat in Dartmouth Square which falls within the vector so well triangulated, Murf observes, "I have that dream-like feeling I've been here before." His happy glance takes in predictable accoutrements, scatter cushions carefully strewn, hanging plants of geranium, ivy trellising through macramé holders, figurines and soft toys reclining on mantelpiece, a poster of Elvis and one of Guernica. "It's positively enchanting. Look, Rolo, how lovely it is." He is driven to poetry, "I could lie down like a tired child and weep away this life of care that I have borne and yet must bear…"

Gobnait waves them to gently yielding sofas. "Would you like tea or," she smiles mischievously, keeping her gaze steady, "something else, or both?"

"Beg pardon?" Murf's brow furrows with quizzical lines of pleasant shock as when a landlord utters those immemorial words, 'This one's on the house, lads,' or The Cart provides a slice of cooked ham on Friday. Largesse flooding down from undiscovered galaxies. "Have I died and gone to Heaven?" he murmurs.

There is one bad moment when Gobnait, without warning and while Murf is still befuddled by good fortune, raises a hand to one of the black pigtails and whips off the wig. But he recovers quickly with a relieved laugh on seeing the finer chestnut curls pop out to grace her face with a subtler more endearing halo.

Reading his mind, she says, "I'm taking off the wooden leg next."

After some trips to the adjoining kitchen the dream materialises of current cake and barmbrack, slathered with butter and blackcurrant jam, scones similarly accoutred, apple tart and cream, all to be washed down by scalding tea from the big Betty Brown teapot. The Cart's was never like this. Maybe even rashers and griddle cakes for *breakfast*. Should one dare to hope?

Ballads in stereo soothe the soul, unshod toes wiggle in the shaggy pile of Curragh sheep, body tension seeps into the poultice of bawneen cushions, and troubled heads are cradled in encircling arms. It is too much for Murf who surreptitiously wipes a tear from his right eye.

Outside, the moon-lit city throbs quietly as the two couples polarise to opposite ends of the couch. Silences, broken at first by muffled snorts and nervous commentary, grow longer and more intense. Murf ponders the logistics of getting Gobnait to bed but doesn't want to rush his fences;

there is much to be savoured here and saved for the future.

It is Fiona who finally stands, smoothing her skirt, to remind them that it's three-thirty in the morning and tomorrow is another day. Gobnait also disengages, though with less alacrity, and tidies up her dishevelled hair. Struggling out of a nest of pillows, regret tugging at his face, Murf complains of back pain, wondering if there is somewhere he might lie down for a while to rectify his tangled vertebrae and disks.

"Why not go to Mrs. McCarthy's in Northbrook Square?" Gobnait suggests, a hairpin between her teeth, face flushed and smiling.

"Wha … How did you know…?" Tongue-tied for once, Murf jerks his head like a swimmer surfacing, to clear his senses.

"We see you some days in Leeson Street." Her lips, smooched clean of lipstick, widen over milky teeth still gripping the hairpin. "It's a small town, you know."

"I'll be damned." Game, set and match to the nurse at the net with the war-paint and the abominably winning ways.

Unusually, there is no post-mortem chat on the way back to The Cart's. A splash of dawn lights the sky although the mist will not clear for several hours. Through the grey gauze, a lingering street lamp throws down a cone of atomised, pollen-coloured light. Gulls interloping from the Liffey bear whiffs of the sea to these always-autumn streets of mouldering ochre stone, wrought railings and trampled dignity. The cherry blossom of Leeson Park will last another week at most before a blitzing breeze dispatches it in one final fling of spindrift. They turn into Northbrook Square with its green park where Loreto girls chase hockey balls and are instructed on the field of play by tweedy referees, and are whistled at by passing louts. Two of whom now sneak soberly by in off-white toga and striped night attire. Murf towards something, Rolo from something, run, but run they must, and never stop. Another day wasted, avoiding what is real.

"Lord, forgive all the little tricks I play on you, and I'll forgive the great big one you played on me."
—Robert Frost

"I don't believe that dangling gerunds are a crime."
—The Present Writer

CHAPTER 2

THE CART USUALLY got low on funds towards the end of the week; this Friday breakfast consisted of a couple of slices of Mother's Pride and watery tea on which floated the fine-grained chaff from the end of the tea caddy. Far better meals were enjoyed by prisoners in a Siberian Gulag. Sitting at the head of the table, Crowley put on his specs and bent fastidiously to the task of spreading margarine on a slice of bread, his head on one side, smiling to himself.

Tim sat chewing vacantly, his craggy, perplexed face clawed by some deep ambiguity. Every now and again a hidden reflex convulsed the circuitry and made him shoot out his arm to scratch the inside of the elbow. These spasms were followed by periods of trance, as he moved in and out of reality.

He was lucky The Cart kept him on in the digs

because no one would share a room with him. His galvanic actions, desperate calls of nature – as irresistible as they were unexpected – and frequent high-strung masturbations, had scared off many a would-be room-mate. Even The Cart in her basement three floors below had heard him in the middle of the night call out from the depths of his celibate soul, "Christ, give me a woman!"

The closest she came to throwing him out was when he stopped suddenly one morning in the middle of Northbrook Square and yelled out for all to hear, "She can keep her bloody breakfast, the bitch!" Hearing him loud and clear, Mrs. Whelan, a rival landlady in the same Square, lost no time in relaying it to The Cart with the rider that of course *she* always served a cooked breakfast to her lodgers. "The men need a rasher in the morning to put a bit of jizz in them." Tim's cardboard suitcase was ominously on the steps that evening and it was only Rolo's intervention that earned him a second chance.

Although The Cart kept Tim on, she lost few opportunities to let him know that he was there on sufferance. It was her blunt way of trying to discipline him and give him some cop-on. It didn't do his peace of mind any good, but she knew no other way.

Since his breakdown which he never talked about, Tim knew that without a digs and an address he would be a vagrant. He tried various ways to improve his stock but these, like the night degree, had no hope of success, His latest venture was selling dictionaries door to door in the evenings. He had to pay the company fifteen pounds, and the area they assigned him to was the Coombe. It had been a standing joke in the digs and Crowley liked to milk it for all it was worth.

The Cart brewed more watery tea in the chaney pot, went to the kitchen door and bellowed up the stairs. By rote, she grabbed a broom and beat a perfunctory riff on the ceiling.

Bleary-eyed, Murf and Rolo appeared in the kitchen and sat at the table. Observing the Spartan fare which was, however, mercifully free of grease, Murf remarked, "It must be Lent again."

"I heard that," The Cart interjected. "And what about that carry-on last night, waking the dead." She stood behind them, fists on hips. Rolo felt the short hairs on his neck bristle; she scared the bejasus out of him.

"Do I detect a note of rebuke?" Murf queried as he spread margarine on a slice of Mother's Pride, working from the crust inward so that the soft but stale centre wouldn't tear or crumble.

"You'll detect the heel of me hand if you bring those yahoos into this house again." She clattered the dented aluminium kettle down on the gas ring to illustrate her point.

"Yahoos?" Murf repeated more in sorrow than in anger, his heavy brows drooping in dismay. "Yahoos? Mrs. McCarthy, you are referring to the cream of the medical crop, doctors with healing hands, God's anointed who suffer that there may be life."

Rolo had a sudden nervous urge to laugh, recalling God's anointed climbing up a drainpipe to see some tit.

"Well, the sooner they get a set on themselves the better," The Cart grumbled. But the sting had gone out of it, compromised as she was between the hallowed pillars of medicine and religion. No one could handle her like Murf. He was gracious in victory.

"And I must thank you for the two quid. It was nice to be able to stand a round for our medical friends on the threshold of their healing ministry. Such small mercies do not go unnoticed." He nodded piously up towards the ceiling, sipped his tea and winked at Rolo over the blue and white striped mug.

"Don't forget your nine o clock lectures." She felt that some advice had to be imparted.

Tim shot out an arm for a scratch, this time rocking Crowley's cup in its saucer.

"Control yourself, man," Crowley warned him, scraping back his chair for fear of spillage. "By the way, I heard you shouting again last night."

"I didn't open me mouth," Tim replied stubbornly, not wanting to be shown up in front of The Cart on whom his filmy eyes were plaintively fixed.

"You did so. You were on about those damned dictionaries again. Rawmayshing about lovely illustrations and hire purchase. How many have you sold up there in the Coombe?" Crowley's lips curled into a slow sneer.

"I've sold enough," Tim said with a hunted expression. He was no match for Crowley. "They ask me in for tea sometimes. They're nice people up there."

"That's not the question," Crowley persisted.

"He's right though." Rolo tried to help Tim.

With studied patience Crowley took off his glasses and laid them on the oil-cloth in a slow arc. "I'm asking how many of those dictionaries he sold yet."

Shifting abruptly, Tim coughed, then gagged. Bile came up. He sat perplexed, hand over mouth, eyes staring.

"Get out!" The Cart yelled. "Go to the bathroom, you bugger."

Tim jumped up and fled, leaving the door rocking on its hinges. The Cart stood wheezing as laughter filled her ample abdomen. "The poor divil," she snorted. "Sure, he's harmless."

"I don't know about that." Crowley was less forgiving and frowned at this unwarranted levity. "He has bad habits … filthy habits. It's disgusting…" His voice descended to a lower, conspiratorial register. "You know what I mean."

"I don't know," Murf said, brightening up. "Explain please for the slow-witted among us."

"You know well enough," Crowley intimated in a delicate lilt. "We can't be more explicit in mixed company." He nodded in The Cart's direction, although her sensibilities were not really at risk. Perhaps Crowley's misplaced gallantry did, after all, reflect a desire to hang up his hat in her house.

"You mean," Murf would not be fobbed off by hypocritical niceties, especially when a lubricious coup offered itself on a platter, "he wanks?"

Crowley picked up his glasses and polished them uneasily with the end of his tie. "I didn't say that."

Rolo stared into his cup trying to read the tea-leaves, his neck craned forward as if waiting for an axe to fall.

"Did you never masturbate?" Murf asked conversationally, brows raised in innocent inquiry. The Cart was unusually silent except for the gentle lap of sudsy water in the sink, but her enormous bulk seemed to wobble more than usual. This was one for her pals at the vegetable stalls in Camden Street.

"Wash your mouth out," Crowley snapped. The superior smile that understood and forgave the foibles of mankind was wiped from his face.

"At least Tim has what it takes."

"What do you mean by that?" Crowley's face was a steel mask, the door of a blast furnace that roared within. From craw to neck a livid rash of colour began to spread; the stud of his starched collar bobbled above his Adam's apple.

"Tim still has lead in his pencil, not like some old codgers who can't raise the latch on a door." Murf looked levelly at him across the table in a charged silence. Even the crockery was still, The Cart's big red hands laced in froth, poised and motionless above the sink.

Crowley recoiled in slow-motion, and appealed to The Cart.

"Do we have to listen to this ... filth in a Catholic house? As we break bread?" His voice went high in martyred ecstasy. The Cart's broad back in its knobbed cardigan quivered and shook; she had Crowley pegged as an old gelding anyway, and besides, she liked a bit of bawd. It would keep her going in the butcher's haggling over the price of tripe. With no support from that quarter, Crowley left the table.

"We're paying our taxes to educate animals. Pigs!" he spat out. "My God, what have we come to?" His parting shot at the open door through which Tim had also fled exposed his cherished bigotry. "This is not England!" He collided with a couple of bank clerks on their way in for breakfast.

"You sanctimonious old die-hard twit," Murf threw after him. "Go and watch your blue tits."

On the way down Leeson Street, Rolo tried to plan out his work for the day, on the assumption that there might be a book or two available in the library. The thought of all those arid formulae and bodies moving, touching and swinging in the most devilish ways imaginable did not appeal, but this was the course he had chosen, a hard science to stiffen his back-bone. Theology or Divinity would have been a doddle by comparison. He tried to psych himself up as he limped over the canal bridge.

No one really knew what Murf was studying

and it wasn't readily apparent that he knew either. When pressed, he would say "Arts" with a wave of the hand that might have indicated the liberal nature of the humanities or his own vagueness on the subject. He did take an exam in English two years before when he was at a loose end and low in funds. After the essay paper was passed out he conferred briefly with a neighbour in the exam hall and established that King Lear had a problem with his daughters. The invigilator intervened and Murf could not afford to ask for any more information about the plot. Nevertheless, he dashed off five pages, introducing the original notion that Lear was an incestuous old fart compensating for sexual inadequacies resulting from an unhappily directed lightning bolt during the storm sequence. When he ran out of facts on which to drape some more ideas, he went to the bathroom. The invigilator who accompanied him stood outside the stall as Murf flicked hastily through some previously stashed Shakespearean cribs.

Murf had no incentive to get a degree because his stepfather was willing enough to pay his fees as the price of keeping him away from the family business which he had taken over in every sense. Murf slipped easily into the role of remittance man, at least for the time being. He hated his stepfather, Fanning, who had preyed on his father's widow and business, eventually taking both over. In a way Murf's exploits helped sublimate his anger in a relatively harmless way.

But he knew that, sooner or later, there would be a showdown with his stepfather and that no quarter would be given.

In the main hall he headed for his personal radiator and, to his consternation, found it occupied.

"Hop it. Squatter's rights." He jerked his thumb and waited until the cuckoos moved off with face-saving scowls and swaggers. Settling himself against the friendly pipes, as an invalid might lower himself with grunts into a warm spa, he lit a Gold Flake and squinted through the smoke at life's pageant. Rolo made a move towards the winding staircase that led to the lecture theatres.

"Don't bother," Murf counselled. "Remember this is the last day of the Rag."

"I've got to go to this class." Rolo winced in his struggle to resist the call of the wild. "Besides, there's a roll-call at this one."

Always ready with an antidote for good intentions, Murf said, "All you have to do is put in an appearance for the roll-call, and then duck out. It's par for the course. The lecturer probably won't turn up anyway. They're all skivers and malingerers. In the meantime, I'll cadge a newspaper from the porters' office and have a leisurely read in the crapper, my usual stall, third from the left, without threat from Tim's bionic bowels. Always start the day with a clean system for there is shit aplenty in the unblessed streets. Though maybe not to-day which promises to be splendid." He paused to let the bait float for a while on the shimmering surface.

"I can't afford to flunk Mechanics again." Rolo's face was screwed up from guilty agony of choice. He ran a hand through his hair which flopped back lankly like wet straw, as split and divided as the ambivalence in his head.

"Oh, come on," Murf crooned silkily. "The Rag is an august tradition, and remember, it's for charity too. Africa depends on us. Think of the foreign missions. Remember when Ashur robbed the black- baby boxes in Hartos for more drink? Surely, it's up to us to set the record straight. If not us then who is going to step up? Who?"

"Save it for The Cart or some gullible victim you want to do a number on." There was a surprising edge to his voice and a tremor of panic. His conscience was the battle-ground where crusaders and infidels faced each other in mortal combat for his immortal soul and a B. Mech. Eng. His attention strayed suddenly across the hall to a familiar figure in a sheepskin coat. "Who is that guy? He's been following…"

Murf turned quickly aside with the head jerk of a Tango-dancer, "Stand there, Rolo. Don't let the fucker spot me."

"What's going on?" Rolo demanded petulantly. "Who the hell is that?"

"Tell you later. Clery's at one. Be there or be square." Murf sidled towards the door, keeping behind his sheepskin tail, and disappeared rapidly down the steps.

The lecturer did actually turn up and made his usual request for the people at the back of the room to put down their newspapers. After the roll-call, Rolo decided to stay. Today, consider if you will, a seconds pendulum being carried to the top of a mountain. It loses a minute a day. So far so good. What is the height of the mountain if the radius of the earth is four thousand miles? Oh God, is there no reprieve? The problems keep coming like plagues of locusts to pick my poor brain-box clean. What is the sensitivity of a false balance when the centre of gravity is adjacent to the point of support? Lord, why was I at the back of the queue when grey matter was being ladled out? Give me now my share. Am I being punished for abandoning my vocation? Call me again and I will come to the more welcoming pastures of Theology and Divinity.

Rolo approaches the lecturer after class to clarify the method of calculating the component velocities of the cattle train going north to Belfast and the canal barge going west to Sligo.

"Look up Chapter 4 in Goldstein," The lecturer grunts, disappearing in a chalk-peppered flurry of gown; he has to be on the first tee at Elm Park in twenty minutes. Statutory lecturers, like vampire bats from sun, scurry away from awkward supplementaries, to unwind after their heavy teaching load of fifty minutes a week.

No point in going to the library, Rolo thinks. 'Goldstein' would definitely be out. So much for the island of saints and scholars. Maybe Murf was right to drop out; it was exceedingly hard to opt in. Frustrations piled up in guilt-ridden layers in this academy where work connoted a plodding second-rate mind, and achievement was a dream in the bottom of a glass.

He spent some time in a deck-chair in Stephen's Green amid red and yellow snapdragons, bobbing ducks and fluttering spring dresses. Like everyone else in the park he moved from chair to chair to avoid the man rattling his satchel for ten-pence pieces, and finally came to rest under the bronze bust of James Clarence Mangan in the shade of a gazebo wreathed in vines. Stop worrying these problems to death, he thought. Forget about the exams looming up like a huge brick wall thrown across his path. Relax, and let the gentle hand of spring press a cold compress to his brow in this fragrant bower. Now, gently sneak up on that relative velocity problem and caress the solution from its murky innards. A monkey climbs a pole at four feet per second, right, and a dog is running around the pole at ten feet per second, okay. Now what is the velocity of the monkey relative to the dog? Gently … easy now … yes, it's coming … at last a glimmer…

"Tenpence please." The deckchair man rattled his satchel.

"Damn! I nearly had it then." Rolo winced painfully as the answer slipped away, the quick-silver of a half-remembered dream. "I'm leaving."

"I saw you playing musical chairs. Tenpence please."

Rolo paid up and headed for Grafton Street, tormented by ineptitude and laziness, realizing for the first time why sloth is a cardinal sin. He had been slothing regularly now for two years, although no longer taking much pleasure in it. On the contrary, he was consumed by not putting his talents – or was it groats – to better use. Now his chickens were coming home to roost, many of them with fowl-pest.

Thoughts of priesthood come bubbling up. Just the job for gentle souls of modest intellect and a yen for creature comforts. A rambling presbytery complete with house-keeper, legacies from grateful parishioners, the respect of the community. Holy orders not to be sneezed at. As an altar boy, pink and scrubbed, in surplice and soutane after a steaming bath drawn by Mom, remember the wimpled nuns during the Corpus Christi procession, admiring how I swung the thurible, saying, "Ah yes, he'll be a priest, a vicar of Christ. He has the nature." Such softly luring prospects of ease for a holy person with that sense of inclusion and cloistered safety … out of the swell of the sea…

But no, I must resist these blandishments for I am not as soft as they thought, and must find my own way in the real world.

At school, I envied that bombastic creep, Sennet, for his moxy and firm opinions about everything, all no doubt gleaned verbatim from his Dad. With cruel aptness he was nick-named "His Master's Voice." Nevertheless, he had that certitude a Dad imparts, a toe-hold in the void. While, Dadless, I had to slough my thin skin and embark upon self-conception. Murf helps though he, I fear, appearances notwithstanding, is still a little wet behind the ears. Two soggy pots bearing our Maker's thumb-prints, we languish in the kiln, awaiting the flash-point of creation. A little more heat would not go amiss, to finish our protective glaze.

The shop windows of Grafton Street, like fish tanks in a giant aquarium, caught his eye. Behind the sheen of glass, tailor's dummies stood with frozen gestures and puffed out chests, dressed to the nines with price tags dangling. In rustic delis, sausages and cheeses hung from tenterhooks in chic affectation. Further down the street the displays go further upmarket, silks and jewels and tangles of gold, all strewn, like oriental plunder on damascene plinths, while all about the escaping essences of Bewley's coffee-grinders, redolent of Rio and brown-limbed beauties, taunt the senses.

Noon-day mass-goers converging on Clarendon Street Church halt in holy tracks as I do when a squad car screeches after a rusty banger cornering on two wheels. All stand rooted in amazement like those tailor's dummies, spiky fingers spread and stretched, and quickly cross themselves on seeing, from the boot of the car, a bloodily dripping arm protrude. There is something familiar about the car. My God, it's Ashur's Mini.

What now affronts as I turn into O'Connell

Street? A huge crowd around Clery's, gazing up at a figure on the roof, teetering over the edge. A large civic guard in belted greatcoat, silver-crested buttons half smothered in his meatiness, bawling upwards through a megaphone.

"Don't jump for God's sake. We'll have someone up to you in a tick. Don't demolish yourself on the pavement. Aisey does it, like a good man."

Heedless of the guard's kind words, the figure leans over the edge to preview the plummet into eternity. Gasps ripple through the spectators and squeamish heads are jerked aside. A little woman with a wicker shopping baset tugs at the guard's greatcoat.

"Do something, you galoot, or that poor soul will come crashing down. Give me that microphone." Lunging up to grab the loud-hailer she got no further than his mid-section. But her efforts were applauded by a rising swell of guttural support.

"Restrain yourself, Missus," the guard said sternly. "We're in the middle of an emergency." He bellowed up again, "This is the Garda Síochána speaking…"

"Say 'guards' for God's sake," someone advised. "He mightn't be bilingual."

Ignoring this interruption, the guard continued, "Come on down like a good man and don't lose the run of yourself. We don't want this to get out of hand … or cause the filling of forms…" He paused to re-set his cap which was sliding off the back of his head.

"Talk him down, Godammit," a senior officer grated in his ear. "You're making a dog's dinner out of it." He slapped a leather glove against his blue-bottle pant's leg. The guard filled his lungs and aimed the loud-hailer.

"The Super himself says you should come down. It's for your own good. You could fall up there and hurt yourself."

Shading his eyes, Rolo spotted another figure on the roof, a good distance behind the jumper. He couldn't quite make him out but there was something distinctive about the way he drew languidly on his cigarette.

"No, no, no, no…" Rolo thought. "No…"

The superintendent shifted uncomfortably, "Use psychology," he hissed. "Did you learn nothing in Templemore? Tell him nothing is that bad, that it's all in his mind and he'll feel better tomorrow. Go on now." He gave the guard a sharp nudge.

"Righto, Super. Hey you up there. Nothing is that bad. It's all in his … your mind … what's next? You'll feel better tomorrow or the day after…"

The jumper was now perilously close to the edge, leaning over at an impossible angle.

"God save us," the guard improvised desperately as a collective groan escaped from the crowd. "A cup of tea will put you right, whatever ails you … a good feed … even a helicopter … There's nothing as bad as thinking makes it a whole lot worse … Jasus, he's coming down in pieces…" A bit of cloth resembling a sleeve fluttered down, followed by a hand that bounced off a window-sill before hitting the ground.

"Mother of God," the little woman clutched her throat. "I'm fainting."

"He's disintegrating!" someone shouted.

Rolo covered his mouth not knowing whether to laugh or cry, for one thing was certain, there would be repercussions.

The guard jammed the loud-hailer to his mouth and thundered, "Pull yourself together, man. We have pills and medicine down here. Don't lose the head … Aw, Jaysus, he has."

The plastic head spun as it plummeted down in a smooth arc, bounced off a double-decker bus and rolled on to the pavement. Then the headless trunk of the dummy came crashing down through the blue air, trailing a long rope behind it.

The guard was on the squad-car radio, "Send an ambulance. He took a bad fall…"

The Super's gloved hand descended on his neck. "It's a prank, you eejit." He wrenched the mouth-piece away from him and began to muster his troops for an assault on Clery's emporium.

Rolo limped furiously across the street and slipped in through a side entrance of Clery's. He took the service lift, and just before the doors closed he saw the guards assemble in force on the ground floor. Hopping on his good leg, as if to make the lift go faster, he had no thoughts of claustrophobia, or of that pot-holing accident many years ago.

Murf had just got off the spiral staircase leading from the roof and was grinding a Gold Flake butt underfoot when Rolo jumped out of the lift.

"Going down?"

"Christ, you've done it now," Rolo blurted. "Don't use the lift. There are guards all over the place."

"All right," Murf agreed. "We'll lose ourselves somewhere in the store."

Clattering down the nearest fire stairs, they found themselves, like bandits seeking sanctuary in a convent, on the Ladies fashion floor. It was a tranquil, cloistered place where browsers idly perused the lingerie on display, turning over a label here, a price tag there, holding up diaphanous articles against their persons, smiling and chatting in a timeless way with assistants who wore pencils in their meringue coiffures.

Rolo peered frantically around. "We don't exactly blend in here … Shit, there they are…" He grabbed Murf's sleeve.

"He's one of them," The Super called out to his men. "I saw him on the roof. Get him."

The guard, desperate to prove himself, lumbered through racks of clothing, careering off display stands and show cases. In the undergarment section he came to grief as stacked boxes of corsets, girdles and figure-moulding devices toppled all around him. Stays popped and elastic snapped; a surgical stocking draped itself around his neck. As he threshed about, women scattered in all directions.

"Get moving," the Super urged him on.

Floundering in whalebone, nylon and polyester, the guard gasped, "I'm … implicated in elastic stuff, Sir, but I'll get 'em." Nearby, a scantily clad lady cowered in pink baby dolls. "Excuse me, Miss ….I didn't see anything ..."

Murf and Rolo ducked into a changing room, causing a sudden exodus of ladies in various stages of undress. The guards converged on the cubicle.

"We're trapped in here." Rolo looked desperately around for a rear exit, a disguise, anything. His gangly frame twitched with an irresistible urge to be elsewhere.

Outside, the guards formed themselves into a circle, a formation known as 'the ring of steel'.

"Let them get out of this," the Super said with grim satisfaction.

"We could lob in some tear gas, Sir." The large guard tried to demonstrate his ability to think clearly in a crisis.

"Don't be a bloody fool," the Super replied, grasping his Sam Brown belt to restrain himself.

Peering through a curtain, Rolo saw the phalanx move closer in a manoeuvre known to the force as 'tightening the ring of steel'.

"How's the house?" Murf asked nonchalantly.

"It's no joke," Rolo said miserably. "They're moving in. It's over." He sat down on a footstool, covering his head like a repentant chimp.

"We've had some good times together," Murf said. "No regrets?"

"Shut up. We're in deep shit."

"Well, they're not taking me alive … On a count of three … Go!"

They burst through the curtains, feinting left and right, zig-zagging through the millinery department towards the relative safety of Rainwear – for the guards were still heavily concentrated in Underwear. Murf hurdled a hat stand and sent a cheval mirror crashing to the floor. Rolo followed in the slip stream trailing his bad leg. Two guards launched flying tackles, missed, and embraced each other with expressions of surprise. Rolo vaulted over them. The ring of steel dissipated in a move known to the force as 'the ring of smoke'.

Regrouping as best they could, the force surged on in hot pursuit as Murf and Rolo burst into the restaurant famed for steak-and-kidney pud. Startled diners stopped in mid-chew and sawed the air with cutlery. With dander up, the large guard sent a waiter flying and the tray went into orbit around the room, raining kidneys. Rolo's bad leg caught in a serving trolley. Brandy sloshed into a pan of crêpes and flames leapt up to singe the ceiling. Murf shouted "Fire!" and diners stampeded for the door. Rolo was knocked over in the scramble for survival and a free lunch, and Murf tried to drag him through the swing door to the kitchen. They were finally cornered near the huge tureen of *potage du jour* – asparagus or maybe leek – and manacled.

They waited in the College Green Barracks while the duty Sergeant wrapped up the case – of a stolen bicycle – he was working on.

"You're sure about the brake levers?"

"Yes, the two finger kind on the dropped handlebars." He studied the latest identi-kit picture made up by the Sergeant. "There's something still not quite right about this picture … I've got it … There's no chain guard." He stepped back from the counter hatch with a triumphant hop.

The duty Sergeant was dumbfounded. "Sure, a chain guard is a standard feature on the Raleigh semi-sports model."

"Ah, it got broke and I had to take it off."

The Sergeant adjusted the celluloid identi-kit and showed the new picture to the owner.

"That's it to a tee! That's the spit of me bike." The owner was as pleased as if the bike had already been recovered and returned to him in pristine condition.

"Ah Myles," Murf murmured under his breath, "You should be living at this hour." He leant back against the wall.

His and Rolo's statements were taken in triplicate in a bilious green room. Rubbing wrists to ease the legacy of handcuffs, they heard a familiar voice from the room next door.

"Ashur, it was just a prank. For charity you know."

The door burst open to admit the large guard, who, without preamble of any sort, went straight for Murf and planted a haymaker on his chin. "Make a fool of me in front of the Super, will you?"

Murf picked himself up. "You don't need any help from me." He cried out and doubled up as a knee rammed into his groin.

The Sergeant who had just come in grinned indulgently and said, "You're a terrible man, Paudge."

"You … can't do this…!" Rolo protested.

"Do you want the other knee in the spondulicks?" Paudge bore down on him with menacing, lowered head.

"I … have a lame leg," Rolo was suddenly scared. There was something sinister about the way these almost lovable duffers could turn so brutal, like innocent children pulling the wings off insects. They were disquietingly not true to form. He had read somewhere about a bull goring a matador to death because the bull had bad sight and couldn't follow the cape. Paudge had the same kind of freakish wrong-headedness.

"A lame leg is it?" Paudge repeated. "Then shut your mouth or I'll give you the match for it."

Murf felt behind him for a chair to sit on, but it was kicked away by Paudge's large boot. He crashed to the stone floor. Rolo knelt beside him. "I want … to speak to … the US Consul…"

"Oh, he's tied up, "the Sergeant said, "with the Cold War."

Other guards, hearing the commotion, had come in to see the fun. They stood around grinning, scratching bellies and necks through open tunics. There was an overpowering sense of meatiness in this stone abattoir, huge carcases of beef swaying lazily on hooks. Rolo felt queasy in the pit of his concave stomach as he propped Murf against the wall on which hung truncheons, handcuffs and pictures of passing-out parades in Templemore, the cradle of the force. Muted sounds of drunken roaring came up from the cells, echoing along the stone passages of this fortress. Somewhere in the basement an old pro screeched, "They're interferin' with me again." Ashur, in the next room, had fallen quiet for the moment.

The Sergeant logged his ledger with painstaking accuracy, his tongue like a slab of raw sirloin between his teeth. Supported by Rolo and with blood trickling from his face, Murf answered questions in a thick voice. It was sad to see him chastened so. Not even he, with all his wiles, could have anticipated the perverseness of the force. Like the blind bull's matador, he was at the mercy of truly unpredictable events; no brilliant pass of cape or dandy feint could save him now.

From what could be heard next door, Ashur, dripping unction, was doing rather better.

"Ashur, 'twas just a last fling, Guards … before I start on the doctoring … I'll be at your beck and call…" He was excelling himself, and it was easy to imagine his puppet's peg nose quivering with Gombeen sincerity. "Well, let me have a look at your back, Guard ... Yes ... yes ... Ashur, that would be the strain and tension of the responsible job you do ... Bed rest for a week and hot toddies would put you right ... If you pass me a piece of paper I'll give you a cert for a week off work ... No, better not take any chances with a ventricular hypothesis like that, a fortnight..." This was followed by sounds of boots scuffling and reams of paper being pushed across the table.

Sensing that finesse buttered no parsnips here, Murf, as evidenced by a jutting under-lip, was growing Bolshie. The Sergeant, looking up from yet another form, snarled, "Your address? I won't ask you again."

"Seasca cúig..." Murf began, but a knuckled back-hander from Paudge sent him reeling across the room.

"That was one of your best," the Sergeant congratulated him. "But go aisey now. He's entitled to answer in the official language of the State. There's a circular on the use of Gaelic above in the day room."

"But we've none of them strokes and dots on the typewriter," Paudge pointed out. He flicked through a file that was just handed to him by a young guard. "He's got a record. Drunk in charge of a motorbike and speeding in Stephen's Green. Boys, this is great news."

"It wasn't proved," the young guard said. "He refused the blood test. Said he was a haemophiliac, a bleeder."

"Oh a smart little bollix, a messer of the first order. He must think he's Brendan Behan or someone." He advanced on Murf and pushed him around again. Rolo looked on helplessly as Murf took his lumps like a trooper.

"Now, are you going to answer the Sergeant in the Queen's English or do you want another rap in the molecules?"

Rolo felt faint; this couldn't be happening just across the road from the Triune Poly and the Book of Kells. What had happened the island of saints and scholars? Answer came there none. Rolo eventually gave in, divulging addresses and phone numbers, singing, as they say, like the Vienna Boys' Choir.

The Sergeant pored over the information for a long while in some bewilderment, then raised his head slowly. "Paudge, I think he's tryin' to give us a bum steer. He says his father's name is Robert Fanning. Sure, it couldn't be Fanning if he's called Murphy."

"Well, you little gobshite," Paudge grated. "We'll have to teach you a real lesson." He stalked him around the room, lunging and grabbing. "Oh yes, boy, we'll have to settle your hash for once and for all." One of his haymakers caught Murf on the side of the head and knocked him against the wall.

"Stop!" Rolo shouted, limping forward to intercept the lumbering nemesis. "It's his *stepfather*, his *stepfather*…"

"Stepfather me arse." Paudge didn't want to be foiled.

"My own sentiments exactly," Murf croaked from the other side of the table.

"Check it out!" Rolo yelled. "You have the number. For Christ's sake, check it out." He was scared of more fisticuffs, sickened by that grinning baboon and by Murf's obstreperous carry-on. The Book of Kells just across the road ... Insanity drove him mad. He experienced the sudden battle-frenzy of Cuchulainn and Achilles. "Just pick up the fucking phone and call him, you dumb bastards!" It was the guards' turn to be nonplussed by this abrupt change of character. It was the element of shock that saved him, that and the trembling that soon replaced the battle-frenzy – a series of shudders they thought might be the onset of hysteria.

The Sergeant dialled the phone, keeping a weather eye on him, not wanting a nervous breakdown on his watch. While waiting for a connection, he said to Paudge, "This must be Fanning of Fanning's Builders' Providers, the lumber baron of the south-east."

"Bastard, you mean," Murf said half-aloud.

The Sergeant got through, and after some preliminaries, said, "Yes, he is in trouble again ... Yeah, disturbing the peace ... I'm afraid we'll have to throw the book at him..." At that moment something strange happened; the Sergeant seemed to have some kind of epiphany or was caught in a fairy-blast. His eyes grew round and the colour drained from his face, realizing the extent of Fanning's political connections. "We can fix it … if you like … it wouldn't be a problem, Sir … No? … No? … You're sure? … And you won't be putting up bail? I see … Very good, Sir … He did resist arrest but he's quietened down now … Very good, Sir. Thank you very much. Good luck to you now, Sir."

The obvious lack of parental concern brought a benighted smile to Paudge's broad features. For a while he had expected a different outcome but it worked out well in the end and the prey was nicely separated from the pack, cornered and alone.

Imagining Fanning's side of the conversation, Murf groaned, "Rotten shit."

"That's no way to talk about your oul fella." Paudge hit him, almost playfully, with a big bear-paw. Murf fell over again, his strength gone, will to resist ebbing fast.

"Leave him alone," Rolo cried in a breaking voice. "I demand to speak to … the US Consul…"

"You can fuck off with your Consul."

"Right," The Sergeant said slapping the ledger shut and pulling a sheet off the organ-like typewriter. "I've got all the particulars. Now empty your pockets."

"You can't arrest Rolo," Murf said in a daze. "He did nothing."

"We're not arresting anyone yet," the Sergeant explained. "Just holding you until the court hearing is arranged. Less paper work that way."

Paudge gave Murf one more punch 'for luck',

and made a threatening dart at Rolo.

Murf peed in a bucket in the corner of the cell, appraising his bruised balls. A mouse darted brazenly between his legs and disappeared under one of the bunks which hung on chains fastened to the painted brick wall.

"How are you feeling?" Rolo asked him.

"I'll live, no thanks to that fat shit, Paudge."

"I never imagined the guards would be so rough." Rolo shook his head from side to side, still badly scared.

"They'd have done whatever Fanning asked … but he didn't ask. Just hung me out to dry."

"Why is that?" Rolo inquired.

"It's no mystery why he hates me." Murf said, "But why he has the guards in his pocket, I don't know for sure. I have a theory. But I haven't figured it out yet. Listen, why don't you call a lawyer? You shouldn't be here."

"Well, it's no worse here than the library." He attempted a lopsided grin of the skin-deep variety. "In fact," he added, glancing at the graffiti, "there's more to read here."

They spent some time perusing the filthy Limericks and drawings engraved on the painted brickwork but failed to summon a laugh.

"I see Jimmy Stapleton spent a night here," Murf observed. "That must've been the night he borrowed the Chaplain's car."

"Are you going to put your John Hancock there?"

"No. Why do you ask?" Murf looked at him closely.

"I just … thought…" Rolo finished with a shrug. He was never sure to what extent Murf liked to cultivate his image. He was something of a poseur – but wasn't everyone? "Why did you do it anyway, the dummy and all that? I mean, it was funny. It was," he repeated, trying to tone down any implied criticism. "But, what I mean is … well … where is the percentage?" This was dangerous water; they both knew it. Murf gave the only answer possible, the ostensible one.

"It was a bet. That I couldn't gum up the traffic in O'Connell Street for an hour. Twenty quid. And I won. All right?"

"And that was the point of the exercise?" Rolo persisted. "Twenty quid."

"No. The point is that there is no point."

A rat-faced neighbour in the adjoining cell made his presence felt by rattling the bars. He told them they'd have to be released soon when they fixed a trial date. He was in a worse fix, having been done for burglary. It was a very poor state of affairs when the IRA could get away with murder while ordinary criminals like him were being banged up for trying to feed their families.

"It's tough all around," Murf lay on the lower bunk and instantly fell asleep in a foetal position, cradling his tender privates.

They were released a couple of hours later and signed for their things. The Sergeant handed Murf the summons to appear in court. "Court Number Four, tomorrow at three p.m. sharp." He looked sternly at Rolo. "There's no charge against you but you should keep better company. Now, be off, the pair of you." It all seemed official and almost avuncular, in line with the popular image of the guards, but completely at odds with the reality behind closed doors.

Blinking in the still strong sunlight of College Green, two lifers sprung from dungeons dark and deep grope their way by the high green railings of the Triune Poly, one trailing a leg, the other crouched protectively over a tender mid-section.

"You should see a doctor," Rolo said limping on large splayed feet and scrabbling in the tin of Old Holborn for the makings of a smoke.

"I'm all right." Murf tried to straighten up an inch at a time. Double-decker buses thundered around the huge rib-cage of the Bank of Ireland, loaded with commuters heading home early for the weekend. Intrepid cyclists wove their way through long lines of cars revving angrily at traffic lights. Gagging and spluttering, the city was voiding its system of fur balls and foreign bodies for the coming day of rest. Buskers and pavement artists stored tin whistles and chalk, and counted the day's takings. Passing by the pigeon-spattered bronzes of Moore, Burke and Goldsmith, Rolo had a brainstorm.

"Didn't Gobnait say she was on casualty this

week?"

Murf paused and brightened, and creaked himself up another notch or two. "Now, there's a thought…"

More particulars were taken down at the hospital where Murf described his malady as general discomfort resulting from a tumble off a bicycle.

"Good God, what are you doing here?" Gobnait looked good in her white starched uniform with Vincent's pin, and a little pert cap nesting in her curls. "My immediate diagnosis is that you've been dragged through a hedge backwards."

"It was the only way I could get to see you." He looked her up and down. "I like the uniform. It leaves Running Water's buckskins in the shade."

"Hmm." She looked at the form that had just been completed and said to the Admissions Sister, "It's all right, Margaret, I'll take care of this patient." She led Murf to a curtained cubicle that resembled a palm-reader's booth at a carnival, and invited him formally, in front of pews of casualties, to step inside.

"Do I have to?" He threw a wink at Rolo as he went in.

Gobnait felt his bruised nose with cool fingers, her breath warm on his cheek, and looked up each nostril with a pencil torch. "You did complain of sensitive nasal passages on a previous occasion."

"I did?"

"Oh yes."

"The old hooter is not my best feature," he mumbled as their warm breath mingled and formed a layer of condensation on the torch's lens, rendering it useless.

"Well, it's not broken," she said. She wondered what had happened to him but somehow this was not the time to ask.

"There's more." His arms slipped around her neat starched waist.

"There's more?"

"Yes."

"Where?" Her breath was coming faster.

"It's a little embarrassing."

"Maybe I'd better get the doctor?" She knew why she was whispering, but did he? Through the frosted glass window set high in the wall, a fading sun bronzed the whiteness of the cubicle, gilding a cherished fantasy. Her lips brushed his cheek.

"I don't need a doctor."

"Well I am a nurse." Her lips now hovered over his.

"Perhaps, you could do … an exploratory?" The timid request, sent on a hushed wing of prayer, was granted.

"That would seem to be indicated."

"I'm glad you concur, Nurse."

"All right. Drop 'em."

Murf stepped out of his trousers with alacrity, flinging them athwart the curtain rail, and presented himself for inspection. Gobnait's tongue slid between her lips.

"They look … tender. Is there … much pain?" Her voice, murmurously low, was distanced from her thoughts.

"Hard to say just now … perhaps palpation … might be indicated." He swallowed hard.

"A good suggestion…" Her face flushed at the excitement of this in her place of work, almost in full view, just a curtain between them and the whole casualty ward. And the matron not far away. She felt a pang of pure risk. The devil high in her, as she cradled his balls with a soft curious hand.

"Does it hurt … here … here … Ah, there. You poor thing … and such a sore swelling…" Her hands settled into a more deliberate engripment, and performed an effleurage upon the rude protuberance. He grappled with her uniform until it slid off her shiny body to the polished floor, half-standing in its starchy crumplement. She straddled him on the examining couch and shinnied up his trunk until, firm in her mount, she gave from her everted mouth, that long slow sigh of commencement. The tempo quickened with racking shudders, helpless groans, eyes fluttering backwards to some lost world of pleasure in this heated, inestimable gamble of the flesh. His feet, overhanging the examining couch, threshed the curtains of the cubicle.

Outside, Rolo sat in a pew surrounded by the hastily bandaged casualties of building site and factory floor, trying to ignore the breathless song of consummation, hoping in fact that the ground would open up and swallow him.

"The doctor must be on his way," a man with his arm in a sling opined. "About bloody time too."

"I beg your pardon?"

"Didn't you hear him shouting? Rude bastard, keeps us waiting and then starts shouting."

"I didn't hear anything," Rolo lied desperately, squirming in the pew. The curtains were fluttering so badly now they could come down any second, and the tortured sounds of copulation were reaching fever pitch.

"Are you deaf or what?"

"No, but … these old buildings … acoustics play tricks…" Rolo kneaded his hands so hard together that little particles of rolled dirt formed in the lifelines. Consummation was devoutly to be wished. Please God, make it fast, none of this macho lingering.

"Don't tell me about acoustics. I've been renovating the bleeding Abbey Theatre for the last…"

"It must be most interesting work. Did you put in baffle pipes…?

"There's something funny going on." He rubber-necked around the ward and to Rolo's horror, pointed a triumphant finger at the cubicle. "In there."

"Where?"

"Are you blind as well as deaf? That cubicle there." He stretched out his good arm again and pointed with stabbing gestures.

"Oh there? That's a serious case, I believe." Conscious of listening ears in the pews behind, he had to elaborate. "Very rare, a pendulum isochronism … I believe. They have to use a Kater's fulcrum … in cases like that … Very noisy…"

"It sounds like a stomach pump to me."

"It could be that," Rolo agreed with alacrity and great relief. "They sometimes use a stomach pump in these cases. Are you a medical man yourself?"

A finger tapped him on the shoulder. He turned carefully around and looked into the purple face of a wino who ventured his opinion. "That's no stomach pump, and I should know."

"Thank you." Thank you, Lord, for this expert help and advice when it is least needed. Maybe you could use a small portion of Your omnipotence to look in on the library one day and by miraculous intervention persuade them to lend out a book or two. Sorry, don't mean that, just a feeble joke in this vale of tears in my extremity. Could You at least hasten Murf's extremity or create some diversion?

Renewed in faith, Rolo asked, "Do you know by any chance who won the three-thirty at Leopardstown today?" No reaction from these punters who are now riveted on the noisy dancing curtains in the corner. What more can I do? Lead them in community singing? "Fa-ith of our fathers … living still, in spite … of dungeon, fire and sword…" The broken-armed man dug him in the ribs.

"God help that poor fella in there. The pain must be something cruel."

"Yes, it is. They don't give an anaesthetic in these cases." Thank you, God, for the innocence of these men who prefer a pint of stout to the other.

"What are those yelps?" Anxious-eyed, the man hopped up and down in sympathetic suffering. "They're killing him. I'm getting out of here!" He darted out of the pew and shot through the swing doors. Others followed in a bandage-trailing exodus from the casualty ward. Only the wino remained, swigging from a bottle of Red Biddy, feeling no pain.

"Where are all you people going? Get back here at once!" Oh God, the Matron. The jig will soon be up with this white behemoth on the rampage.

She summoned a student nurse to her presence and grilled her. "What is going on in there? And why are all those patients leaving?" Without waiting for an answer from the timid trainee, she turned and directed her luminous bulk towards the rocking cubicle.

Seized with panic, Rolo jumped to his feet, not knowing what to do. There was no time for subtlety. He had to interrupt her march. If he could only reach one of the fallen crutches … No time … In desperation he hurled himself at the Matron's feet and locked his hands around her ankles. His last thought was that he should have been a priest.

"God above, man. This is no time for a seizure." She bent over him slapping his face. "Please extricate me. I'm on my rounds."

He lay there with a death's grip on her stalwart ankles, his cheek resting on a huge white brogue, and eventually opened his eyes when he surmised a reasonable tranquillity in that special area of the ward. "Where am I?" he asked in a small voice. "Did I faint again, Mother?"

"What's the matter with you?" Matron grabbed him by the scruff of the neck and stood him upright on liquorice legs.

"Just a phobia…" He began, when to his undying relief, he saw Nurse Gobnait emerge from behind the curtain, smoothing her uniform.

"Good evening, Matron."

"What's going on in there?" Matron fixed her with a gimlet eye.

"I was … em … taking a patient's vital signs," Gobnait said lightly.

"Let me see." Freed from her shackles she surged like an albino whale towards the cubicle and barged in. Gobnait squeezed Rolo's hand in hope, and they stayed rooted until Matron re-emerged, the instruments around her neck dangling over the great cliff of bosom.

"Nurse, you should know that in thirty years in this hospital I have not witnessed anything like this." She stood with her large brogues, like canal barges, spread far apart. It was only the red flush of her face that distinguished her from an Alp. Oh, no, Rolo thought, offering up a silent prayer for Gobnait who bowed her head waiting for the blow to fall.

"This," Matron continued, "is the most extraordinary phenomenon I have come across, and in casualty of all places. What have you got to say about it?"

"I … I'm not sure exactly." Gobnait stared at the polished floor ruminating on the high price of fantasy, knowing the truth of the old Latin tag, *"Post coitum animal triste est."* Rolo racked his brain for some excuse. Come out, Murf, you bastard, we need you in this hour of need.

"You should have reported this immediately," Matron said with only a shimmer of rebuke.

"I … what?" Gobnait looked up in confusion, the white cap still somewhat askew in its nest of loosened curls. Matron pointed to the cubicle with a plump fore-finger.

"That young man in there has no visible pathology. Agreed?"

"Agreed … I think."

"And yet his blood pressure is 200 over 120."

"It is? Yes, of course, it is." She kicked Rolo on his good ankle.

"And," Matron continued, intoxicated by her findings, "His pulse is close to 160 per minute. This is unprecedented. What a metabolism!"

"I did think he was hyper-active," Gobnait said, sailing close to the wind, too close for Rolo who was just beginning to breathe again.

"Well, my dear, don't you see? This is one for

the books. Bleep Dr. Mahony immediately. He is researching abnormal endocrinology."

Murf finally appeared, pulling on his jacket and rummaging in the pockets for a packet of Gold Flake which he offered around before plucking one out for himself.

"I feel fine now, Nurse. Thank you kindly."

Too excited to tick him off for smoking in the ward, Matron turned to Rolo as if he might prove to be another medical find. "You may well have the same symptoms. Do you fall down often?"

"Just every now and again."

"Come with me. I want to check your signs. He was sucked helplessly into the vortex of her white force-field, and would have given a gallon of blood had she asked. But Murf intervened.

"We're leaving now. Thank you."

Matron rounded on him, her eyes like blancmanges not fully set, bulging with incredulity.

"You can't leave now. We've just bleeped Dr. Mahony."

"Well, unbleep him then."

"You can't unbleep a doctor." She was offended and puzzled by the suggestion. Her loyalty towards doctors knew no bounds; patients were an awkward necessity for playing hospitals. Her doctors were all that mattered.

"Well, I'm off now." Murf threw a covert look at Gobnait who grinned in recognition of the coded glance. "Thanks for the treatment, Nurse. I'm a new man."

"You can't discharge yourself." Matron was horror-stricken at the thought of this medical phenomenon slipping through her fingers, and not making himself available for experimentation to Dr. Mahony. It also seemed unconscionable that such a rude lout should be the possessor of that remarkable metabolism.

"I can discharge myself," Murf said, "though it's better with two. Good evening." She stood there, a beached leviathan, mouthing.

Buses squished by on the wet street gleaming like black PVC, slashed here and there by orange headlights, pavements mottled with sodden leaves. Lights went on in terraced houses, yellow rectangular openings in brickwork that soaked rain into its pores and turned raw umber. Drenched trees along the canal had the colour and hapless texture of boiled spinach. Pubs filled up for the evening, with sounds of greeting, settling in, scrapes of stool and clinks of glass. "All right so, another pint. You'd be drowned out there in that downpour."

It had been, as Rolo used to say at the end of his school essays, an eventful day. What would Mom say if she heard he had been in a cell? Maybe he should let it slip out in a letter, to prove how stretched now are those apron strings as he, on his own two feet, takes the rough with the smooth in this blustering town, and how he is forging his own little soul on that Joycean anvil. But still, another day wasted because it was a consequence of the day before, which was also wasted and gone up in smoke.

Murf had his own thoughts which, oddly, did not focus on Paudge, but on that infinitely more evil genius, Robert Fanning, who had conned his gentle Dad and finally, as had always been his intention, taken over the family business, lock, stock and barrel. Well, there was one chattel which didn't come with the deal. Even if Murf's mother had fallen under Fanning's spell, his sister, Maura, had not and she kept Murf posted on developments. Look out, Steppop, your number will be called soon. But first things first. Have one's day in court and win.

Their footsteps pointed towards Northbrook Square and The Cart in *loco parentis*.

"Sharks die if they stop swimming against the tide."
—The Present Writer

CHAPTER 3

DWARFED BY THE cupola of the Four Courts, they stood in the vaulted universe, called to account for earthly sins, feeling small and dirty peering up under this huge hooped skirt of Justitia.

Among the officers of court, fat barristers, and tipstaffs who flit about the corridors that radiate from this grand circle, one stands out in his bulk and lethargy: Paudge, leaning against a pillar, nursing a paper coffee cup in a ham-hock fist. From behind the doors of Court number four came an occasional buzz of spectator reaction, generally of a disapproving kind. It was like waiting outside a football ground hearing the collective intake of breath as a goal is missed, a pass fumbled.

A couple of barristers passed close, deep in negotiation, like two farmers at a fair. They heard one of them say, "Oh forget the rights and wrongs of it, how much does your fucking client want?" The other one said, "Make me an offer and, remember, I know the fucking judge."

Murf straightened the stringy tie he'd put on for the occasion.

"Let's go in and meet our fate."

"We're not up yet. There's still time," Rolo said edgily.

"I want to read the room."

They slipped into a pew near the back of the public gallery to hear Judge Prendergast in session. As at mass, a familiar though intimidating sense of liturgical tradition drifted off the polished wood, grave oak bench, and spike-railed dock.

A wild-eyed itinerant stood in the dock, accused of assault and battery. He was not sure what was going on in the grainy courtroom full of posturing and empty words, and would have much preferred to have had a few wallops from the guards and an order to move on. Judge Prendergast took each ball early on the rise and, though slow and ponderous in his returns, showed a penchant for puncturing egos.

"So, in summation," he said as the clock struck eleven, "the prosecution claims the attack was unprovoked and that the defendant was polluted." He looked down sternly at his audience. "By that, let the record show, is meant intoxicated."

"Footless, Your Honour," the prosecution put in helpfully.

The judge clutched the front of the bench and bent menacingly towards him.

"You, Sir, have had your opportunity to browbeat the jury, a jury which has taken you two hours to select. Please do not now intrude upon my summation."

"Obliged, Your Honour. Merely amplifying…"

the irrepressible counsel responded.

"Well don't! Not in my court!"

Having been sentenced to the maximum allowable by law, the dazed itinerant was led down through a trap-door in the dock to the underground passage that connected the courts to the Bridewell Prison.

"That judge is a tough old goat," Rolo whispered uneasily. The sight of the prisoner sinking through the floor of the dock had the potential for nightmares and the recollection of pot-holing disasters.

"Pompous twit, though," Murf said. "*My* court. *My* summation. He likes to play God. Maybe I can use that. Let's slip out before the tumbril comes for me."

In the bathroom, Murf produced from an inside pocket a satchel of Helena Rubenstein make-up and started to apply dark mascara under his left eye.

"Good old Gobnait," he crooned, puckering into the mirror. "Just muddy up the old physog a little bit. Hmmm …some rouge for the mandible perhaps and a ball or two of cotton wool for the gob." He hummed as he worked, standing back periodically to get perspective on the total effect.

"No, no … This isn't going to work," Rolo pleaded with him, hopping from foot to foot. "It's too obvious. You'll go down." He had an image of Murf sinking through the frightening trap-door of the dock, never to be seen in daylight again.

Murf grinned crookedly, looking punchy

already. "It's worth a try. His Honour is half blind. Did you see the way he had to peer at the papers in front of him? And with any luck Paudge will get his pantaloons in a twist." He groped through the make-up kit, fished out an eyebrow pencil and proceeded to blacken out two front teeth.

"Not two," Rolo groaned. "That's overkill."

"Stop worrying. Here, put this bag in your pocket and get out of here while I visit the water closet for the last time as a free man. Let me know exactly when I'm called. Exactly."

Sitting in the stall in that heightened sober moment before a major play, Murf knew he had to win this one. There was much at stake. Fanning would like to see him swing and so pluck a thorn from his side. A criminal record would be grist to Fanning's mill, give him the opportunity to say in all sincerity, 'We gave Murf every chance even though I told you it would do no good.' And with much head-shaking and bleating about black sheep, ease his step-son out forever from the family circle. No, not this time, Fanning, not ever.

Dust dislodged by the previous case descended slowly to the cracked parquet floor from whence it had come. Judge Prendergast, still presiding, pored over a new sheaf of notes and continued to do so after Murf was ushered into the dock to stand on the bolted trap-door, a palpable reminder of the gallows.

Guard Paudge who was rehearsing his evidence, looked up from his notes and went slack-jawed on seeing the contusions glow and glisten on Murf's countenance, already creased with an expression of holy forgiveness for those who knew not what they did. Paudge's eyes narrowed to slits and he made a sudden move towards a uniformed colleague who guarded the dock. But it was too late. The judge who had begun to read out the charge noticed the unseated bulk cluttering up his courtroom.

"Guard, I take it you are the arresting officer in this case. If so would you please sit down. We are not playing the National Anthem." Turning towards Murf, he said, "You may opt for a jury if you wish." His tone indicated that he regarded a jury as a most disagreeable form of tokenism and a slur upon his own ability to judge.

"No thank you, your Honour. I … don't want to … cause any inconvenience…"

"Very well." The judge jotted something down. "You heard the charge. How do you plead?"

"Guilty, I'm afraid." His whisper was made more plaintive by a slight lisp caused by the wad of cotton wool in his jaw – an unexpected bonus.

"I'm sorry. You'll have to speak up." The judge cupped a hand behind his ear and craned forward. My God, Murf thought in alarm, what if he's deaf as well? Maybe, like Paudge, he's so bereft of faculties he can't be manipulated. The one lock that bested the great Houdini was a broken one. The nightmare of the irrational was upon him.

"I'm guilty as charged, Your Honour," Murf said loudly. "But … I meant no harm." It was difficult to do the Uriah Heap bit *fortissimo*. All his delicate nuances would be missed.

"This is a very serious charge," the judge said, still not showing any sign that he heard him. Was it conceivable that he had been dispensing justice for twenty years without ever having heard a word of mitigation, a special plea, a choked sob? Murf was rapidly losing confidence. It was like playing Hamlet to a house of rugby supporters.

"…disturbing the peace," the judge droned on, scanning his script, "by throwing a tailor's dummy off the roof of a city centre emporium, terrifying citizens, causing guards, doctors, Samaritans – all of them hard-pressed, concerned people – to rush about on a fool's errand. What if someone had died of a heart-attack? The charge would be manslaughter then. Do you follow me?" The thin pompous wimp, not unlike Crowley, continued to pontificate from lips that skirmished under the shade of an aubergine nose, like two worms mating.

"Yes, Sir." Murf gouged his fists remorsefully into his eye sockets, taking care not to smear the mascara, although he wondered if his Honour could see anything more than a blur. He was reminded again of the matador gored by a half-blind bull. If the bull had been sound in wind and limb, the matador would have been able to manipulate him with fancy passes of the cape, and saved his family jewels.

"What are you studying?"

"Divinity." Murf shook his head with even

greater remorse since a divinity student should have known better.

"Good Heavens. In my time, Divinity students didn't take part in the Rag. This is an appalling sign of the times. Guard, I am ready to hear your evidence."

Licking his thumb, Paudge flicked through his notebook and began, "Your Honour, the tailor's dummy was abducted from F.X. Kelly's drapers in Grafton Street. Then it was attired in apparel for the purpose of making it resemble a human being. Then the whole caboosh was dangled over the roof of Clery's to make the onlookers think an act of dangerous suicide was being perpetrated…"

"I think I understand that much, Guard. Was there much damage to property?"

Well, Your Honour, the dummy plus the three-piece serge suit plus the shirt and boots came to £128 and fifty pence. There was more damage done in Clery's…" He paused to flick a few pages of the notebook. "The damage to Ladies' innerwear and corsetry came to £102." He looked up from his notebook. "A Beangarda checked that out."

"Is that it?" the judge asked.

"Well then, there were helpings of steak-and-kidney pie knocked over, and…"

The judge held up a hand and addressed the defendant. "What charity is the Rag supporting this year?"

Although not normally silenced by ignorance, Murf hesitated, giving Rolo who cowered in the gallery, a very bad moment.

"Foreign missions," he said at last. "And the Black Babies," he added.

Paudge, looking more confident now, rebutted this, saying that no monies had or were being collected for any known charity and that the 'Black Babies' fund was been wound up because the name gave offence. In his opinion there was no excuse at all for the upset caused to hundreds of innocent victims. He scored heavily and was pleased to see his Super dropping into the courtroom.

From his vantage point on the bench the judge looked pinched and solemn like an old weather-cock feeling in his scraggy wattles the first frosts of winter.

"I agree with the guard," he snorted. "This action was distinctly unamusing and was designed for no other purpose than to disrupt the populace going about their daily business. I would not dignify it by the term 'prank'. It was a dangerous and misguided act directed against the citizenry."

Holy Christ, Murf thought, he's going to put on the black cap soon. Can he not see my lumps and bumps? I must project more for this myopic fart although it goes against my subtle grain. A lot more ham would seem to be required. With a strangled cry, he slumped in the dock and grabbed the spiked rail to support himself.

"Are you feeling all right?" At last he had the attention of the bench.

"Yes, your ... Honour..." He grimaced to

show the missing teeth and distend further his swollen jaw. The judge peered over his glasses.

"You don't look very well."

"It's nothing … Sir … just a little … concussion."

"A what?"

"Concussion, Sir." To add plausibility he turned his eyes and squinted at the clerk of the court who sat four feet below the learned judge. "But I … deserved it…"

"Deserved what?"

"The guards were only … doing their duty … I deserved everything … I got."

The judge leant out over the edge of the bench. "Are you saying they punished you in some way? Is that what you are suggesting?"

Murf looked at Paudge and the Super, and hung his head. The die was cast now. He felt exhilaration spurt into him – his meat and drink. Racing drivers could keep their hair-pin bends, sky-divers their 'chutes, this knife-edge was his.

"I don't hold it against the guards … your Honour … They had no choice…" He spread his hands in a gesture of cosmic understanding. "They said … the courts were too … what's the word … lenient. I suppose they have to … take the law into their own hands … sometimes…"

Rolo, who had already bitten the nails of his left hand down to the bone, began to start on the right, as the judge addressed the arresting officer.

"Guard, is this correct. Did you lay hands on the defendant while he was in custody?"

Like a coal tip beginning to slide, Paudge shifted his weight and settled back on the inadequate seat, his buttocks straddling it like mule sacks. His denial was vehement.

"Not a tall, your Honour. We didn't lay a finger on him."

The judge turned to Murf, "What do you say about that?"

Swaying again and passing a hand weakly over his face, Murf replied, "Well, it doesn't matter now. I seem to be recovering quite well … since I was discharged from hospital … to be here to-day … And anyway, how were the guards … to know about the internal bleeding …?"

"We can always check with the hospital."

"Yes, Sir. It was St. Vincent's. They will have the records. My vital signs were off the chart, apparently … I just … managed to make my way to the Casualty Ward after," he paused with a dramatist's instinct, "being released from College Green Barracks."

"Is there anyone in the courtroom who can corroborate this serious allegation?" The judge's earlier tone of incredulity had deepened to a bass note of serious inquiry.

"Yes, Your Honour. Mr. Rolo Sangster."

Rolo leapt a foot in the air as all eyes turned towards him. There was a sudden commotion in his chest that threatened his rib cage.

"I will not ask you to take the stand, Mr. Sangster, as we have dispensed with learned counsel in this case," the judge began, "but could you please tell the court if the defendant was admitted to hospital immediately following his period of incarceration?"

"Yes, Sir … yes, he was," Rolo answered by rote, unaware of the gasp that arose from his neighbours in the public gallery.

"And what kind of treatment did he receive in the casualty ward of that hospital?"

"What kind of … treatment?" Rolo repeated in a strangled voice. The courtroom began to spin and sizzle like a roman candle. Through the buzzing in his ears he dimly heard the judge repeat the question. In some recess of his befuddled mind a word formed miraculously, like a pearl in the most anaemic oyster on the ocean floor. "Extensive," he croaked. "Extensive treatment."

"You may be seated," the judge said heavily. He addressed the court at large," Strictly speaking, I can't admit this evidence but I am obliged to follow it up myself." Turning to Paudge, he asked, "What is your reaction to what you have just heard? Did the defendant come to harm in the barracks? Remember, you are under oath."

Paudge looked uneasily from Judge to Super and found no comfort in their stony expressions. Gripping the arms of the seat, he raised and resettled his haunches as if trying to achieve some modicum of comfort. "Sometimes there might be the odd …accident in the barracks. The table in the day room often gets in the way … when there's a bit of … activity. I've banged me own kidneys off it from time to time…"

"We're not here to discuss your kidneys. Did you assault the defendant while in your custody?" With a sharp movement the judge plucked his gown by the lapels and pulled it around his narrow shoulders.

Paudge again shifted his weight and while composing a reply in the dusty silence, emitted a loud belch.

"Your reply. Now!" The dignity of his court was on the line with this clod-hopping flatulent guardian of law and order. There was already that dangerous warbling sound of choked-off laughter that could erupt at any time and turn these grave deliberations into a circus.

Sensing that his back was to the wall, Paudge began with much throat-clearing and followed it with a rush of improvisation which was not his strong suit.

"Well, he might … have missed the chair … once or twice … And the floor in the station is hard enough … The Department wouldn't approve a bit of carpet for us … not even a bit of lino … And the walls and tables … sometimes get in the way, like…"

"So," the judge pounced. "He did come to harm in your custody." It was an inference rather than a question.

Paudge glanced at Murf who screwed up his face and flinched as if dodging a blow. Paudge began to stammer, "I d-don't know, like … he wasn't very healthy c-coming in … maybe he had a turn. I-I think he had drink taken … M-maybe,"

At last he found a nice phrase, "he has a weak constitution…" Like gas escaping, laughter seeped around the courtroom, signalling the danger of an explosion to follow.

"So now we have it," the judge thundered. "You, an officer of the law, have perjured yourself in my court. And it is clear to me that you beat the defendant. We are lucky the defendant is not suing the State." He extended a quivering finger." I want you and your Superintendent to see me in my chambers when we recess for luncheon." He turned to Murf. "I am not condoning your behaviour but I have no option but to dismiss the charges brought against you."

The gavel came down and as soon as the judge left the bench, Murf flung a victorious fist into the air and gave the two-finger sign to Paudge who writhed under the Super's scorn. A spontaneous burst of applause came from the mob now standing in the gallery. Murf turned in the dock, bowed from the hip and blew kisses at his boisterous fans. The trap-door would not open for him on this good day.

In the bathroom as he wiped off the make-up, Rolo slapped him on the back.

"What a day in court! You gave me some bad moments. I still can't believe you brought it off." His delight was tempered by a surge of delayed shock.

Murf grinned happily, his front teeth magically restored, although for him the real thrill was already over. "It came close at times, didn't it? But you see how it pays to read the room."

"And what about Paudge? Did you see his face as he followed the judge out?"

"That was a bonus all right," Murf agreed although it was clear that he didn't harbour a grudge against the ursine public guardian. He had bigger fish to fry.

A stockily built man came in, dawdled a while in front of the mirror, re-arranging some thinning wisps of hair, and then approached one of the urinals. He did a double take when Murf began to wipe off the mascara and spit out balls of cotton wool. The man jogged Rolo's memory by his build and general demeanour. When he did up his flies and left, Rolo said, "You never did explain about the guy who was tailing you."

"Oh, him? I owe him some merchandise. All will be revealed in the fullness of time."

Rolo watched him scrub off the rest of the make-up, peering into the mirror with an artist's dedication. There was something eternal about the sight of Murf going about his chameleon business. He needed the cut and thrust, the leaping weirs and cataracts of white water, to hone his skills and escape from the trouble he deliberately brought upon himself. It was hard not to wonder about the purpose of such inventiveness; what parsnips did it butter? Could it not be put to more profitable use?

They walked along that stretch of quay where Christchurch Cathedral looked across the river at the Four Courts, claiming a higher moral authority, and the Ha'penny Bridge threw a span, delicate as a wishbone, across the khaki water. Bookshops with outside troughs of well-thumbed offerings mingled with dusty antique shops in which brass and tarnished silver glinted in the gloom of aspidistras, cats and cobwebs, modest treasure sunk several fathoms deep. Auction houses smelling of worm-eaten furniture and mangy carpets, boasting also of coal scuttles, brass fenders and ships' bells, took the place of pawn shops finally ousted by dole and welfare payments. Between the trees along the embankment, yellow flags flew, indicating that some Papal potentate was visiting this frontier post of the spirit.

After re-charging his batteries on the radiator in the main hall, Murf said he had some business to attend to, and, with Rolo in tow, headed downstairs to stock-take his locker. Rummaging through the contraband of this steel boutique, he mused aloud, "I'm very low on French ticklers. It's worse than I thought."

He dipped into a cardboard box on the bottom shelf of the locker, pulled out a random selection of ordinary condoms and studied the packets.

"Damn, these are due to expire in a month. I suppose I could shift them, but still, one must try to maintain standards." He scribbled the results of the inventory on the back of a Gold Flake packet.

A group of black-suited clerical students, walking in formation, passed by on the way to their lockers, to stow bicycle clips and black berets, oblivious of the tawdry business being conducted next door.

"So what's the problem?" Rolo asked. "You can always go to Belfast and replenish your stocks." He stepped back to let a stray seminarian pass.

"Finance, old son. My debt-equity ratio has gone woefully askew. I am, in fact, up to my oxters in red ink."

"What about the twenty quid you won? That would cover a gross or so."

"I need more than that," Murf said in the throes of calculation. "I'm behind with a big order and those French ticklers don't come cheap. They've gone up in price by fifteen percent in the last fiscal year. I should buy shares in the London Rubber Company." He shut the locker door and bolted it. After the clerics filed out he explored some neighbouring lockers but, apart from the odd clerical grey gabardine coat, there wasn't much to hock.

"How much do I owe the Chaplain?" He sat down on the wooden bench and stretched out his legs.

"Don't touch him up again. He's broke too."

"You're right." Even Murf was reluctant to exploit the good-hearted Chaplain who was a generous creditor to the impecunious and a sucker for a tale of woe. There would be no joy in fleecing the Pascal Lamb.

Murf rubbed his chin which had been well shaved for his day in court, "I suppose we could hit the Medical Library again."

Rolo pointed out the hazards of such an exercise, pointing out that the Cuffe Street dealers were already choc-a-bloc with 'Grey's Anatomies', texts which were too hot to handle in any case.

Deep in thought, Murf passed a hand through his hair. At this time of year even the Freshers were becoming too sophisticated to be separated from their digs money. There were slim pickings in this financial winter of discontent.

"It's so unfair," Murf said with an unaccustomed air of self-pity. "DeLorean can get away with millions and here I am trying to save my little business that has nothing to do with dope, and is actually a social service if you think about it. And I'm staring insolvency in the face for a measly fifty quid or so." He stood up and began to pace among the rows of lockers, warming to his theme, and advocating the rights of the little man. "I should get a grant from the Government. Look at all those lame-duck industries they support, and here I am, an independent trader, providing an important service, and do I get a subvention or hand-out or even a thank-you? Not a bit of it."

It wasn't just the fate of his business that bothered him; there was also the danger of retribution by impatient creditors, made imminent by the appearance of the gumshoe in the sheepskin coat. He threw himself down on the bench again, fumbling for a Gold Flake. By the time he had taken three good drags of the cigarette, he had recovered his ability to think under pressure.

"I believe," he said, "we are going to the dogs."

In the early evening glow of floodlights they passed through the turnstiles of Harold's Cross dog track and split up to mingle with the punters, earwig in the bars and stands, and pick up whatever morsels of information were thrown to the winds by the more dedicated dog-fanciers. A good night at the dogs, Murf reckoned, could get him out of trouble and provide a little seed-corn for his flagging business in prophylactics.

With a folded Evening Press under his arm and a racing sheet in the back pocket of his corduroys, Murf worked the stands, hovering behind groups of huddled savants, trying, in the swirl of fevered comment, to separate the bullshit from the buckwheat. He had not been to the dogs for some months and needed to bring himself up to date. Tips at the dog track were closely guarded because the odds were sensitive to rumour, hence this kind of earwigging was rather frowned upon.

Rolo worked the bars and the enclosure over by the Tote, craning his long neck for tips, like a kingfisher stretching towards a pond of tadpole. At the rail of the enclosure a group of cognoscenti clustered around a small voluble man in a tweed cap who discussed the next race with the fervour of the young Messiah lecturing the elders in the

Temple. In his eagerness to learn from the Master, Rolo leant too far forward, his bad leg gave way, and he stumbled into the outer ring of the seminar, whereupon the young teacher interrupted his discourse to inquire, "What the fuck do you want?"

"Beg pardon … bad leg."

"Yeah, well there's no free tips here. Go on, bugger off out of it."

Because the irate guru reminded him of a librarian, Rolo couldn't help asking, "Do you by any chance have 'Loney's Dynamics'?"

"He's not running. Shag off."

As Rolo moved away he had the mild consolation of seeing these punters consult their programmes for this unheard-of dog. On his way back to the rendezvous he watched the greyhounds being exercised by their handlers behind the traps on the starting line. They were lean and mean, aristocratic and aero-dynamic. From muzzled snouts to pinched-in haunches they were sculpted for speed, their waist-coated midriffs seeming to float on finicky legs and padded paws. They were a strange disdainful breed whose origins were unknown; they promenaded with a hauteur that would be made ridiculous when they were fooled into chasing an artificial hare. Unlike the sport of kings, the average punter here had little interest in the runners themselves but only in their form and price. It was gambling in its purest aspect, as angular and charmless as the dogs themselves.

"Well, what do you think?" Rolo asked when

he met Murf to compare notes.

"I'm not sure. There's a lot of conflicting opinion about. But given the odds, I think 'Cold Warrior' should be worth a flutter." He took a pencil from behind his ear and made some notes on his already crumpled programme.

"My advisors suggest 'Grassy Knoll'. He's supposed to have good form and he likes soft going."

Murf nodded. "Yeah, I heard him mentioned in dispatches." He consulted the form sheet. "He did all right at Shelbourne and New Ross, but the price isn't great, four to one and shortening. Tell you what. Let's do 'em both for a place. Modesty to begin."

They joined the crowds heading towards the Tote and queued at windows to place their bets. The sky was darker now and the floodlights made the grassy park inside the track rail look like an incandescent space ship. Rolo had a sudden feeling that he might be an alien life form, 'alone and afraid in a world he never made.' He pocketed the Tote stubs and pulled his jacket tighter around his shoulders.

On the way back to the stands he stopped dead in his tracks and tugged Murf's sleeve.

"I hate to bring this up again, but your sheepskin friend is here."

Murf groaned in exasperation. "That's all I need. That bastard just won't give up. It's going to be difficult to concentrate on the doggies with that goon hovering about."

For reasons of prudence they had to position themselves a safe distance from the finish line. The dogs were led into the traps, unleashed, de-muzzled and given a final rub-down and word of encouragement. 'Cold Warrior' was jumpy for a while in the confines of his trap but finally settled like the others, snouts quivering until the electric hare whizzed past, and they were off. The dogs went streaking towards the first bend, legs barely touching the turf, then whipped horizontal again as the strides lengthened out. At the bend 'Grassy Knoll' was hustled, skidding in an angular ball, to the outside. He pawed air for a while in frenzy but recovered and regained traction on the turf. 'Cold Warrior' had a better line on the inside rail but lost his position as he went wide to cut off the hare.

"Get back, you bastard!" Murf yelled, his advice lost in the roars that swelled the stands. And, suddenly, after a final colour-blurred spurt to the line, it was all over. The hare was slowed and the still-pursuing dogs foiled in a net.

"I think we did all right," Rolo hopped on his good leg. An announcement confirmed that 'Cold Warrior' was second, though 'Grassy Knoll' was unplaced and presumably still running. Murf did a quick calculation, faster even than the sudden, and to some, unsatisfying orgasmic rhythm of this sport.

"We're fourteen quid to the good if the odds held." He rubbed his hands and punched Rolo on the shoulder. "Not a bad start at all."

They joined the crowds heading for the bars

under the stands. It was an irresistible movement like one of those tectonic heaves that sweep up mountains and forests in its path. At a distance they saw Ashur who was dejectedly tearing up his stubs, and decided to catch him later.

They stood ten deep in the bar lost in research. Murf's baggy jacket came into its own; the capacious pockets held at the ready the research materials, wager stubs, stake money, Gold Flake and matches. From the breast pocket protruded the neck of a foaming bottle of stout. Rolo, less practised in these arts, had considerable difficulty in re-lighting a pinched-out butt of Old Holborn that hung crookedly from his lip, and had to swallow particles of tobacco dislodged by the first pull.

Murf diligently studied the runners in the next race and looked up with a happy face.

"I think we're on to something here." He tapped the flange of his nose with a nicotine-stained forefinger. "I know this hound, 'Tricky Dick'. He used to course near my home town. There's a bit of the wolf in him but he's a winner, no doubt about it."

"I'm not really at the races here," Rolo confessed. He had nothing to contribute except a caveat. "Why are the odds so good? Eleven to one is kind of generous if he's the dog you say he is."

"Good point," Murf conceded graciously because he had the answer. "This crowd of Dublin gurriers doesn't know the first thing about coursing which as you know is a blood sport beloved of culchies, clergy and mountainy men in remote parts of the country between deliveries of poitín. So," he spread his hands in a gesture of humble exegesis, "this dog is your classic dark horse." He rewarded himself by unsheathing the bottle from his breast pocket and taking a long pull.

The bar emptied quickly in another of those geological surges, indicating that the Tote was paying out. Erratic punters rode the glacier. Murf gave Rolo the stubs and he went on his own to collect the winnings. The odds had actually improved and he picked up £16 and loose change, enough to stake them for the races to come. They operated a common chest and though Rolo was a silent – if not a sleeping – partner, he did all right when Murf declared a dividend. He fought his way back through the crowds, almost all men, wearing caps, and with Guinness stains on upper lips.

There was no sign of Murf when he got back; perhaps another geological shift had carried him in another direction. He bellied up to the bar for another stout which he sipped reflectively, feeling the warmth of the medicinal compound spread through his narrow frame which had a limited capacity for alcohol and a hair-trigger mechanism for its ejection. Life really could be all right at times, he thought, as he contemplated the creamy head on his drink; it was still solid even though sinking – a sign of quality. Even those damned problems in mechanics could be solved in this mellow mood – if one could only recall them. A

monkey climbing a pole on a barge going north …
or was it west, and a dog?

Craning towards a sagely nodding group, he
heard the name 'Ho Chi Quinn' being mentioned,
though not often or favourably enough to threaten
the odds. It occurred to him that life was
symmetrical; you could pick a winner but get a
poor price, a windfall of cash could make one
miserable, you could dream of the future and not
wake up. Then maybe there was no point in
having a purpose since it would all just even out in
the end. He overheard a runner called 'Moon
Landing' being mentioned in high encomium with
the rider that he had been 'nobbled out of it' in
Greystones the previous week. Maybe he was
being deliberately held back until a more
remunerative pay-day came along. Opinions in the
bar would become more dogmatic, and be
expressed more forcefully, as the night wore on,
and even now, it seemed to Rolo, needed to be
taken with a grain or two of salt.

When the buzzer went for the next race there
was still no sign of Murf. The bar cleared
magically, leaving Rolo standing alone with a
froth-lined glass and a decision to make. He would
have to get the bet down soon, but what if Murf
was getting the latest word on 'Ho Chi Quinn' and
'Moon Landing' from trainer or maybe even
owner? He waited as long as he dared, then went
to the enclosure where the dogs were being shoe-
horned into the traps. It was now or never. Feeling
stressed, he rushed to the window just before it

closed – the sight of the hatch being pulled down reminded him queasily of the library – and with a plaintive cry caught the attention of the clerk. With no time to think, he put ten pounds on 'Ho Chi Quinn' for a place. True to form, he had hedged his bet, but what else could he do in the absence of his mentor?

His moment of suffering was well compensated by the gods of symmetry, because after the streaky flash of blurred colour came back into focus, it turned out that 'Ho Chi Quinn' had been pipped at the post by the presumably unnobbled 'Moon Landing'. But with an each-way bet they were still in the money, maybe not a king's ransom but certainly a squire's perks, and enough perhaps to re-stock Murf's contraceptive larder. He bent over the rail, faint with relief, then straightened up as the good news sank in, feeling proud of the decision he had made. With a slight swagger, he allowed himself to be geologically carried back to the watering hole from whence they had all come three minutes earlier.

He had just, in celebration, raised another ebony fluted glass to his lips when he saw Murf staggering into the bar, hair wilder than ever, coat and tie askew, hands gripping the lumbar reaches of his back as if to unclench some seized-up disks and knotted vertebrae.

"My Godfathers, what happened to you?"

Murf eased himself gingerly on to a barstool which a kind man, recognising a fellow sufferer, had vacated with the consoling comment, "My dog's still running too."

His face a crinkled mask of pain, Murf grunted, "Be a good man, Rolo … and get me a bottle of stout … for my nerves." He twisted his torso against the hand-braced back and let out a yelp, followed by a sigh. "That's a bit better. Lord, it's been an odd sort of day and I am sick at heart. Things got … out of hand and somewhat physical for a contemplative type like me. Lord, was it for this the Wild Geese fled?" He reached shakily for his drink like an invalid for a cane, raised it weakly to his lips and drained it to its lace-like lees. "Aaaagh, this life which I must bear … till I feel in the warm air my breath go cold … and hear the sea breathe o'er my dying brain … its last monotony. Rolo," he looked up sadly, "I have just had the shit kicked out of me."

"Our sheepskin friend?" Rolo sympathetically placed another bottle before him.

"The same. And two heavies, punching out my kidneys. Is there no trust any more? Have we really fallen so low in this distressful country? Bloody Vets. I'm surrounded, Rolo, by ham-fisted yahoos … Gobnait alone might be able to ease my burden…" He caught him by the sleeve and leant closer. "Listen, don't let this get around, you know."

"Don't worry." Rolo grinned inwardly. 'Characters' had their reputations to think of, even more than the righteous pillars of church and state. Listening intently to Murf's continued ramblings – his way of dealing with and concealing the effects of shock – interspersed with the odd snippet of Shelley beaten into him by the Christian Brothers, Rolo pieced together the sorry tale.

The Vet syndicate had paid in advance for a gross and a half of French letters a month ago. Murf who had blown the money instead of re-stocking, was unable to deliver and had been lying low ever since, until tonight when the angry celibate Vets had finally run him to earth in the bathroom of Harold's Cross dog track.

Another brace of bottles later they checked their winnings on 'Moon Landing', and Murf congratulated Rolo on his decision-making ability, adding generously that he himself might well have done 'Moon Landing' to *win*, thus landing himself in even more serious trouble vis-à-vis the coitally-barred Vets.

"One more good result should do the trick," Murf said, splitting the take, having resumed their places at the counter. "We have enough already for regular condoms but they insist on French ticklers." The irony overwhelmed him. "What do Vets want with French ticklers? They have as much savoir-faire as pigs in shit. Talk about casting pearls before swine … Anyway, another ten quid or so and we can make ready for another trip to our separated brethren in the North, and save more precious ovaries from pollination. That leaves the question of a car. Speaking of which, who is it who this way comes?"

Ashur came innocently into the bar with head bent, studying form.

"Hello lads, any luck?"

"Fair to middling. And fortune smiles on you, I trust?" Murf had that steady look in his eyes, the sort of unabashed hypnotic stare of a king cobra ready to strike when it spots a mere pin-head of exposed pink flesh.

"Ashur," he tossed his head. "They slowed the hare in the last one and codded my dog up the yin yang. He went so wide he's probably in Ballyfermot by now. I have a real goer in the nine-thirty though. His owner is putting a stack on him."

"Which dog is that?" Rolo asked too straightforwardly.

"Ah now, I wouldn't want to lead you astray," Ashur said deviously

"Little fear of that," Murf said with a debunking laugh. "'Khruschev's Pal' is a certainty in the nine-thirty. No one can touch him."

Ashur ridiculed the idea. "Not at all. Ashur, he's got no form at all."

"That's because," Murf said bluffing, "He has been deliberately kept under wraps for a big purse. And this is it. I spoke with the trainer just ten minutes ago. I can tell you this," he looked around wary of prying ears, and leant closer to Ashur, "'Khruschev's Pal' is the next 'Master McGrath'. The legend begins this very night." He turned aside and had a drink; that was his last word on the subject.

Ashur looked uncertain. "I don't care how good he is. He couldn't have the class of 'Colonel

Ripper'.

Murf made a mental note of the name and changed the subject. "I didn't see you in court to-day."

"And why would you?" Ashur grinned happily at his gombeen coup. "Didn't I give sick certs to half the guards on the force. Heh, heh, Boys, it would be a good time to pull a job with all those flatfeet on leave." He stretched his arms with a shudder and sighed in satisfaction. "You know, I feel really good. Just been to confession and made a clean breast of it all, carnal thoughts, immodest actions, nocturnal pollutions, the lot. A good confession cleans out the system better than a dose of salts. Mick and the other lads went off after mots to-night, but I said, no, a good clean outdoor activity is just the job for me. And here I am."

"I can certainly see," Murf began with wasted sarcasm, "that you are indeed in a state of grace and well in control of the base appetites. Were you to be struck this second by a Jovebolt, you would wing your way straight to a high place in heaven, bypassing the fires of purgatory." He took a pull of his freshly poured stout and looked over the rim of the glass at the light drizzle that began to fall, hazily, through the glare of floodlights. Softer going, he thought, must remember to check out 'Colonel Ripper's' preferences in the matter of turf consistency.

"There's many a true word spoken in jest. The eyes are the windows of the soul." Ashur, already the country doctor, seemed to be practising these pisherogues to enrich his bedside manner. Sporting a new tweed suit, he was clearly working on his image as a father-figure of medicine, higher-ranking in the village order than the bank manager and school master, on a par with the parish priest, and second only to the inbred descendent of the squirearchy. He even declined a proffered Gold Flake with another platitude about physicians healing themselves.

Murf felt with a twinge of sorrow that Ashur, an erstwhile protégé in the art of frivolity, was now lost to him, turning his face towards the establishment without a murmur of remorse. Here, at the track, a sort of Assumption was taking place before his moist eyes. With an effort, Murf turned from sadness and looked for some residual value from this glory-bound soul.

"Isn't it strange and comforting how helping one's fellow man produces a warm glow in the eternal soul?"

"Ashur, you've hit the nail right on the head again."

"I was thinking," Murf followed up quickly, "now that you're a fully-fledged doctor with such a wonderful opportunity to do good, whether you would like my assistance in the matter of ... aaam ... providing a structured programme of birth control. Only for those in need of course, and safely within the marital fold..." Murf's smile faded as Ashur shook his head almost sadly, burdened as he was by the weight of sanctity.

"No can do. Ethics you understand. I couldn't

be handing Johnnies out to all and sundry. I'd get a belt of the crozier or be hauled up before the Medical Board. Think of the headlines: 'Country doctor blitzes parish with rubbers, makes money out of contraception. It's not on, Murf. They'd have the Ashurian balls for book-ends."

"Could we at least discuss terms?" Murf asked anyway though he felt sure he was flogging a dead horse. This recent convert was hot in pursuit of a comfortable life and the promise of obscene cheques from the National Health for dispensing Valium and writing sick certs for patients with hang-nails.

"I have a reputation to think of now. Funny how it all changes. One day a student kicked shitless by everyone, then suddenly a doctor, and the population queuing up to kiss the fundament. A bit like the 'Ugly Duckling'. Heh, heh." He rocked gently on the balls of his feet as if practising that country doctor habit of warming the backside against a splendid fire set by a devoted housekeeper.

"Once a quack, always a quack," Murf said darkly.

"That's good, "Ashur chuckled; on the threshold of luxury, he was immune to taunts. Then, he committed the cardinal sin of patronising Murf with advice.

"You should think of getting a set on yourself. You're no spring chicken, you know."

Manfully, Murf restrained himself for the moment, thinking of the Mini he had yet to wheedle out of this tight-fisted twerp who no doubt still had his first communion money. He white-knuckled the edge of the bar and swallowed hard so that his Adam's apple bobbed and plunged like a ball-cock in a flushing cistern.

"Oh you're right," Murf said in self-deprecating tones. "By the way," he forced a winning smile, "do you remember the time when you lost the cadaver and I covered for you? I got a replacement for you from the College of Surgeons and smuggled it into the dissecting room? God, I can still smell the formaldehyde…"

"And don't think I wasn't grateful," Ashur said infuriatingly. "But Johnnies on demand …? Can't be done, I'm afraid."

"Forget about that silly idea of mine. I can see how it would compromise you at the beginning of your healing ministry."

Rolo looked on, not quite sure what line Murf was taking. It was like watching a tennis match being played by phantoms with an imaginary ball, but the moves were good and the spectral finesse fine. It would go to five sets.

"Right so. Glad you see it that way." Ashur was about to move away and Murf went to his fall-back position quickly. This at last was the strike.

"Let us borrow your Mini for one last trip to Belfast."

Rolo moved aside to let the psychic sparks fly.

"Gor, I dunno." Ashur needed time. He bought an Evening Press from a newsboy and over-paid him by mistake as he debated the issue with himself. "I just had a spray job done on the old bus. Sahara Gold metallic paint. She's looking neat and tasty."

"We'll be careful, don't worry. You know, Ashur, I need to make this trip for my customers, of whom you were one and a desperate one at that, if memory serves. And did I ever up the price or take advantage? No, I did not. Remember the night before the Meds Ball, you were taking Lucy Morton, and you came to me on bended knees. Did I turn you away even though I was down to my last dozen Thai Trojans, and the Ags were beating my door down for a pre-paid order? Did I turn you away? No, I did not. I had standards then and I still have them. If you don't want to lend me the Mini, fine. But I won't let my customers down. I'll go north on a bicycle if I have to."

"I didn't say I wouldn't," Ashur said with a poor grace, annoyed at having been put on the defensive. "Is Rolo going with you?" This appeared to be the clincher.

"Yes."

It bothered Rolo that he wasn't even consulted, but it was a compliment of sorts that Ashur wanted him to go along.

"Well, all right then. One trip, no more. And if you're caught at customs you won't leave me holding the baby. Heh, heh. I want your word on that."

"You've got it."

"Just to be clear, I know nothing about the

Johnnies. OK"

"Don't worry. You won't be implicated in any way."

"And," Ashur held up a finger. "You'll leave a full tank of petrol in the car…"

"Yes."

"All right so. By the way the gears are jumpy. Do you know how to double de-clutch?"

Murf gave him a withering look, "Does your Granny know how to suck eggs?"

Murf wasn't quite as happy as he should have been after this minor coup. He still rankled as a result of Ashur's patronising tone. As a 'chronic' of some standing, Murf had long experience of callow youths whom he had taken under his wing, and who finally graduated and moved on the better things, leaving him behind. It was beginning to get to him. Life was moving on. As much as he hated the notion of treadmill and bandwagon, he was occasionally tempted by an urge to jump on board himself. But what could he do with a year of Divinity, six months of baby Latin, Coptic, Sanskrit, English and Geology? This whole mish-mash of soft options did not amount to a row of beans.

And now the Ashurian gravy-train was pulling out of the station, leaving him behind on the platform twisting in a cold wind. His ambition was to wrest the family business from the clutches of Fanning, as much for the memory of his father as for himself, but it seemed to be taking on, as time went by, the wispy substance of a dream. At twenty-five he was beginning to feel the need for some direction, even if it led to confrontation with the real issues he had been avoiding.

Ashur, who had been scanning the headlines of the Evening Press, said, "I see where a Protestant arms dump was discovered in Belfast. Rocket-launchers and armour-piercing missiles no less." He whistled softly. "Some fella called Mayhew is supposed to be supplying them. I suppose the IRA will start stock-piling now. Ashur, the whole bloody thing is escalating up there."

"Mayhew, Mayhew, where did I hear that name before?" Murf asked vacantly.

"Don't you remember," Rolo prompted. "Crowley was having a go at him one evening back in the digs."

"Listen," Ashur said. "They're on the brink of civil war up there. Be careful with the Mini for God's sake. I need it for house calls. Heh, heh."

Of the races remaining, they had one winner – Ashur's 'Colonel Ripper', who did after all like soft going – two places and three no-shows, and came out ahead on the night to the tune of fifty-five pounds, safely above the critical mass required for the shopping expedition to Belfast. The dogs, quivering and sweating, were bundled up in rugs and whisked away like prima donnas being ushered out the stage door to waiting limos. The floodlights were doused and the abruptly voided stands sank into the night, bearing on their bleachers the confetti of lost hopes.

"These our revels are now ended … and our

little life is rounded with a dream," Murf misquoted from his one term of English, during which one lecturer turned up and was pissed out of his skull.

"Well, we did it," Rolo said as they filed out through the tall iron portals joined at the top by a ranch-style hoarding.

"Yep, we did it." Murf seemed unusually thoughtful.

The surface of the canal was covered with a frothy scum of algae, penetrated here and there by pram wheels and bicycle frames. The pub at Portobello was letting out its clients, some of whom draped themselves athwart the white-tipped timbers of the lock-gates and added their measures to the turgid waters cascading through the sluices. Sodium street lamps, many of them smashed from use as cock-shots, covered the ill-used canal with a sickly pall. The last buses shot in convoy over the hump of the bridge, desperate to get out of town before being stopped by inconsiderate passengers.

Through a lighted window in a modest Georgian house, Rolo spotted a classmate poring over a pile of texts and tapping like a nervous hen at one of those new-fangled mechanical calculators. He felt the old familiar heart-scald of guilt, counting again the dwindling days to the finals, one of which had just gone up in smoke. The inherited conscience of William Penn that gnawed quietly at his soul now bit clean through a nerve-ending and he jumped in psychic pain. What he needed was a start upon the path of virtue and clean living; if only he could get a run at it, or at least get his splayed feet out of the blocks. Confession had done something for Ashur; could that be an option for him?

Their digs-bound faces were inclined and cast in black and amber shadows.

"That's this country all over! Not content with a contradiction in terms, it must go on to an antithesis in ideas."
—George Tyrrell

CHAPTER 4

ACCORDING TO LEGEND, The Cart's husband never had a lie-in on a Saturday morning. In consequence, the lodgers were hounded out of their beds at the stroke of eight and now sat dumbly around the table in the kitchen, poking encrusted sleep pus from eyes, poring over iron rations, denting, if not quite breaking, their fast. A fly on the ceiling would have seen them as petals of some huge ugly flower, craning centrally towards the stamen.

Crowley with his specs on meticulously sliced a sausage aswim in grease, skewering it with a tinny fork to stop it slithering off the plate. The Cart stood behind the busy trough, wielding a skillet, and commenced the refectory lesson.

"I don't want anyone coming in late to-night and waking the house, mind me now. Don't spend your digs money on beer. Them that has exams better get their noses into the books. My husband could show you how to work, God rest his soul. And for God Almighty's sake, aim straight and flush the toilet. I'm fed up to the back teeth mopping piss off the floor. And watch that hot-water geyser. If I find any more medals or foreign coins in it, I'll throw the lot of youse out. Tim! I'm talking to you. And whose car is that out there?"

Everyone looked in relief at Murf, electing him as spokesman.

"That would be a vehicle on loan to me from a kind medical colleague." He was in good spirits, ready to embark on a profitable venture to Belfast. He put down his cutlery which had done all the little that was asked of it. The blade of the knife was curved inwards from regular sharpening on the doorstep, and the yellow bone handle was pock-marked from repeated licks of the gas-ring. The grease on the plate had congealed, leaving a perfect fossil of a Clover sausage, skinless, singular and burnt. The grease in his stomach, however, had not yet assumed the inert state and was still sliding around, seeking a way out or some chemical transmogrification.

"It shouldn't be parked so near the neighbours," she complained although she quite liked the idea of her arch rival landlady, Mrs. Whelan, thinking that her boarders had cars. She let the gauze curtain flutter back and went to brew more tea.

"That will soon be rectified when Rolo and I finish these elegant comestibles. A spot more tea if you would be so kind, to warm the innards for our imminent field trip." Apart from some lingering muscle pain around the back and ribs, he felt in fine entrepreneurial fettle on this good day with cash in his pocket and a Saharan Gold car waiting for him in the dappled shade of Northbrook Square. He had hoped to call on Gobnait, but that pleasure would have to be postponed until he got those mountainy Vets off his back.

"What … field trip?" She towered suspiciously over him, pouring out Musgrave's Oriental Infusion into a mug as big as a bidet. "I hope it's to do with work."

"What else?" he asked rhetorically. "We go North to inspect at first hand the flora and fauna of the Quasi-Jurassic period." He shovelled four spoons of sugar into his tea; it was the only form of energy to be had at this Spartan table.

"Hmmmmngh!" It wasn't clear whether this primal honk suggested doubt, outright disbelief or weary resignation, but it did mean silence for a time.

Crowley, still rankling over the charge of masturbation or impotence – though hardly both – looked out the window at Ashur's newly painted Mini with its smart 'Doctor on Call' sign, designed to frustrate traffic wardens rather than minister to the sick, and remarked huffily, "That crock wouldn't get you as far as Dundalk."

Murf refused to be drawn on such a promising day, as crisp and fresh as the dew-drenched heart of a winter lettuce, and merely murmured, "Oh I don't know about that. It's a game little car by all accounts."

Tim stretched out an arm and pulled up the sleeve for the first elbow scratch of the morning and asked who the doctor was who owned the car, and how much he earned. It was as if he needed to know how far down the totem pole he was, as measured by his own meagre pay-packet.

"Dr. Hyde and a mint," Murf replied unhelpfully.

"Don't know him," Tim answered vacantly, having slipped out of reality again. With jerky movements he tried to light a Woodbine with black-headed matches and wasted several in a failed attempt.

"Don't smoke them things in here," The Cart snapped, and then chuckled, as Tim, dropping the remaining matches, fled up the stairs.

Crowley sent his eyes heavenwards as if praying for the afflicted, "I suppose he's gone to sell dictionaries in the Coombe."

"He did sell some last week." Rolo rushed to Tim's defence. Tim had followed him into the bathroom the night before and confided the good news to him.

"Oh, that's just his fevered imagination," Crowley said. He was glancing snidely at Murf. "What's more important is that Fanning's Builders Providers are doing well these days."

"How do you know?" Murf was surprised.

"Sources," Crowley said enigmatically. Somehow he seemed to know of Murf's angst on the matter. "Robert Fanning is the best thing to happen to the Fianna Fáil Party in years. He's a true republican and should be nominated at the next election." He looked narrowly across the table and was disappointed to see Murf's monumental indifference. He redoubled his efforts. "Fanning is just the man for those shoneens who want to hand Ireland back to the British and apologise for its condition. He'd soften their cough for them. All those bed-wetters and nambie-pambies … There comes a time when real men have to take a stand. Fanning has guts. I liked his speech to the Ard Fheis last year…"

"We'd better make tracks," Murf interrupted, keen to hold his peace. He wondered how Crowley knew so much about Fanning since he was not as yet much in the public eye. Some political connection, he presumed.

The snub-nosed golden car bounded through the dozing, bedraggled streets, crossing the Liffey at O'Connell Street and taking traffic lights in its stride. Murf manoeuvred it well through the road-mending debris of Corporation workers who had downed tools for the week-end and left gaping holes and mounds of spoil unguarded in a creative though treacherous slalom. Traffic was light enough and within twenty minutes they passed the turn-off for the airport and followed the open road to Northern Ireland.

The open windows of the Mini sucked in the country breeze with its blended tinctures of heather, fuschia and woodbine, overlain with the earthy smell of turf smoke. Dense unruly hedges flashed by, streaked with yellow furze and primroses, broken every so often by crooked gates and wooden tables sometimes bearing milk churns for collection. Rolling patchwork hills beyond the hedges held little in the way of crops or cattle; husbandry came a poor second to disability benefit and farmers' dole. From the fallow fields drifted a sense of quiet despair; even the birds went to town to scavenge, led by raucous magpies and rooks. Once in a while they passed a lone house on a hill, a plume of turf smoke rising in the blue air. Rolo was intrigued to know what was going on in those lost outposts which held for him small mysteries.

Hell bent on driving, Murf had his foot to the floor and only eased off when they approached one of the many small towns of painted concrete, each one dominated by its own church spire.

"This car does have a jumpy clutch," he said after crashing gears at a cross-roads. "And the synchromesh is banjaxed."

"Shall we get there by candlelight?"

"We better get there before the chemist shops shut or we're in big trouble. Ooops, a hitch-hiker. Too late to stop. A long-haired Bolshie anyway."

"Do I detect a note of censure?" Rolo sat back in the passenger seat, enjoying the trip, his long legs buckled up so that his knees almost touched the dashboard.

"Those fellows are just playing at revolution. It's just a pose…"

Rolo had to work hard to stifle a guffaw.

Murf threw him a sidelong glance, "Why are you giving me that toothy grin? I'm not a rebel. I haven't any ideology. Damn, I don't even have views. I don't give a two-penny damn about anything," he added passionately.

"Why do you rock the boat then?"

"The devil finds a use for idle hands, haven't you heard?" Murf took a corner at speed, sending one of Ashur's golf balls cavorting noisily in the glove compartment. Because it reminded Rolo of a problem in mechanics he opened the compartment to silence the moving sphere, and spied a copy of Dale Carnegie's 'How to Win Friends and Influence People'. It didn't surprise him all that much that Ashur was reading self-improvement literature.

"Don't kid a kidder," he said to Murf, who changed down to pass an articulated truck that hogged the one-lane secondary road.

"You Americans are always plumbing the depths of the old psyche, confusing yourselves with analysis and related mumbo-jumbo." Murf changed up and attacked an open stretch of road.

"I wonder if we're not all a bit insecure…" Rolo began.

Murf took a hand from the wheel and held it up to silence him, "I know that malarkey, compensating for something or other, trying to find the right identity. Look, I've seen 'Playboy of the Western World' too." Distancing himself from these poor platitudes did not prevent images of his father's gentle face floating to his mind.

"So?" Rolo was unusually persistent. He felt that maybe the time was coming for his friend to take stock of himself rather than of his prophylactics. But he wouldn't put it as crudely as

Ashur had done at the track. Maybe Ashur hadn't yet started on Dale Carnegie.

"Rolo, be a pal and light me a Gold Flake. Fags in left pocket, matches in breast pocket." He slowed the car and wove carefully through a herd of scrawny cows, probably half-starved during the winter in hope of early grass. One large product of this hand-to-mouth husbandry leant against Ashur's Sahara-Gold Mini and raised her tail in a meaningful way. Murf honked and swerved as the golden oranges began to fall with ponderous deliberation. The cow, disturbed in mid-motion, executed a capriole and kicked the Mini right in the door panel.

"Shit, that's all I need." Murf accelerated out of danger.

"Aren't you going to say something to the farmer? It's his responsibility."

"Unhappily, no. Farm animals have the right of the road. If the farmer claimed that poor old Daisy had a whiplash or dried up from trauma, we'd be on a hiding to nothing. Better let the hare sit." He drove on puffing furiously at the cigarette Rolo had handed him. The day that had started so well was beginning to go sour, and was saved only by a whimsical thought.

"Now that you've seen close up the bovine derrière, you might, like me, wonder why the Vets want French ticklers."

Leaving Dundalk, sometimes called 'Gundalk' because of the guerrillas who hid out there on their way south from the border, Murf returned guiltily to the subject.

"Did you ever hear the story about the woman who smoked cigars. Everyone said it was a bad case of penis-envy but she insisted that she just happened to like cigar tobacco. No one would believe her. Well," he hammered a finger against his chest, "I happen to like me."

"No, you don't."

"I like me. I should know."

"Who are you trying to convince? If it's any consolation, I don't like myself very much." Rolo's desire to help was infuriating.

"I don't need consoling."

"Uh – huh."

"And I like Gobnait, tobacco, booze and steak and chips and…" He swerved to avoid a grey squirrel that paused quivering on the crest of the road, then darted into the hedge on the other side.

"And your stepfather?"

"Rolo."

"What?"

"Put a sock in it."

Rolo started to laugh. It could hardly have been otherwise. Even on the Day of Judgment, Murf would read the room and don one of his many hats to out-manoeuvre the Angel Gabriel. If he took off one mask it would only reveal another one, and another one after that. Rolo continued to laugh quietly to himself as they approached the customs post and joined a line of buses crammed with Dublin housewives on a shopping spree to buy a range of lower-taxed goods in Newry or

Belfast.

Clip-board in hand, a customs official examined their papers and kicked the tyres of the Mini. Going north on worn tyres and returning on new ones was a well- known ruse. The official then went through a standard list of questions with them.

"We're clean," Murf said lightly. "There's nothing worth smuggling north anyway." He was preaching to the converted. The official waved them through with a tip of his cap, and went back to his prefab to hold a lonely vigil with his tea-pot.

But there was yet another hurdle before reaching the pearly gates of Belfast, a military check-point, to test the nerves and fortitude of north-bound pilgrims. A British soldier in flak jacket, nursing an automatic weapon in the crook of his arm, questioned them about their itinerary and its purpose. A Tommy from the West Indies, he spoke with a Cockney accent.

"To visit friends at Queen's," Murf stated his business and for ID produced his dog-eared student card.

"You're a long way from 'ome, mate," The Tommy said.

"I could say the same about you, mate."

Rolo was hypnotised by the mouth of the machine-gun and the ventilation holes along the casing of the barrel. He wanted to get out of there fast, and involuntarily stabbed an imaginary accelerator pedal with a platypus foot.

"Facq orf, ya bleedin' Mick," the Tommy said.

Having taken the Queen's shilling, it did not apparently follow that he had to speak the Queen's English. Because of the unpredictable synchromesh, Murf had some difficulty putting the car in gear. As he wrestled with the stick Rolo rocked back and forth, urging the car forward, and didn't draw a decent breath until the engine engaged and they leapt ahead to safety, leaving that obscene machine-gun behind.

"It gets to you when you see it up close," Murf said. "It's the Black and Tans all over again. Imagine him asking where I'm going in my own country?" He slowed the car. "I think we should go back and tell him off."

"No, no ... Bad idea," Rolo said in alarm. "A Smith and Wesson beats four aces."

"Might is right. It makes me sick."

It was early afternoon when they cruised into the city centre, but because of military restrictions on parking, actively supervised by patrols of Sappers and sniffer dogs in armoured vehicles, it was not far off four by the time they got down to business. Because of time constraints they decided to split up and so cover more ground. Rolo didn't care much for this and he entered his first chemist's shop – one of the Boots chain – with a mild tremor. His hope of self-service was soon dashed; he approached a white-coated avuncular chemist and said diffidently, "A gross ... of condoms ... please."

The chemist cupped his ear. "Beg pardon. How many?" His voice, like a sonic boom, rattled the jars and bottles that lined the shelves of this emporium.

"A gross ... twelve dozen..." Rolo's voice was prayerfully quiet as if he was reciting an Act of Contrition at the altar rails after confession.

"Twelve dozen ... a gross?" the chemist repeated, verifying the order. Leather-clad females dabbing perfume on their wrists broke their concentration on the relative merits of scents, and cocked their ears.

"Yes," Rolo grated, hoping his voice would carry far enough but no further.

The chemist went deep behind the counter where Rolo couldn't follow.

"A-ahem, excuse me...!"

"Yes?" The chemist turned back from the glass case but did not come any closer.

"Half should be ... of a special kind..."

"What kind is that?" the chemist bellowed.

Rolo wanted to crook a finger and beckon him closer but politeness prevented it. How often had he wilted from the bad breath of people who stood too close, but now this apothecary held his ground a mile away and seemed to recede further into the back of the shop. He got it out fast.

"French ticklers ... six dozen."

"Any particular colour?"

"Skin ... I mean natural..." Trying to keep his dignity afloat, he heard smothered snorts of derision wafting over from the cosmetics counter. Belfast lasses, reared under the gantries of the ship-yards, didn't suffer fools gladly.

"Very good. That would be six dozen of the French ticklers, natural hue." The chemist liked to get things right and leave nothing to chance. "Ribbed or plain?"

"Half and half and the rest ordinary." That didn't give too much away, Rolo thought with some relief but, O Lord, the chemist was filling his capacious lungs again.

Right, that would be three dozen of the French ticklers, natural hue, ribbed and three dozen of the same lads only unribbed. And six dozen of your ordinary common-or-garden rubbers. Right?"

"Yes!"

"Any Sheikhs or Trojans. We've got a good line in Hustlers. Super-sensitive, I'm told…"

"No! No, thank you!"

Eventually he managed to shove the packages inside his bomber jacket and crept towards the door. One of the raunchy leathered lasses, waving a lipstick at him, asked for a date, and all the repressed mirth came cascading cruelly out.

In a shop two streets over Murf was faring better, chatting up the lady chemist who waited on him in faint disbelief, rejecting his suggestion of a discount for bulk orders and feigning ignorance of the advertised superiority of Snuggies over Spartans. Holding a sample up to the light and viewing it with the careful eye of a watch-maker, he mused aloud.

"I wonder if these might be a tad snug? One does not wish to impede the hoped-for frisson or cause gangrene in the midst of frolics."

The lady alchemist, realising she had a southerner on her hands, a papist with heretical leanings and a certain savvy, removed her glasses, shook out her pinned up hair, with a slight predatory curl of the lip.

When Rolo entered the shop he thought he saw them disappear behind the counter and heard Murf say, "What a good idea ... a dry run so to speak..."

Heart in mouth, he sidled down the nave of the shop and found himself in the kiddies' section where he loitered among sticks of barley sugar, bulbous soothers, disposable nappies with wet strength, and plastic bibs with moulded guttering. It occurred to Rolo as he leant against a display stand of bottle warmers and formula feed, mustering as much nonchalance as he could, that he seemed to spend a considerable amount of his time these days waiting for Murf *in flagrante*. The junior shop assistant offered to help him choose some requisites for baby. He said he was just browsing but he bought a stick of barley sugar anyway.

He walked up and down outside sucking the twisted sugar-stick. An armoured car passed by, helmeted heads protruding from the turret like duck decoys, camouflaged with ivy and laurel leaves. In this city-centre shopping area the incongruity was funny and sickening at the same time. A few spindly-legged kids yelled "Brits out!" and "Stick yer rubber bullets!" No one knew for sure when a word, a stone, or a hair trigger might unleash a sudden fury and touch the tinder of remembered wrongs. The Saracen passed like a many-headed monster; this was a peace-keeping presence with an explosive temper, ready to turn on these youths scrabbling in the scree of history, under the shadow of Stormont. How much more heart-stopping interruptions of daily life could these people take?

When Murf finally appeared, Rolo's prurience got the better of him.

"You didn't … did you?"

"It's true, you know, what they say about Orange women. All true."

"What, what do they say?" Rolo fell into step with him.

"They have extraordinary … Hell, what time is it?"

"Four-thirty. But what …?"

"Hit the street. We have to get another gross before close of business."

They met at the car about an hour later and did a swift count and preliminary sorting of the merchandise. There was more than enough to fill the Vets' order. Murf removed his shirt and started to tape the little packages all over his upper body. Rolo looked on in amazement.

"Oh come on," he laughed. "There's no need for this. I mean it's not heroin. This isn't 'Midnight Express'."

Murf used his strong teeth to sever a piece of tape.

"Look, we have to get past those pious Willies

at the customs. The last thing I want is to have this lot confiscated after all our trouble. Get your finger out and start taping."

"I'll do it if you tell me about Orange women."

"Well, she made me say 'Sod the Pope' before we got down to business."

"You're kidding."

"Maybe, maybe not. Tape up. We must away to our southern sanctuary before our souls go mortally astray in this Godless place." Finishing his self-mummification, Murf opened a bag and extracted a couple of nudie magazines which he placed in the glove compartment.

"That's the first place they'll look," Rolo said derisively.

"Right first time. It's a diversion. The customs man will confiscate these little beauties and assume we're a couple of neophytes. He'll be so pleased with this little haul of soft porn that he won't look any further. He'll just rush back into his little hut as fast as his little legs will carry him. It works, believe me."

"You seem to have everything taped." Rolo enjoyed his ghastly pun.

Dusk was gathering in little folds of pink-edged clouds as the golden Mini sped into the sunset, gamely eating up the miles and giving impudent lurches every time Murf changed gear. Rolo felt uncomfortable and crinkly with all those packets of Gallic epistles taped to his peach-skin torso. He straightened up as they slowed for the army checkpoint which was a good mile inside the border.

"Where are you coming from?" The soldier, a white Brit this time, nursed a vicious looking sten gun against his fatigues.

Murf answered by rote, looking straight ahead, "We were visiting friends in Queens. Anything else, Captain?"

"Don't Captain me, mate. I didn't ask for this sodding duty."

"I understand. You're just obeying orders."

"Facquing Micks." The soldier looked up from Rolo's papers and said, "You're a Yank."

"An American, Yes."

"Stone the bleedin' crows. That's all we need. Who did you meet in Belfast, prods or papes?"

"You've really picked up the local lingo very well," Murf said darkly.

Rolo tried to comfort himself with the thought that Murf wouldn't do anything that might jeopardise his valuable cargo.

"Don't get smart with me. Answer the facquing question." The soldier bent to confront them through the side window, the gun falling with a hideous clatter into the crook of his arm.

"Atheists , as a matter of fact." Murf's eyes narrowed. "Now if you would stand aside we will be on our way." To signal his intent he put gentle pressure on the accelerator and revved the engine which was in neutral. As if reading too much into the hint, the car took on a life of its own, jumped into third gear and crashed through the barrier, splintering the red and white pole.

"Halt!" A shot rang out.

"Holy shit," Rolo cried. "He's firing. Stop the car!"

"I can't. The fucking gears are seized." More bursts of automatic fire ripped through the Mini, shattering glass and metal.

"Get down!" Murf shouted, wrestling with the gear lever which was stuck in third. Rolo crouched but couldn't telescope himself enough to get out of the line of fire. A couple of bullets whistled viciously between the seats and embedded themselves in the dashboard near the St. Christopher plaque which read 'I'm with you up to 60 mph. After that you're on your own'.

"For Christ's sake stop! We're being shot to shit."

Murf stood on the brakes, slewed the car into the ditch and put up his hands. Soldiers appeared from nowhere and pulled him out. A priest, I should have been a priest, Rolo thought as he was flattened against the side of the car and roughly frisked. A tough boy once caught him in a head-lock in the school yard, stole his cucumber sandwiches and broke his glasses. The only consolation was that his little sailor suit was torn beyond repair. Despite desperate entreaties, Mom complained to the Principal of the school and Rolo was shamed beyond understanding. He was never roughed up again but he became a recluse in the schoolyard, moping from the fountain to the bicycle shed until the bell went.

"Wot 'ave we 'ere?" A burly Sergeant

interviewed them from behind a steel desk. "A couple of Fenians right in our laps." His jawline was a frightening reminder of Paudge.

"They made a break for it, Sah. Crashed through the barrier." The soldier nudged them forward with his gun barrel which was more effective than a cattle prod.

"It's all a mistake," Murf said with a sickly smile. He lowered his hands to strengthen the plea for understanding. The gun cracked him twice on the elbow and he raised them again. "The car has a jumpy clutch. Check it out."

The Sergeant nodded to one of his men who fetched a torch and went outside.

"We're n-not IRA," Rolo stammered. "Call the US Consul … We were just visiting B-Belfast…"

"Maybe if I could have a word with the CO…" Murf suggested.

"You're speakin' to 'im," The Sergeant replied. "You don't think Her Majesty's Defence Forces would waste a real officer on red-faced Micks?"

"I suppose not," Murf said. "Anyway, you lads are doing a great job."

The Sergeant got to his feet and put his fists on the desk. "Enough blather. We can detain you for as long as we like. Emergency powers, mate." He ordered them to be searched.

"No-ooo." In alarm Rolo backed away from two privates who approached him. They were bound to discover the merchandise he had taped all over his body. If he had become a priest he might now be relaxing in a deep, button-backed armchair, feet encased in calf-skin slippers after a round of golf, ringing the bell for tea and hot-buttered muffins, before turning to his sermon for the Ladies' Sodality.

After much manhandling, during which he tried to defend his secreted wares and called upon the US Consul about whom the British Army apparently didn't give 'a facq', his shirt came away in strips, scads of tape were mercilessly torn from complaining peach-fuzz, and the small packets fell, like St. Theresa's vision of souls descending into hell. Having done their work the privates stood around gazing at the mound of rubbers rising up from the rough deal floor-boards.

"Wot 'ave we 'ere?" the Sergeant asked rhetorically. "Well I'll be blowed." The penny dropped. "They're smuggling these little beauties into the Republic. That's rich, 'init lads." The soldiery guffawed with their leader.

The Sergeant explored the find with a large boot and slapped his knee. "French ticklers," he croaked. "For Micks? Ahahaha, wot next?"

Rolo was reassured by the sound of laughter however crude, and almost cracked a grin himself, but Murf took a dimmer view.

"All right, so now you know. If you return our property we won't detain you any longer." Murf did his best to appear dignified. The Sergeant turned his beefy face on him, gouging the laughter from his eyes with a baker's kneading fists, and shook his head.

"'E wants us to return 'is property, lads. But

we can't be party to immoral acts in the Republic. No, these little frenchies are now the property of the Crown." The militia turned briefly to the picture of the Monarch hanging on a nail behind the desk as if consulting a higher authority for the right of seizure.

"Oh, come on, lads," Murf said with a forced conspiratorial smile. "You know how it is. You're all men of the world. This is a matter for Customs anyway, although I doubt if they'd be as sharp as you. Let's have them back and we'll all be happy."

The Sergeant sat down and put his boots on the desk with a clatter. "We'd be even happier if we shared out these little spoils of war. Right Lads?"

A murmur of endorsement broke from the nodding soldiery. The Chief was excelling himself, improving morale in this lonely outpost. And that, roughly speaking, was the Sergeant's last word on the matter.

Bereft, they left the barracks, skin smarting under tattered shirts. Murf switched on the engine and the car responded with a leap out of the ditch as if apologising for previous tantrums.

"It's too late now to go back to Belfast," Murf said glumly. "This is a fucking disaster."

"It could have been a lot worse." Rolo was beginning to breathe more easily and the stinging weals on his chest from where the tape had been wrenched were being cooled by the night air whistling through the Mini, which now resembled a colander on wheels.

"How could it have been worse?" Murf asked

petulantly. "Tell me how. Our capital is gone. We've been robbed and abused by that scruff back there. Ashur's car is riddled with bullets. And the Vets will nail my hide to the barn door. How could it be worse?" The plaintive question soared to the stars that came twinkling out and could be seen through the nearest bullet holes. He gripped the steering wheel and bayed at the crescent moon, clearly visible through a hole in the roof. "What more can they do to me?"

When he stopped at the customs post he answered the questions with churlish indifference; for once he really had nothing to declare. He didn't even look at the official who shone a torch inside the car.

"Aha, what have we here?" The official's face flickered with sinister triumph in the torchlight as he fished the nudie magazines out of the glove compartment and had a quick flick through the carnal gloss to whet the appetite for later. The diversion worked like a charm except that there was nothing to divert from, thanks to Her Majesty's Forces.

"God in Heaven," Murf groaned. "Now they're taking 'Oui' and 'Playboy' from us. This is the last straw." He got out of the car with vengeance in his soul. Having taken on the British Army, the Department of Customs and Excise held no fears. "Why don't you take the shirt off my back? Why not," he led the goggle-eyed official towards the ventilated Mini, "take the fucking car as well?"

The custom man's eyes grew wider as he took in the condition of the car, cracked windscreen, smashed front grille that now resembled a camel's mouth, and the variously punctured body. He dropped his clip-board and began to stammer.

"I-I'm sorry … I d-didn't know…" His trembling hands fled to his face as if to shield his vision from worse horrors. Murf, who had been holding him by the lapels, relaxed his grip in puzzlement, wondering if the Department was recruiting mental cases or whether border duty was beginning to take its toll.

"It's all right."

"Are you … sure?" The official looked at him with moist, doe-like eyes, his under-lip atremble. "I wouldn't want ye going away … with bad thoughts of me … I don't want to search ye at all … and I'm dreadful sorry for stopping ye in the first place…" He ground his hands together like a stricken penitent.

Murf thought of all the runs he had done through this very customs post. He had been searched, grilled, dogged and badgered, and now when he had absolutely nothing to declare, he met the greatest push-over of all time, almost weeping in the non-discharge of his duty. What a wasted opportunity! A monumental sense of injustice flooded his being; if only he had something to not declare. He wanted to call all the smugglers who ever drew breath and shout, 'It's OK, Joe's on to-night!'

The customs man offered back the magazines

which fluttered in his outstretched hands.

"I'm so sorry. Take these back now. Never let it be said that Jack Hanlon ever …deprived the IRA of a bit of a read … Or searched anyone coming back from … a mission … in a riddled car. Remember me to the lads in Dundalk." He leant closer as a wisp of cloud covered the moon. "God speed the cause."

Murf brightened instantly, a flicker of light returning to his sad eyes, a bat-wing touch of a smile on hold. "But how do we know for sure that you're a friend?" he inquired sternly.

The official recoiled, a stain of fear spreading across his face. "Aw God, man, ask anyone. Sure, I'm always being lifted…"

"Lifted is it? We know that game. Brought to the barracks in the dead of night, for what? To spill your guts? You could be an informer."

"God in heaven. Never. Me? Never in a million … Me info … infor…" He couldn't say the word which lay like molten lead on his tongue. Murf consulted Rolo with a look.

"We should, mebbe, take him for a ride?"

Rolo who wanted no part of this, stared straight ahead through the cracked windscreen. It would be time now for supper in the Presbytery, a glass of hot milk and some Marietta biscuits…

Jack Hanlon took one look at his rigid, staring face, figured him for a psycho killer, and groaned, "I'm loyal to the cause, lads. Good Christ, I'm as loyal as they come … Me whole family was always on the right side … fellow travellers …

Sure, I'm loyal to a fault…"

Murf let him bleat on and then said, "Prove it."

"How? Just tell me how. Anything, man … anything…"

"Did you confiscate any contraband to-day?"

"Pucks of it. Come into the hut and have a look. But," he added crestfallen, "No arms. 'Twas a slow day for the arms. There's a hunting knife if that's any good to ye … A real pig-sticker…" He gave a nervous grin describing the knife, to show that he was a comrade in arms.

"I'd better check this out." Murf bent to the window. "You stay there, Pat. You know what to do if this is a set-up." He straightened up, tapped a forefinger to his temple and confided to Jack Hanlon, "He's half-saved. But a good man on a job if you take my meaning."

"I do … I do. A good man on a dark night I'd say to be sure…"

They walked into the prefab hut, leaving Rolo staring in fear through the Swiss-cheese holes of Ashur's Mini for signs of military activity. Murf could not get away with posing as an IRA man. It was a nightmare, and he was getting in deeper and deeper with that lunatic who was so twisted up inside he could not see the danger under his nose. Maybe – Good God, why hadn't it dawned on him before? – Murf was deranged, literally out of his mind. The astuteness he sometimes showed was nothing more than the cunning of the truly mad. Rolo sat rigidly not feeling the cold night air swirling through the orifices of the car.

He heard a sound, was afraid to look, but saw out of the corner of his eye a shadowy figure beyond a copse of trees, herding pigs south over the border, smuggling in broad moonlight. He closed his eyes and kept them closed, hoping the hallucination would pass. He wondered about the relative velocity of pigs going south, and thought he might be losing his mind. He longed to be in the library, and that proved it.

Reflected lights appeared on the shattered windscreen. He looked around to see a huge vehicle pulling in at the customs post not ten yards behind the Mini. His first thought was of an army truck crammed with SAS troops, but when the dancing bilious spots cleared from his eyes, he saw that it was a tour bus filled with returning shoppers, singing and drinking beer.

Customs Officer Jack Hanlon came out on his own from the hut and went towards the cab of the bus to talk to the driver. Rolo went on tilt, wondering if a message might be passed, a coded cry for help. In a trance, but with the instinct of a hardened criminal, he struggled out of the Mini to prevent the Customs Man giving a tip off.

"I'll be with you in a second, Barry," the official said to the bus driver.

Rolo crept up behind him and, not recognising his own voice, croaked, "Wave him through. Get rid of him."

Jack Hanlon froze from the proximity of the low-voiced assassin. He waved feebly to the bus driver.

"Go on, Barry … It's all right … No check to-night…"

The bus driver didn't need a second invitation to be gone. Before the bus disappeared into the night Rolo caught a glimpse of the back window stuffed with transistors and stereo-sets; the tarpaulin-covered roof-rack bulged with spin-driers, micro-wave ovens, dish-washers and TV sets. Electric cables and extension cords dangled down like tendrils.

Murf emerged from the prefab carrying three plastic British Home Store bags. He said to his benefactor, "The lads in Dundalk will appreciate this. But mind now, not a word to a sinner."

"No Sir. It's just between you, me and the wall … and," he looked fearfully at Rolo, "your quiet comrade there."

It was the first chance Murf had to survey the damage to the car which really was a mess. Apart from bullet holes and broken glass and dented metal, the door of the boot lolled open, shot out of shape, the bumpers front and back were bent and twisted like spills of silver paper, two windows had disappeared completely, the tail lights had been shot out. Inside, the stuffing dribbled out of the upholstery like the larvae of white maggots. What could he tell Ashur? He caught Jack Hanlon by the sleeve and asked.

"Is that your car over there, the Datsun?"

"Ah Sir, ye wouldn't be thinking…"

"I may have to commandeer it for the cause. This Mini is too hot. The Movement will see you all right."

Jack Hanlon's face crumpled like a dry sponge. "Ah Sir, she wouldn't pull the skin off a rice pudding and she'd be no good at all in a getaway. The shocks are gone on her and she's leakin' oil by the new time. And," He was ready to confess, for an officer of Customs and Excise, the unforgivable sin, "she's no tax on her."

Murf consulted his quiet operations chief. "Leave it," Rolo said in a choking voice, although it occurred to him that they were so far gone that car theft wouldn't make much difference. "Leave it."

"You're lucky my friend has a kind heart." Murf sat into the hapless Mini.

"I can see he has," Jack Hanlon said with great relief. "He's hardly a gunman at all … except when he has to be…"

They hadn't quite lurched into second gear when Murf started to grin.

"God never closed one door but he opened a window." He wiped his eyes with the back of a hand. "Just look in the bags. Go ahead, take a peek."

Rolo unclenched a catatonic hand and reached back. The first bag was a rubber cornucopia, teeming with at least five gross of assorted condoms. He remembered a long time ago being at a church fête in Cheltenham, PA, Mom picking lint from the collar of his velvet blazer as he tried to guess the number of rubber balls in a basket. Because of pimples he wasn't allowed coke or soda pop, nor was he allowed stand near the booth where the nice girl was selling kisses. It was hard now to imagine how he kicked against the goad of such cosseting. He was sheltered even from the cloudless skies.

"It seems," Murf began, still chortling, "It seems … Oh Lord," he snorted. "Start again. A group of liberated women tried to bring these contraceptives down today, as a protest. Freedom to control their own bodies or something … quite laudable of course … The Press were there in force and our good friend, Jack Hanlon, dutiful to the last, confiscated the lot. One woman's poison is another man's meat. Can you believe it?"

There had been three hundred and fifteen balls in the basket. He had guessed four hundred and cried because he missed the prize, which was an iced cake. Mom baked him a special cake that night to make it up to him. It was supposed to be all for him but his sister scoffed half of it and gave him a clip around the ear when he complained. Still, they were minor tribulations in retrospect. He had not risked life or limb as he had just done, fleeing in a bullet-ridden car with a truckload of stolen Durex, and a guerrilla army no doubt in hot pursuit.

"Don't you want to know what's in the other bags?"

"What's in the other bags?" He used to have a real leather schoolbag with chrome buckles and a luminous yellow strip to keep him safe from traffic as he trotted home to Cheltenham on his little legs to be greeted at the door by Mom with outstretched arms.

"You name it," Murf said. "Transistors, toasters, a food mixer – we could give that to The Cart – a pacemaker, two hearing aids, multitudinous dirty books and mags, and the pig-sticker of course. Jack gutted the place, thrust the lot on me. I don't know … this place gets weirder and weirder." He paused for breath, then lit a Gold Flake and looked across at Rolo. "You're very quiet."

"Mmmmmn." Mom was such a good cook, too. Her home-made toffee was wonderful and then there was the pecan pie, always left to cool on the window sill of the kitchen…

"No more shrink-talk anyway. That's a relief." Murf stared ahead at the dark, winding road, grinning to himself. In his book it had been a most successful day, made sweeter by the final coup at the customs post. It occurred to him that success could only be truly savoured when the whiff of defeat tickled the nostrils.

Gobbling up the miles, wind whistling through the perforated car like an Aeolian harp, they reached Drogheda by nine-thirty. From then on a light drizzle fell. Since the wipers didn't work anymore they had no option but to knock out what remained of the windscreen. That was when it really got cold. It was like a wind-tunnel in the unglazed auto. Rolo's hair was blown back like the wings of Mercury and his prow-like nose was as red and moist as a slice of watermelon. The wounded Mini performed well, however, and with great heart, lurching through turbulences with that final burst of energy that sometimes comes before total collapse. This last splurge of the adrenals got them to Balbriggan in jig time, but the cold had gotten the better of Murf who pulled off the road when they left the town behind.

"We're going to die from exposure," he chattered, beating his arms against his sides. A quick rummage in the boot of the car revealed nothing of a thermal nature; Ashur had not yet acquired those plaid woollen rugs that grace the laps and warm the genitalia of the tweedy set at rugger matches and point-to-point race meetings. Murf fought his way through a hedge, ripping his trousers on concealed barbed wire, and stumbled over the furrows to a barn that brooded quietly on the dark side of a hill. After much fumbling, misguided footsteps and smothered oaths, he found a couple of old tarpaulin covers probably used for protecting haystacks. They draped these makeshift stoles, speckled with chicken shit and rodent droppings, about their shoulders and drove on through the punishing night.

Just north of Malahide, Rolo rallied a little from his shock-induced detachment to suggest in a cool and neutral tone, "I think there may be a car following us."

"There is no fixed meaning anyway, so fuck it all."
—The Deconstructionist Handbook

"Thus we live, forever taking leave."
—Rainer Maria Rilke

CHAPTER 5

NEWMAN HOUSE WAS the unlikely venue for the transaction with the Vets who stood around Murf in the Pax Romana room and checked the contents of the bag he had handed over. These beefy ones in lambswool coats and cavalry twills were living proof that silk purses could be made from sows' ears. Their Dads had made fortunes out of the Brucellosis Eradication Scheme by the simple device of turning this mild bovine influenza into a self-perpetuating epidemic. Artificial insemination had also stood them in good stead.

Their spokesman eventually grunted, indicating that the tally was correct. Murf felt relieved that the debt was paid at last and that he was finally shut of them. But he had another problem now. Ashur had thrown a conniption fit over the state of his Mini and would not even listen to the argument that the car had acquired a certain cachet from being shot up by the British Army. When it was pointed out to him that used rubber bullets were worth four quid each on the open market, it had no effect whatever. So Murf was expecting a large bill, if not indeed a writ, from that quarter. He was finding it increasingly difficult to keep ahead of the game. For every step forward there were two backward ones, all in the middle of a minefield.

He strolled through Iveagh Gardens, which basked in the first small mercies of summer. Girls lay on the grass, legs tucked daintily under flared cotton dresses, open books nestling in laps, unperturbed by the bare-chested hearties who pranced among them tossing rugby and Gaelic balls to each other. Over the incoherent buzz of insects came the sharper more definite sounds of tennis. Through the delicately shaded lime-green light, Murf nodded at some familiar faces and, with an unaccustomed twinge of sadness, realized that by late summer, when *their* exams would be over, he would probably never see them again. Good-bye Mr. Chips. To cheer himself up he thought of Gobnait. She was on night duty this month which meant she would be at home right now and probably in bed...

By one of the fountains he met up with Rolo who had just put in a strenuous hour, trying unsuccessfully to extract Budden's 'Motive Power' from a librarian. In the manner of hard chaws they greeted each other with curt nods, and traversed in silence the gravelled pathways that swirled around the fountain in the pattern of a Celtic Cross.

"There's a guy over there … by the tennis courts…"

"Don't say it," Murf interrupted. "I don't believe it." He furrowed his noble brow and let his dark head sag. Who was it this time? It couldn't be the Vets, and Ashur was on hold at least for a while. And surely not the IRA or Ulster Volunteer Force – all that was merely Rolo's fevered imagination at work. He was punchy from pursuit.

"Who is it this time," he asked wearily, refusing to make the effort of looking up.

"I think he's a member of the Student Council." Rolo screwed up his eyes in an effort of sun-dazzled recall. "McDonnell, I think…"

A tall gangly figure emerged from a hedge and approached across a lawn, skirting a flower bed of snapdragons and wallflowers. His face, amorphous in the strong light, did not become any more defined as he drew near, but it did hold a certain smug twist of something to be imparted rather than shared. Murf continued to walk and McDonnell fell into stride with him, this accommodation being part of his stock-in-trade as a budding politician.

"I have to talk to you alone," he said, squinting his blah-like face as if trying to knead it into some kind of recognizable shape.

"Spit it out, McDonnell."

"All right. The President wants to see you."

Murf looked up for the first time. It was more than he expected or wanted, but something in his expression accepted that the time had come, the noose was tightening.

"What's it about?"

"The future of the Rag. It seems you went too far." McDonnell shrugged his sloping shoulders indicating that he was merely an honest broker. "The Guards made a formal complaint and threatened to ban all Rags in the future. We – the Student Council, I mean, – have urged the President to look for a compromise."

Murf pinned him with a gimlet eye. "What kind of compromise?" he asked slowly in a voice that muffled the sound of a safety catch being released. A Gaelic football rolled towards him and he neatly chipped it away.

McDonnell twisted his neck as he tightened the knot of his tie which bore the logo of some club or other. He probably had a wardrobe full of club ties to demonstrate his allegiance to everything good and true.

"The Guards finally agreed to let the Rags continue *if* the College handles the disciplinary side of the recent episode in a meaningful way." McDonnell shrugged slightly again as if to disassociate himself from this deal which had been struck, and which, by the shape of his lips, he seemed to consider distasteful.

By instinct Murf had been circling his man, whose pale glutenous face showed a nest of blackheads in the flange of his nose.

"So, I'm to be delivered up on a platter to save the Rag, is that it?" Murf knew that he had been set up by this white worm who was pretending to be nothing more than a messenger. He immediately bracketed him with Fanning. Was it possible that all politicians crawled from under the same stone?

"I wouldn't put it like that," McDonnell said silkily. He was good, Murf had to admit, as nuanced as the different shades of pale that whispered across the characterless planes of his face. Already a group leader in the Fianna Fáil Youth Movement, he was, at twenty-one, a regular little soldier of destiny.

"You've picked the wrong fall guy." Murf stuck an accusing forefinger in his face.

"The President has pulled your file and is not impressed. You have not, apparently, covered yourself in glory in this institution. I believe … you have sold allotments in this very garden to botany students…"

"This is rich, coming from you." Murf wasn't quite able to muster the detachment needed for sarcasm. "I know all about that machine you're part of on the Council. I know all about those jaunts to the Continent on expenses. And the rigged elections. Don't lecture me on morality, you shit." Somewhere at the centre of Murf's angst was the same feeling he had that night at the track with Ashur, the sense of being left behind by more purposeful protégés. He glanced at the high vine-covered wall that formed the northern perimeter of the gardens, and felt imprisoned.

McDonnell did not react. "I'm just delivering the message. You're to see the President in his rooms at three-thirty to-day." He turned and walked away. His henchmen materialised from the shrubbery and formed a protective circle around him – a giant condom.

"Fascist pricks!" Murf spat out, watching them march down the crunching gravel drive. "Behold the future Government of this distressful country, Rolo. My God, was it for this that Pearse and his comrades gave their lives?"

Try as he might, Rolo couldn't quite fight off the feeling that Murf's exploits had finally caught up on him, incongruously in this fragrant sanctuary. This could even be the thin end of the wedge. What if the IRA heard about the incident at the customs post? Had there been a car tailing them from Balbriggan into Dublin?

Murf walked on in silence, head lowered like an animal cropping grass. Rolo respected the silent rite of rumination, knowing that a superior instinct for survival was at work. Why the hell did he spend so much energy on diversion, knowing that he would have to break the laws of entropy to extricate himself from the consequences? Like the pendulum he would never come to rest, but oscillate forever. If he was sent down now, as seemed possible, Fanning would write him off as a waster and send him careering into that void where he would have no distraction from himself.

Murf stopped to watch one of the gardeners weed a herbaceous border and then asked Rolo if he could lend him a quid.

The President had an earnest sort of face, made

even more forthright by the reassuring pipe that stuck out under a pelmet of salt-and-pepper moustache. Murf had seen him on TV – some Sunday evening programme about values in modern society, that sort of thing. His faded jacket was covered by a rather intimidating gown not unlike the one worn by Judge Prendergast. This was the big one, Murf knew, requiring the performance of a lifetime.

The President sat behind a large desk littered with framed photos of his family, and signed off some letters with a flourish. They waited for the Chaplain, Father Burn, who was to be a sort of angel's advocate in this kangaroo court, and who now lumbered in, face shining like a cox's pippin, effusive in his apologies.

The President began the quasi-judicial proceedings, giving a few quick puffs to his pipe to keep it in good heart. He outlined his understanding of Murf's part in the Rag and subsequent events. Not having had time to read the room, Murf's antennae were working overtime in search of clues and trinkets of meaning.

Having explained the nature of the compromise reached with the Guards, the President went on.

"I looked at your file, Mr Murphy, and I have to say that your record is atrocious in terms of academic achievement and general behaviour. Do you follow me so far?"

"Y-yes, Sir." Murf looked grave and somewhat distracted. His fingers nervously shredded the frayed cuffs of the gardener's jacket which he had just borrowed for a couple of quid.

"I'm afraid that in all the circumstances I have no option but to expel you from this university. As you know, you would have been sent down last autumn after your fifth failure, were it not for a technical Grandfather clause. I have your transcript to hand." He briefly held it up by a corner and let it drop with the semblance of a shudder. "Now, however, your conduct warrants expulsion. Stealing cadavers from the College of Surgeons, selling library places to naïve first-year students, etc. These actions are egregious and unacceptable. There are even rumours of a clandestine trade in prophylactics which would of course run counter to the Catholic ethos of this university. But since this is hearsay we will not take it into the reckoning." He lay back and ran a pipe-cleaner up the shaft of his Meerschaum pipe with the same verve he had just used in gutting Murf. "Do you have anything to say?"

Murf shook his head slowly. "No, thank you." He pulled a handkerchief from his pocket and blew his nose. "It's just that … I haven't been feeling myself lately … But it's a personal matter … It has no bearing…" He gave a long noisy expurgation into the frayed handkerchief, forcing the blow through the dry bore of his nose which made his eyes water – a small bonus.

"Murf," the Chaplain said gently, his eyes big as boiled eggs with concern. "Maybe you should share this with us. It may have a bearing."

"I don't believe in … special pleading." His sinuses hurt from the dry nasal gawk. "The President is right. I'm no credit to this institution. I've even borrowed money from you."

The Chaplain pounced on this cue. "But you've paid it back, every penny. I have your … aam … account right here. Now come on, Murf. Please say something in your own defence. Some young men mature late. Remember the prodigal son."

Murf gave a wan smile in appreciation of the priest's Panglossian faith.

"I'm afraid the Rag stunt … well, I didn't really know what I was doing…"

"Oh, and why is that?" the Present inquired glacially.

"Too much drink … I'm afraid."

"That's hardly an excuse," the President countered.

"I couldn't help noticing," Father Burn cut in, fearful of the implied criticism, "that you are wearing a Pioneer pin."

Murf looked down in surprise at his lapel and spotted the glinting pin. Who would have thought that the damn gardener who stuck him for two quid for a loan of the jacket would have been a teetotaller? He coped as well as he could with this unexpected turn.

"I've no right to wear this," he said with self-loathing. "I've broken my pledge … Just one lapse, but nevertheless…" He plucked out the little shield and threw it in the waste basket, looking wistfully after it. He hoped the action was not over the top.

"What caused you to break your pledge?" the Chaplain prompted softly, right on cue. "There must have been a reason. Does it by any chance relate to the personal matter you mentioned before?" The priest was so keen to see good, he could, Murf thought gratefully, be pushed down a sewer and think he'd been saved from walking under a bus.

"Forgive me ... I'd rather not say..." Murf waved a hand in a feeble gesture of dismissal. "It doesn't matter ... now."

"Please, Murf," the Chaplain insisted gently, "You must tell us, however difficult it may be for you." He leant forward earnestly and stifled a cough as he entered the exhaust stream of the President's pipe.

"I had to ... numb the pain..." Murf covered his face and turned sideways to give them a view, for the first time, of the black diamond patch tacked on to the sleeve of the gardener's jacket. The powerful symbol of mourning produced a shocked silence, suffused with respect, shame, and thoughts of the travesty of justice there might have been.

"I'm so sorry," the Chaplain said wretchedly. "We had no idea you were bereaved."

The President shifted uneasily and offered his condolences. The pipe was laid in the ash-tray; one didn't smoke at a time like this.

"You should have mentioned this earlier,"

Father Burn said in lugubrious tones. "May I ask whether … I mean a close…?"

"My stepfather, Father." Murf couldn't bring himself to say his father, even though that would have been the clincher. It might also have been the truth. He pulled out the handkerchief, this time with a rosary beads entangled in it, and blew his nose a little more sparingly than the first time. In hushed tones the President excused himself and left the room for a moment.

The Chaplain said of his departing back, "We're fortunate in our President. He's an understanding man."

"I know, Father."

"At times of bereavement we have to resign ourselves, Murf. It may be hard to accept it now, but time can and does heal." The priest rummaged in the waste basket and retrieved the Pioneer pin. "Here, wear this with pride. One lapse is of no account. The power of forgiveness is as infinite as our Maker is wise. Never forget that. Remember 'The Hound of Heaven'? 'Rise, clasp My hand and come'…?"

Murf was touched by the priest's sincerity but he couldn't allow himself to weaken now. He was away on a hack, on the pig's back; it had worked like a charm.

"Do you think the President will buy … I mean re-consider?"

Father Burn reached across the desk and patted the hand that still clutched the moist handkerchief. "Don't worry. He's a decent man. Speak of the devil…" he quipped out of a full heart as the President resumed his seat. He was followed by a secretary bearing a tray of coffee and biscuits.

"Well, Mr. Murphy, I'm afraid we've been rather hard on you," the President said. "I hope you don't take it amiss. It's sometimes difficult to get all of the pertinent facts." He passed the plate of biscuits, and Murf chose a Kerry Cream, a fig-roll and two ginger snaps which he balanced in the curve of the elegant Beleek saucer on his knee. He felt like an actor after a successful opening night, a warm glow in the innards, the hectic flush of footlights still in his face. He suddenly recalled winning the balloon race at the school sports and his Dad proudly bringing him for a treat – lemonade and custard-cream cakes – to Baker's café near the tholsel. His feet dangled over the chair, not even reaching the first rung, but he had that same inner warmth that allowed him to be himself. His trophy for the race was an alarm clock made in Taiwan. He gave it to his Dad on his next birthday and it had pride of place in his office for what Murf thought then would be forever.

"I understand." Murf had to snap out of his reverie. "Sometimes there are so many facts that one has to choose between them. I believe Karl Popper has drawn our attention to this dilemma." Knowing that the President had written on Popper, Murf had done some research during lunchtime by button-holing a cleric in the Annex. He didn't need to name-drop now but thought it would be a pity to waste the fruits of his research.

The President smiled and the dottle gurgled happily in the bowl of his Meerschaum. "It is a pity you don't apply yourself more, Mr. Murphy. You do seem to be most intelligent." The Chaplain beamed his agreement.

"Oh, I doubt that," Murf demurred, "Though I do tend to believe that exams are a rather inexact test of ability."

"Interesting viewpoint." The President seemed to be taken with his opinions and keen to pursue them. "How do you find lectures and other teaching aids in this college?"

Murf sipped his coffee reflectively and helped himself to several more biscuits from the proffered plate, including a couple of chocolate-covered Goldgrains. A Cart lodger could not afford to pass up any offer of supplementary nutrients.

"The system is basically good," Murf said judiciously. "But some lecturers could make more of an effort, as could librarians who for some reason don't seem to be interested in locating books." He thought of the frustrations of Rolo where the library was concerned.

"But then", the President said, "There are some students who never return books and even pawn them."

Murf nodded gravely. "I'm aware of that. Vets and other ingrates. And the worst offenders are members of the Student Council." This was sweet and heady wine. He even adopted McDonnell's distancing trick; he was simply a disinterested observer, quite above it all. "We expect more from our future politicians somehow. We don't expect them to fiddle expenses and rig elections." He spread his hands resignedly. "It's not clear where we should look for good example anymore, barring the church, of course." He was rewarded by a smile from the Chaplain.

"I thought the student body were satisfied with their council of representatives," the President put in.

Good Heavens, no." Murf risked a mild chuckle of incredulity. "Still, who am I to cast the first stone?" A sudden thought occurred which he could not let slip by. "Some might say that this institution has had its share of blueshirts…"

The grimness that settled over the faces of his interrogators showed how deeply the bolt had gone home. He had done for McDonnell and his henchmen with that *coup de grace*. Strange the power of a word – blueshirt, informer, Provo. His satisfaction was multiplied when he saw the President pluck a pen from his Connemara marble desk set and make some notes.

The President looked up from his desk to ask if the American, Mr. Rolo Sangster, had been involved in the Rag stunt. Murf went on tilt. Was it possible that, having failed to nail him, the President was casting around for another scapegoat to deliver up to the Guards? Rolo wouldn't stand a chance. He wouldn't, Murf thought with grim humour, have a leg to stand on. And the B. Mech. Eng. meant so much to him.

"Absolutely not," he answered hotly. "He is a

very fine character … who tries to work hard … I mean the very thought of…" He started to block badly; sincerity was rough going. Fortunately, the Chaplain rowed in to defend Rolo.

Murf pushed back his chair, thinking of celebrations in Hartos which could commence immediately after the Holy Hour. He could see the creamy head rise intriguingly to the top of the glass and feel the foam part magically around his upper lip.

"Before you go, Mr Murphy," the President said smiling, "I should tell you that I have just been on the telephone to your Stepfather. It seems that his demise has been exaggerated. He assures me that he is fit and well, and he advises that we should discount anything you might say on any subject. Mr. Fanning and I have met before." He lay back in the swivel chair, tapping his teeth with the stem of the Meerschaum. Apart from the tapping which could have been the timing device on a neutron bomb, a pall of silence lay over the room. Murf's mouth hung open. Even if he could come up with an excuse he would not be able to do it justice, for his stomach was full of snakes. The Chaplain groaned, "Oh Lord," and looked down at his black shoes; the red apples of his face had lost their sheen.

Murf could hardly believe he'd been bested. Academics were supposed to be gullible and naïve. They never had to live on their wits. The President of a university was the archetypal fuddy-duddy, lacking in street smarts and should have been a push-over. Why couldn't people stay in their proper pigeon-holes? Was there something in the water to account for such mutations? The matador should not be gored by a bull; the bull should not be blind; the President should not be savvy. The world was going to hell in a hand-basket. If there were no predictable categories anymore what was the point of living?

Murf was going to suggest that Fanning was lying but how could one lie about not being dead? He changed tack.

"I must have…been misinformed … or I picked it up wrong…" This was pathetic and he knew it.

The President held up a hand. "Don't embarrass yourself, Mr Murphy. The jig, as they say, is up." He gave an alarmingly frank and almost boyish grin. Gone was the begowned formality, the gravitas of high office. Even the Goddamn pipe was set aside. "You know, Murf, you can't con a con. I started my career on a building site before I got the call to academic life. It was good training in chicanery. You're not bad, but your technique needs a little work." He put his feet up on the desk and lay back.

Murf looked at him in awe, knowing too late that he was in the presence of a master.

"May I ask what put you on to me?"

"Well, the rosary beads for one thing. It was a bit over the top. But when you work with props you have to be very careful. Only women use mother-of-pearl beads." He swung his feet off the desk and became more business-like. "In a way we'll be sorry to lose you. We do need some characters around the place but, unfortunately, we're not auditioning right now. So that's about it."

"That's it?" Murf repeated as a question. The roguish fellow-feeling with the President was swept aside and the shock waves kept coming. "I'm out?"

"'Fraid so." The President stood, ending the meeting. He tightened the gown about his shoulders, thus ringing the curtain down. The finale had come and gone; there were no bouquets.

On the way out Murf looked back once to see the Chaplain's sad face, and was sorry to have undermined his irrepressible faith and trust. Something maybe to be said for innocence after all, though it does get exploited by shrewd bastards like Fanning, to whom I have now handed my head on a platter. What had Rolo said about self-sabotage? No matter, as I walk in wonderment down this curving staircase for the last time and see life going on all around me as if nothing had happened.

"What a waste," the Chaplain murmured as he made to leave the President's office.

"Yes indeed. But standards must be maintained. We'll soon be in the Common Market. The deadwood has to make room for the diligent. We have to turn out European men and women, not arrested pubescents lingering in the Celtic twilight. No more *Sturm und Drang*, Chaplain."

Pratfalls were no good, he thought, when the audience demanded wit.

"No real harm in him," the Chaplain continued, "compared with some of our more successful citizens who go from boardroom to boardroom carving up the usufruct. 'Greasy fingers fumbling in a till…'"

"A venal world, Father," the President conceded. "There are, as you say, those who gain much by doing very little. The country is in the grip of entropy." He hung his gown carefully on the back of the door. "We're teeing off at three with Bishop Quinlan and that pro-contraception Senator, both single-figure men. I hope you've been working on your short game."

"I have," the Chaplain admitted, or rather confessed.

The President buzzed his secretary and asked for his car to be brought around to the front gate.

By the time he'd reached the bottom of the staircase, Murf felt dizzy. Hard to second-guess the unpredictable and Protean. With everyone behaving out of character one's insights were stymied, intuition poleaxed. Either he was losing it or the world was changing faster than he could dance. He'd lost, as they say in West Cork, the pattern of himself. Pity the poor chameleon who must try to hide in a kaleidoscope of ever-changing colour.

Can't face Rolo; he'll take it so badly. Unsettling to see his jaw drop and eyes grow round behind the specs. Besides, it's like looking in a mirror … or watching my Dad shave with that old cut-throat which he stropped with gentle strokes, whistling 'Ten Green Bottles' through the lather. I will arise and go now … to where peace comes dropping slow … and live alone in the bee-loud glade. But first clean out my locker and then decamp, for ever and a day.

The black and white squares of the main hall traversed all day by smart young women, porters' office walled with keys and pigeon-holes, my favourite radiator shining still, bulletin boards of welcome and upsetting news, all soon to be memories. Open this hold-all and stuff the booty in. Not much to show for five years, half a locker full. Bankruptcy must be like this. Should have a closing-down sale to liquidate these miserable assets. Here they come, these worthy clerics like mallard ducks in formation, to stow bicycle clips and black berets. See how life goes on despite calamity. Maybe they would buy my remaindered stock of Gallic epistles. You never know with all this liberalism coming in. Buy one and never be father, Father. Paternal in name only. If a man burn it is better to take unto him a woman, or harlot in the Hebrew version, than to take himself in hand like poor Onan. Just the few left. Half-price these seed bags for seminarians. Going fast, just a few left now.

"Good Heavens, take those filthy things away. You are a tool of the devil!" Senior seminarian seems shocked. Unhappily not, mine lacks a trident. Come, kind clerics, spread some dues around.

"What are those things he's selling?" The infant cleric runting behind the herd seems keen.

"Quiet, Anselm, you haven't come to that chapter in Apologetics yet."

How quickly they melt away, shooing Anselm in front, protecting him, mouthing pious aspirations. Am I so untouchable? But that was a cheap shot, scandalising those innocents, one of whom might be a future Chaplain. Mind must be going. Grief can derange, they say, cause the cerebellum to slip its moorings and float off into a sea of fantasy.

Might as well remove my name-tag from locker and put it with the other mementoes in this bag. Now up these steps for the last time. Farewell Annex of coffee fame and heated talk, and favourite stall of graffiti that leaves little to the imagination. Never to borrow the porters' newspapers again or wait by these Doric columns to waylay rejoicing exam-passers. Or plot to keep poor Rolo out of the library where he was a victim of librarian abuse anyway.

Now under these portals take a last look at the 'Ad Astra' motto neatly carved in limestone. Never made it to the stars and never will for I have been truly canned. No-one sitting on these steps under apple blossom suddenly out will know I've gone. Or care. For I am a busted flush with bells on. Hard world beyond these portals, so they say. We'll soon see. Best years of one's life in here, so also do they say, which means the rest must be truly shit.

Stop this self-pity. Remember that young lad who lost his Dad in Croke Park and stood for hours biting his lip in panic. Until found eventually. And swore never to stand still again. To hell with them all. Freedom at last. Bring on anarchy, the only way to flush away complacent fat shits. Oh, death where is thy victory? I should be living at this hour. And so I am. Don't leave yet without one last exercise of freedom, one final fling.

So this is the library that has hounded Rolo so, and these the knitting Harpies. Rest my hold-all on the counter while lighting this Gold Flake. Dear me, it doesn't take much to distract these studious folk whose faces now uptilt in pale hope of some diversion. Comforting to know one's reputation does after all precede one. Sense of *déjà vu*, oddly in the future.

"Extinguish that cigarette immediately! Don't you know where you are?" It seems the crotchety old bun-headed Fury is alive. Which clacks more, her dentures or knitting needles? Test her mettle by dropping a little glowing ash on the counter and see a further pinching of the mandible, and hear an extra murmur of excitement from this captive audience, starved of spectacle and the thrill of disorder.

"Get out of here!" The crone doesn't give up. Must push her and the system further. Ask for a book. But which? It's been so long. Five years in tertiary education and can't think of a single book. Poor show ... Ah, but I've got it.

"Run along and fetch me a copy of the Oxford English Dictionary. As my old English teacher used to say, 'When in doubt, get out your dic.'"

"It's out." The crone cannot resist the reflex of long practice.

"Really?" Quickly check one's flies. Ham it up for this fun-loving audience now erupting into hoots and whistles. I shall exit well after all.

"You're drunk and disgusting. Summon the porters immediately."

Now to rummage in my bag to treat these poor wretches beating their brains out in frustration. Let them have all three remaining gross, ribbed and plain, French and basic Anglo-Saxon.

"Here you go, Children. All you Freshers I ever conned, come and get these beauties, brought to you at incredible expense from the Northern frontier. Forgive this interruption and you won't have to interrupt yourselves any more." Heartening to see the prophylactics raining down from vaulted space. And students clambering, knocking over furniture, to get their share.

"Enjoy! Enjoy!" Another launch of little packets brings even more spectacular results and elevates the soul. Librarians look defiled. Or vapourised in this fall-out. Their iron rule is broken for good.

Here the porters come to take me away. More uniforms. Always uniforms. Hands gripping me in unseemly places. This is not a fit exit. Must turn table one more time and leave with dignity. How does that Bogside accent go again?

"Do not be interferin' now, if ye know what's gude for ye. This is an IRA recruitment mission, d'ye unnerstand?" Some hands slide off in wonderment but not enough. What is that semi-secret saying? Our day will come? That's it. And the clenched fist.

"Tiocfaidh ar lá." My God it works! They blanch and fall away, melting like an ice cap in retreat. Now that they are stunned it is time to slip away with empty bag and soul. Regret not using the IRA ploy before. What power it gives.

Still, the cockles warmed by cheers of gratitude from liberated swots, and sight of porters cowering against the wall. But most of all, librarians utterly foiled, besmirched, their strangle-hold broken for good. Yes, this is more like it. A suitable envoi. The echo of departing steps, as out into the world I go. Nothing became my life here as the manner of leaving it.

He trudged up the painfully familiar and sweeping ramp of Leeson Street, only partly aware of the set purpose in his sad steps, until he slipped between the sheets and lay beside Gobnait furry with sleep, blinking in surprise. He pushed Teddy aside and laid his head on her welcoming, lace-edged breast, a vanquished warrior sick at heart, running from the field of battle into the arms of a woman good and true. Where peace came dropping slow…

"Murf, I'm sorry. But I knew you'd go too far sooner or later." She rubbed his back.

To his consternation and undying shame, tears came to his eyes.

"Fuck them all," he sobbed and sniffled, "from a great height." It wasn't just the expulsion. They had seen through him, right through the carapace to whatever miserable soft flesh lurked and shrivelled within, and winkled him out, to wither and turn to dust. Visibility was painful as would be growth, if it came to that. And then there was Fanning, the outright winner.

Smoothing his hair, her hands, as she woke up, became more playful and inquisitive, discovering that he was not completely down and out, until gradually the miasma of sleep and distress receded and each dissolved into the other in the narrow warm bed.

His Dad would read as he walked by the canal, waving to greet friends without looking up from the book which he held straight out in front of him. Sycamore seeds spiralled down as Murf, trotting in tow, kicked up drifts of rusty leaves with his new vulcanised wellington boots which bellied out around his thin calves. He also kept an eye peeled on the hedges because his Dad asked him to pick blackberry leaves, not the blackberries, only the leaves. It was an unusual request but Murf didn't question it.

They stopped once to see a dead fox slung

over a road sign.

"No more chicken dinners for you, old son," his Dad spoke sadly to the fox as if it were alive and human.

Their walk usually led them to Bramble Well to take a drink of spring water, then home by the back road, past the Quaker's graveyard with the humps of earth under which the coffins were placed standing up, or so they said.

In town, sun beat on concrete walls, making mica glisten, giving expression to the dun surfaces. From imagined faces in the walls, the hum of telephone wires, the heat shimmer over tarred roads, came a feeling of stealth, tranquility so scary it made him shiver. It was as if the present balance of things was too delicately poised to last, and that a raindrop moving slowly down a leaf could bring everything to ruin.

"What are the blackberry leaves for, Dad?"

"Oh, it's just a little experiment. Promise me that you won't tell your mother."

"I promise."

Sometime later he was taking in the dustbin and he noticed the blackberry leaves stuck to the bottom. Wet and colourless, they looked as if they had been boiled. He had turned eighteen before he understood the significance of the boiled leaves.

"You're miles away." Gobnait gently disentangled herself. Murf came out of his reverie horrified. Couldn't even pass it off as brewer's droop or ever laugh at Crowley again. The beginning of the end, impotent at twenty-five.

Should put it in the Guinness Book of World Records: Hard chaw in mid-twenties, sober and with no known ailments or performance anxiety, experiences first failure in the sack. From then on he remained unresponsive to all female blandishments and stayed celibate for the rest of his unhappy life. Needless to say, there were no young Murfs.

"Relax," Gobnait said soothingly.

"I am relaxed," he replied bitterly, not wanting too much kindness. He was afraid to try again; a second failure would put the kibosh on it. It was like the time, before he had learnt to swim, he had fallen into the canal and was afraid to put his feet down in case he *couldn't* touch bottom. He nearly drowned in three feet of water. Fear of fear.

"Is it me?" she asked.

He looked sideways at her, searching for signs of sarcasm, and to his relief found none. He squeezed her hand.

"No. It's me. Shock or something. Memories. I don't know…"

"You're not a machine. " She propped herself up on an elbow, the glow of a bedside lamp bathing her smooth face. "What are you going to do now? I mean about the future."

"I don't know." His answer was as miserable and uncertain as he felt. He couldn't put off the future anymore by filling the hours with pointless activity. But an illusionist without props wouldn't go far. It chilled him to the bone.

"Maybe you could go and see the President

again," she suggested. "Make a clean breast of it."

"No, it's over. Anyway I suppose it's time to be chucked out of the nest." He did feel like a fledgling fluttering in a hopeless, limp-winged spiral down to the forest floor; it was pathetic.

"What about a job? It's not unknown for people to work."

"With *my* qualifications? I suppose I could … go home." The last word was a bitter one, mocking the idea of 'home'. Fanning might take him in as a supplicant or even a penitent. Who ever said the Prodigal Son was happy to go home? He had merely run out of options. He probably wanted to sneak in the back door without any fuss and pretend that nothing had happened.

In a clotting voice he told her something of his family circumstances. She listened intently, sensing that it was rare enough for him to open up like that. The lights of traffic wandered over walls and ceiling in an aimless pattern. The distant street sounds became moist from rain.

"It seems to me," Gobnait said when Murf had unburdened himself, "that Fanning owes you. I'm sure he'd take you into the business."

"Oh God, don't put it like that…"

"I don't mean as a charitable gesture. He has no option. It's your birth-right."

He caught himself smiling at her vehemence. She was a perfect fullback on his team.

"Birth-right," he repeated as if he'd bitten into a lemon.

"Don't confuse it with privilege," she said.

"It's your right. Your Dad would have wanted it. You don't have to ask Fanning. *Demand* it. He sounds such a creep anyway, he wouldn't have the balls to refuse."

Murf wasn't used to this kind of support, and couldn't help liking it. The danger was coming to depend on it.

"He'll know I'm after his hide. And I *will* go over the books."

She pursed her lips weighing this up. "That's a risk he'll have to take. Anyway, use a bit of diplomacy. Tell the old bastard you want to help him, that you've finally seen the error of your ways…"

"Such cunning in one so young," he marvelled. Cosier now in this rumpled bed, he was more disposed to believe that somebody was actually trying to help him, without any axe to grind. Maybe she did like him despite his record-breaking impotence. His preference had been the roar of the crowd rather than the approbation of a single person. Was that in the process of changing?

"Something like that." She jiggled her eyebrows in a parody of scheming. "Remember, your mother will be on your side too."

He wasn't so sure about that. "She's a bit … ineffectual now. Fanning has her in the palm of his hand."

"Yes, but she still has a majority of the business." Gobnait had followed the narrative very well and had absorbed all the salient facts. She closed one eye and snapped out a finger. "Fanning can't be all that sure of himself. And if he's interested in politics, as you say, then he can't afford to rock the boat … with her or with the locals she grew up with. I'm from a small town too. I know how these things work. A blow-in has to be very careful."

Murf's eyes never left her face. "Remind me never to make an enemy of you."

"As if you would." She gave him a peck on the cheek.

"Gobnait."

"What?"

"I'm all right now. I won't be going into the Guinness Book of Records…"

"Oh Lord, I'm on duty at ten."

"But you can't leave *now*."

She raised the sheet and agreed.

In the Westmoreland Street Bewleys, within breathing distance of the irresistible coffee urns, Rolo, who had waited up for Murf for most of the night, could only repeat the word.

"Expelled … expelled …?"

Murf nodded. "The President is no slouch. Boy, I really met my match. It was like running into a brick wall, bouncing back, then stepping on a rake. He got me coming and going.

Rolo sat bolt upright on the wobbly bent-wood

chair, gripping the edge of the glass-topped table. How could Murf not have wriggled out of it? "I can't believe it."

"He had me cold," Murf admitted. "He wasn't always an academic, you see," he added by way of explanation. "Worked on a building site, would you believe it? You just can't take anyone at face value any more."

Prodded by a lady with parcels and a tray of confection, Rolo pulled in his chair to let her pass.

"So what now?"

"Go home, I suppose. Work in the business ... or rather save it from Steppop." Gobnait had helped his mood. The real low had passed and something of the normal swagger had returned to his voice and manner. The wrought-iron lift behind them rumbled upwards to the sandwich bar, weaving as it passed the strands of coloured light that splayed from stained glass windows. Murf spooned brown sugar into his Blue Mountain coffee.

"Are you ready for that?"

"I'll play it by ear." He thought of Gobnait's useful pointers. "I can't keep running away ... And then there's my sister Maura to consider. She's been holding the fort down there for a long time and probably needs a break ... and some moral support."

"You never mentioned a sister before." There was a barb in Rolo's voice. Why was Murf opening up now of all times, when he was at the precise point of leaving for good? Rolo was prickly because he was hurting.

"No? Well it never came up." Murf swung his legs out from under the table, crossed them and lit a Gold Flake. "Maybe I need this jolt. Ashur might be right. I'm no spring chicken any more." He cupped a hand over his mouth and drew heavily on the cigarette. "We're an odd vintage you and me. We have nothing to rebel against except ourselves …and the library of course. Seriousness is coming, social awareness and all that. But not yet. We're out of synch, old son."

"Are you saying it's time to join the Establishment?" Rolo asked by rote. He didn't think this was the time or place to discuss the swings and roundabouts of social history.

"I wouldn't go that far." Murf grinned. "By the way, I have something for you." He rummaged in the duffle bag that lay fully packed under the table and handed him a brown paper parcel. "It's just a book," he said awkwardly, turning sideways to release a stream of smoke.

"Thanks." But it didn't take the sting out of it. Murf had already packed his goddamn duffle bag. "What do you feel about being expelled?"

"I'll manage." Christ, Murf thought, I hope he's not going to start all this again.

"Oh, you'll manage, will you?" Rolo came as close to a sneer as he ever would and brusquely waved away a waitress who came to collect the empty cups.

"What the hell is eating you? I'm the one who's been sacked."

"You're just going to walk away. I see you've even got your bag packed." He kicked the duffle bag under the table to prove his point. "And you probably wouldn't even have said goodbye if I hadn't tracked you down."

Murf couldn't avoid the stare. "What do you want me to say? That I'll miss you or something?" There, he'd said it. Did he want it in blood?

"Yeah, or something," Rolo said truculently, his face burning. There was a sickeningly reminiscent pain in his bad leg that cast him back over the years to that deserted mine.

"It goes ... without saying." Murf shifted on the round perforated disk of the chair. "For God's sake, this is a small island. I'll be only eighty miles down the road. You can drop by."

"How can I?" Rolo asked peevishly. "You don't even know yet how *you'll* be received." He suddenly heard the sound of his own voice and wondered if he wasn't close to nagging.

Murf looked at his watch and then peered through the domed window to see if the weather was suitable for hitching. The sky was uncertain but he would give it a try.

"I'd better make tracks. You'll have a chance to get some work done for a change. Get the finals, old son, and be the best damn Mech. Eng. around. Give my regards to Gobnait and Fiona if you see them. I'll send Ashur some dough for the car." He stood and slung the bag over a shoulder. "I should be able to hitch a ride on Leeson Street Bridge ... So long, Rolo..." He held out his hand.

It was the first time they'd ever shaken hands; it seemed adult and faintly ridiculous. Murf's hand felt surprisingly small-boned.

"I'm sorry I got on your case earlier. I … don't find this easy."

"Me neither," Murf replied, acutely aware of eye contact, of two grown men standing together in a crowded restaurant, saying their farewells. "Give my souvenir of Nelson's Pillar to The Cart. It's under the bed somewhere. Say *au revoir* to Tim and the other inmates … Ah well, at least I saved the Rag. It's a far far better thing I do…"

"Cut it out." Rolo was choked enough.

"I'll be off then." Murf patted him briefly on the shoulder and walked out. Rolo watched him framed in the doorway, looking again at the complex sky which was brilliant overhead but ominously dark to the west, a marquetry of clouds fading fast from pearl grey to cinder, saw him give another heave to the duffle bag and set off in his loping walk towards Leeson Street Bridge.

Rolo slumped back knowing suddenly the distances of small islands, and the isolation. Of course it had to happen some time, and there never would be a right time. Maybe it was for the best but it certainly didn't feel like it right there and then. Murf would finally have to face up to his responsibilities. Rolo might indeed get some work done – he certainly wouldn't have anything else to do – but there was precious little time left. Strange that his leg hurt so much. Was it Bobby all over again, losing a friend? Maybe it was nature's way of distracting him from a deeper pain.

He opened the brown bag Murf had given him and pulled out the book, 'Daily Life in Ancient Rome'. It had been Murf's one and only book and was stamped, 'Property of the National Library'.

Summer came on like a brass band and the city looked to its laurels. The parks surged with colour, girls came out in their figures to sunbathe on the steps of offices, young gurriers splashed in fountains and canal locks to the dismay of reincarnate swans. Women students doused themselves in strong perfume to counteract the smell of male feet in the library. It was evident that socks were not being mailed home often enough to Mammies for laundering. The Cart shooed magpies off the milk bottles every morning. Crowley stopped airing his underwear and some kind soul in the Coombe who had made a killing at the dog track bought a dictionary from Tim. As usual the bank clerks went on strike because it was easy to get work in England during the summer months. Ashur set up a medical practice in a village in Munster, sold the perforated Mini for scrap and bought a BMW which was more suited to his image. There was no news of Murf.

Rolo spent more time in the College of Science than in the Arts block. No one knew him there; he was trying to turn loneliness into a virtue.

Each morning he could see thin-headed civil servants with worn satchels containing sandwiches and novels, sleek Ministers alighting from Mercedes to stride purposefully up granite steps and peer around in hopes of media coverage. On the other side of Merrion Street he sometimes saw demonstrators lining the railings of the red-brick Land Commission whose purpose, like that of a megalithic monument, was shrouded in mystery.

One morning there blossomed on the street a new breed of demonstrator: farmers complaining about the milk lake and butter mountain. They had spent the night on footpaths in makeshift sleeping bags, and kindly Dublin women were, this morning, bringing them cups of tea and slabs of toast. Reporters rooted around with microphones, covering this *rus-in-urbe* symbiosis. The demonstration lasted several weeks and Rolo became quite adept at picking his steps through the sleeping bodies of farmers each morning on his way to the College of Science. No one noticed him.

It didn't take The Cart long to replace Murf in the digs. Rolo's new room-mate was a reticent radio officer with the smelliest feet imaginable. The Cart's temperamental hot water geyser was under no threat from this plump young man who snuffled a lot and whose acne wept. And the irony was that he did send home his laundry fairly often to his mother; Rolo could tell because his jeans had creases ironed into them that could shave gooseberries.

Rolo would lie awake at night holding his nose, trying to bury it in the blanket, and clench his teeth in frustration because there was nothing he could say. And all the while he could hear the moist, mucus-gurgling snores of the pesky radio officer who slept like a baby. Rolo finally devised a plan which was by no means perfect, but was the best in the circumstances. He allowed two pairs of his own socks to get high, and stuffed them under both sides of his pillow so that he could bask in his own pong which was at least preferable to that of his room-mate. The Cart who made the beds about once a week started to complain about dirty divils who were afraid of soap and water. The radio officer never got the hint and poor Rolo could only hang his head in shame, and hope that she wasn't referring to him.

He worked hard and spent lonely lunchtimes in the National Gallery or the Natural History Museum among the stuffed sharks and great red elks. He occasionally saw Fiona and brought her to a film in the Green or the deluxe. But the relationship didn't develop beyond friendship. Gobnait had not heard from Murf, and settled reluctantly for a lower key plodding relationship with, of all things, a Vet.

The exams loomed like a brick wall that one hurtled towards. The stomach-churning day came when the Aula Max and even the Gym were decked out with thousands of tables and chairs. Students roamed miserably about ten minutes before the dreaded hour, visiting toilets, scratching pimples, swallowing purple hearts. From the moment the first answer books were handed out, Rolo seemed to enter another dimension, an alien atmosphere of sticky heat and sweaty concentration, where the horizon squatted low on the breathless land and sunlight was a memory beyond the margin of the closed-in mind. In this chamber of sense deprivation, formulae and symbols flashed like filaments behind his eyes. From time to time there was a vague sense that in the welter of the moment, if there were such moments, he may have made some kind of sense.

And suddenly one morning after two amorphous weeks of sweat, ink squiggles, lined paper and torn acne, as he wrestled into consciousness, the thought came slowly. My God in Heaven, they're over. He dressed quickly, trying not to breathe the aroma of the radio officer's socks, although a whiff of ammonia might have perked him up on this barely credible morning, and went down to the euphemism called breakfast.

The Cart still complained about Murf's rude departure – the fact was that she missed him. So did Tim, since he had lost his protector. And there was no one left who could take a rise out of Crowley or the bank clerks. The balance of power had shifted. The Cart was now impregnable and ruled her supine lodgers with an iron hand though she seemed to miss the challenge of Murf's back-answers.

Rolo, who got a sausage because he'd finished his exams, itched as much as Tim during breakfast and by mid-morning found that his entire body was covered in a rash. He dropped into the Pauper's Ward in St. Vincents where a group of interns drew little circles in biro around several representative spots on legs and chest and went into a huddle muttering long latinised phrases while he lay awkwardly with his pants around his ankles and his pecker shrinking from, and causing even more, embarrassment. He thanked God that Fiona and Gobnait were not on duty. Morbilliform rash, they said, tension-related. Learn to relax, they said. Get out and about more. It was amazing how the impressive latin phrases could dwindle to such homely pisherogues. He was allowed to stand at last and pull up his pants. The huddle of medics moved off, walking in step, chattering.

Murf had sold his body to the College of Surgeons. He had sold it to other medical schools as well. But promised no delivery date. Where was the bastard hiding out? Suppose Fanning had not taken him in, then he could be anywhere.

Inquiries brought Gobnait to the desk in the statued entrance hall with its gilt-framed portraits of healing nuns and steely-eyed surgeons.

"Nice to see you again, Rolo. How are you and how is Murf?" She looked soft and bubbly despite the starched uniform that would draw blood if you brushed against it.

"I haven't heard a word from Murf. How about you?"

"Nothing. He's gone to ground." An orderly passed by and grinned at her; she flashed her electric eyes collusively.

"May I ask you something…? Are you serious about this … Vet?"

"Well, it could develop into something, I suppose."

"Right. I'll be off then."

She caught him by the sleeve. "Hold your horses. Give a girl a chance."

"It's just that … well, I think that you and Murf are … well suited." He shrugged as if to disparage his role as match-maker.

"You rascal. Did he send you?" These two were capable of anything, she thought.

It was nice to be called a rascal; the word had spirit to it. "No, it was just a thought on my part. I've no business interfering. But … you sort of get on well together…" He had to take some initiative because Murf was so screwed up he might not appreciate the qualities of this girl.

"You mean I'm as mad as a March hare as well?" She gleamed with mirth.

Rolo's crackle of a laugh echoed along the polished corridors that radiated from the entrance hall.

"Well," she added, "tell Murf to get on his bike and do something about it. I'm not going to *Keep Myself Forever*." She blessed herself quickly in a parody of convent school nun-speak. "And certainly not until he decides to grow up, which could take even longer. And I'm not going to chase him. So tell him – what is it you Americans say? – to get his ass in gear."

Rolo looked at her in admiration. "I will. I'll tell him that. Good. That's great."

She brushed her cheek against his. He felt warmed by the prospect of a happy ending. Bring 'em together and let nature take its course. Phosphorous on water, much hissing and splashing, but what an exchange of atoms.

Sitting among the great red elk one lunchtime, Rolo contemplated the future. Should he go back to the States or not? Of course he loved his family but still he needed space. He had a longer road to travel but he wasn't sure of the destination. He had agreed to help Crowley on a bird-watching trip the next day, something to do with protecting the peregrine falcons of Wicklow. He needed to get out and about as his doctors had advised – or was it because he had nothing else to do? It seemed as if his future could only be arranged one day at a time.

———

There was that moment of uncomfortable intimacy being on a bus together after months of sidling past each other on The Cart's narrow staircase. As the bus rattled on towards Glendalough, Rolo sneaked a look at Crowley who seemed to be smiling inside his face. He was odd, and quite possibly not playing with a full deck. But despite his baiting of Tim and his bigoted views, Rolo had some sympathy for a man of his age who lived in a rented room with that constant smell of Frytex and lino wax, an habitué of libraries, galleries and all public institutions as though he were rehearsing for that final institutional resting place, the hospice.

Crowly pumped him for a while for the gory details of Murf's undoing and then launched into a paean of praise for Fanning's republican views, sprinkling it with asides about Rap Mayhew's gun-running exploits in the North. The IRA, it seemed, needed more resources if they were to counteract the activities of the said Mayhew. Rolo, who couldn't see any connection or theme in these ramblings – although he would later to his cost – responded only to the extent demanded by common civility.

Crowley turned to the matter in hand. "If we can explain the migratory habits of the peregrine falcon it could unlock the entire ornitho-universe."

"I see," Rolo said as the bus plunged into the startling green of Wicklow.

"Yes." Crowley agreed with himself. "But the most immediate thing is to save the species, which is dying out in these parts."

The first part of the expedition went well. Rolo's lungs tingled from the pure air that came sweeping down from the mountains. St Kevin's ancient monastic settlement with its crosses, little kirks and custodial round towers moved him in a special way for this truly was the heartland.

They started to climb the mountain that rose above the upper lake and soon came to the ledge on which Crowley's endangered falcons lodged. With a rope around his middle, though the climb didn't really demand that, Rolo clambered down to the ledge and edged his way along it. Fred Falcon, as Crowley called him, and his family were at home, though not expecting guests. They seemed rather fierce to Rolo as he peered around an outcrop of rock, but there was something sad about them too, the lone survivors of their clan.

"Are you sure they're not dangerous?" he called up in a hoarse whisper for the umpteenth time.

"No," Crowley assured him paying out the rope. "They feel part of the experiment now. They know we're trying to save the species."

Rolo called for a little more slack and looked cagily at the sharp beaks and gimlet highlights in the watchful eyes as they sized him up. Fred threatened him with a flurry of his strong wings. Crowley said it was just an instinctive opening gambit and was nothing to worry about. Rolo quickly doled out the valium-enriched giblets which Fred and his brood quickly tore to pieces between beak and talon.

"Are they quiescent yet?" Crowley called down after a while.

"Just about." Rolo moved closer. The falcons slept with their penetrating eyes open, pantaloons legs tucked under them. As well as Fred's mate, there were two nestlings whose wings were almost fully developed. Now that Rolo was more fully in charge of the situation, he saw what magnificent birds they were and wondered if nobility always came from predatory skill. The left leg of each bird bore five plastic coloured rings. As arranged, Rolo called out the colours from top down, and Crowley made meticulous notes in his cloth-covered book.

"You say Fred has a yellow ring uppermost?"

"Yes."

"Nearest to the body?"

"Yes."

"That's most peculiar. He must have migrated to Wales and been tagged by a colleague over there. But that means he came back in less than a week. What an extraordinary conundrum." He became quite excited, rummaging in his satchel for further documentary evidence of Fred's comings and goings. "It can't be Fred then," he shouted in a high-pitched voice. "Don't you see what this means? Good God, all the theories are wrong. This is going to shake up the entire profession. Those lazy academics never did enough field-work anyway … You can put on the new tags now."

Rolo got the equipment out of his bag and knelt over the sleeping birds.

"There's not much room. They've got a lot of tags on already."

"Don't worry." Crowley lay on the grass peering over the cliff, his spectacles in danger of sliding off his nose. "The talons have a property of elasticity which is deceptive."

Rolo looked down at the peaceful valley and

lake, the stony churches and the round towers piercing through the trees. He had no fear of heights and his bad leg wasn't bothering him. He loaded the tag gun and started to clip the rings – purple this time – onto the sinewy legs of the sleeping birds. It was easier than he expected. Fred was emerging from his post-giblet snooze by the time he'd finished and looked from the new ring on his leg to Rolo. It was a withering look out of the corner of his rapacious eyes which said, 'Try that when I'm fully awake and I'll have your eyeballs for breakfast'.

"I've finished," Rolo said, keen to make good his escape.

"Good." Crowley helped him up. "Now let's wait until the sedative wears off."

Saving a species, Rolo thought warmly, lying back on the springy turf, feeling the gratitude of nature. The last section of rash had almost disappeared from his side and he thought there might be something to be said for being 'out and about'. A plane passed overhead leaving a vapour trail that frayed slowly and melted into the blue.

"A good day's work," Crowley purred, peering over the edge for signs of stirring on the ledge below. The Society would be astounded by his ornithological breakthrough. Next year they might give him an endowment to work with the coots. "Yes," he exclaimed, "they're coming round. They'll probably want to fly to get used to the new tags. This will be a real treat. Come and look."

Rolo tore his gaze from the breathless sky and

joined Crowley at the cliff-edge. "They can cope with the extra weight of the rings?" he asked.

"Oh, no bother to them. Wait until you see the wing-span … Now! There goes Fred."

And there Fred went with his impressive wing-span and funny little undercarriage of plus-four legs, gliding out over the lake in an arc as smooth as a maiden's brow, to flap suddenly in desperation in a ghastly stall, bomb downwards and disappear from sight into the murky waters that lapped against St Kevin's bed. Whether from loyalty or heedlessness, the same awful trajectory was followed by his mate and the two nestlings. Plop, plop, plop and plop. The entire species wiped out by the pull of that extra tag which augured them into the lake with deadly fidelity, one after the other, as if it were a suicide pact.

Crowley's face was a mask of horror. There was such finality about those plops. He kept looking over the edge in disbelief, then staggered to his feet gasping for air, clawing at his crêpey neck as if it were a clogged snorkel.

"Oh God, what will the Society … say?" He grabbed Rolo with a bony hand. "Not a word to anyone. Understand? Nobody must ever know … I can't even mention the extraordinary migration … Nothing must be said … Absolutely nothing…"

"What about the birds?" Rolo felt sick.

"They gave themselves … in the interests of science." He quickly blessed himself by prodding his narrow chest in three different spots.

"I thought you knew what you were doing? No

wonder they're becoming extinct..." Rolo limped down the mountainside with Crowley at a running crouch behind him, pleading and clawing the air.

"Not a word to anyone, please. Don't mention it in the digs ... I'll make up for this ... Save the coot population next. You'll see."

An odd thought occurred to Rolo. He and the deranged Crowley had been out of their natural habitat. The cliff edge was for Murf, not for them.

From a long way off, even from the other side of the lake, someone might have seen these two strange figures hobbling at a slant against the sky and sensed that all was not well. As for Rolo, he would think twice about getting out and about again in this fair land of amateurs and dying species.

"Critics might say this is a superficial, buddy tale without a deeper meaning and with only the faintest nod in the direction of post-modernism; they would of course be correct – as would everyone else who agreed or disagreed with them."
—The Present Writer

"When a man talks of a 'home' and I discover him to mean a house of detention, I judge that he is trying to deceive."
—Arthur Quiller-Couch

CHAPTER 6

MAKING CONTACT WHEN he had nothing to report wasn't Murf's style. It wasn't that friendship didn't matter but rather that true friends didn't have to engage in idle chatter or, horror of horrors, 'cultivate' each other. Knowing the whereabouts of Rolo and Gobnait was enough for the time being, especially as he was now finally confronting the hidden agenda of his life. So, when he did eventually call, towards the end of July, he had much to report.

Rolo took the call on the pay-phone near The Cart's broom closet and plugged one ear against the background noise of the kitchen. His intention to upbraid Murf for his long silence was foiled by a crossed line, the scrape of plates and his relief at hearing that familiar voice again.

"I'm really on to something," Murf said excitedly. "Fanning's definitely been cooking the books. A little more midnight oil and I'll have him cold. My ship is coming in, old son, and his is sinking fast. Steppop has overstepped himself."

"Gobnait is keeping well and sends her regards." Rolo, a little tired of Murf's preoccupation with Fanning, changed to a subject closer to his heart.

"Good, good. Give her my best if you see her. Tell her I'll be in touch when I've straightened out things here. Tell her she was right about Fanning, right on the money."

Good God, Rolo thought, he's somehow managed to bring it around to bloody Fanning again. A door slammed behind him and the pounding on the stairs suggested that Tim was laying desperate siege to the bathroom again.

"How did the exams go?"

"It's hard to say. The results won't be out for another three weeks or so." Rolo's heart knocked against his ribs at the thought.

"So you're just kicking your heels then? Why don't you come down here?"

This was the best offer Rolo had had all summer, a bonus offer because he could avoid the radio officer's feet and Crowley's constant pleas about keeping the secret of the unfortunate falcons who plummeted to their death in the beautiful surroundings of Glendalough.

"You're sure that would be OK?"

"Of course," Murf replied with a snort that queried the need to ask. "I'll probably be at the office when you arrive. Ask for Murphy's Builders Providers. Anyone will direct you. I'll be the one poring over the ledgers, shouting 'Eureka!'"

Rolo had a grin on his face when he hung up.

And the pain in his leg eased considerably the next morning as he walked to the station swinging a rucksack. He dropped into St Vincent's and left a note for Gobnait. 'Murf sends wishes and is about to get ass in gear'. At the station he inserted the ticket in the automatic barrier but it spewed it out in an electric convulsion, not unlike a vomit reflex. Two porters kicked and punched the recalcitrant machine like their Luddite forefathers.

An announcement, preceded by a flurry of crackling puffs, tried to drum up sympathy for the failure of the 9.35 southbound from Drogheda to arrive on time. The travelling public looked up at the loudspeakers with expressions of martyred ecstasy, resigned to the hopelessness of public transport.

Rolo used the delay to buy a newspaper and a tin of Old Holborn. He also bought some regular cigarettes for offering around. He was after all going on a holiday, or so he thought. Finally, boarding the truant train, he paused in the corridor to blink at the dishevelment. There was the usual evidence of cannibalism: old bus seats nailed to the floor of what used to be a cattle car, shower curtains from the railway hotels screening the passage-ways where sliding doors used to be. Old cylindrical steam heaters boiled and belched under the seats. Strange signs in Irish encouraged the not spitting and the not pulling of the communication cord.

A testy old gent, struggling to heave a case on to the luggage rack, called on two passing porters one of whom turned to the other and said, "Don't bother, he's only a fuckin' passenger."

Eschewing an orange plastic seat transplanted from the bus station, Rolo selected a compartment and finally located a spot of upholstery, repaired with duct tape, from which no spring or foam rubber protruded. He gently lowered himself into that oasis. Further down the corridor a man sat on the toilet – one of the better seats – reading the Irish Times.

The journey of eighty miles began with a single lurch that had the carriages rear up on their couplings in a monstrous mating ritual. The heavy metal clanking eventually sorted itself into a gentler rhythm as they passed under the concrete fortress of Landsdowne stadium, heading towards the sea. Acres of wet sand at Sandymount invited the tide in further but it dithered instead in a tracery of froth. A lone man with a dog dug for clams surrounded by little wet piles of sand. About a mile out to sea four mounted horses rode the gentle swell, their riders giving them an easy rein. It wasn't a saga come startlingly to life, but rather the latest fad in horse training.

The old amber train soon shrugged off the

shackles of urban sprawl and trundled gamely into open country. There were fewer passengers now and Rolo got a better seat near a window.

Murf's home town turned out to be solid, mercantile and busy, with an irreproachable main street, some sets of traffic lights, a one-way system and a certain cluttered independence. Rolo walked from the station to the town centre which boasted a tholsel, a modest square and a statue to the 1798 freedom fighters. He asked directions of a man who had just come from a bookie's shop. The man stood, expanded his chest and resettled the cap on his head.

"Well now, Murphy's Builders Providers, Hmmmmn." He sucked in his breath and flung out an arm. "Next left, then second right up Mary Street, then right again. Do you get me? And it'll be right slap in front of you. Sure, you can't miss it." He peered at Rolo and asked, "Is it himself you're looking for?"

"Y-yes," Rolo answered uncertainly.

"Well, you're going to the right place so. God bless. Good luck now."

Following the directions to a tee, Rolo found himself in the MBP yard which was a bedlam of stacked lumber, fork-lift trucks and screaming saw-mills.

"Excuse me Sir, could you … Oh, I'm sorry…" The young operator in navy ski cap and ear muffs had to switch off the saw mill to hear. "I didn't mean to interrupt … I was wondering if Murf was around?" Rolo was greeted by a smile, a nod and a pointing finger. "In that building over there? Thank you so much." The youth bent to the task of measuring a huge slab of teak and then switched on the evil-fanged saw.

Shaking sawdust and curled shavings from his feet, Rolo crept up on Murf seated at a drawing board.

"Fraud squad here!"

Murf whirled around on the draughtsman's stool. "Aha, you made it. Good man. Welcome to the provinces." They shook hands warmly. Murf was obviously better at greetings than farewells, or else he had let some tense springs uncoil. The weeks of separation disappeared like a puff of smoke.

"I like the threads." Rolo's face gleamed as he ran his fingers along the lapels of Murf's suit jacket. He had never seen him in a suit before; he looked ridiculous, a wolfhound clipped like a poodle.

Murf introduced him around the office, to clerks and brown-coated shop assistants. There was a fine bracing mix of smells: gloss paint, linseed oil, putty, wood preservative. Some big orders were being filled and large trucks converged on the customer pick-up area. Forklifts moved and bleeped in the warehouse, bearing pallets of timber, bricks, paving stones, guttering and rolls of insulating material.

"I'm impressed," Rolo said.

"Not bad," Murf said with some pride. "The old man built it up from scratch." He leant back against the drawing board and stretched. "It's good to get out of one's ivory tower," he said with a straight face. "Come on now, a welcome drink is called for."

As he jumped into a utility truck Murf yelled above the saw mill's scream, "You've met Rolo?"

The ski-capped operator waved and nodded; again there was that iridescent smile.

Murf settled into the driver's seat. "I don't know why she stays here working for Fanning. She has so many options."

"She?"

"My sister, Maura. I thought you'd met her."

"Not really." Rolo looked back in surprise at the slim 'youth' tending that frightening machine. "You're in the office and she's out in the yard doing all the real work."

"Bit of a tomboy, I suppose." Murf glanced in the rear-view mirror and edged the truck into the traffic of Mary Street.

Old age pensioners were on the first tee as Murf and Rolo brought their pints on to the verandah of the club-house and sat watching the elderly golfers skittering balls along the fairway, sending up linear sprays of early evening dew.

"This would appear to be the life," Rolo observed, looking down the vista of fairway to the sea glistening like gun-metal and the jade and purple mountains guarding the other side of the bay. It was a revelation to see the normally impoverished and scavenging Murf in these plush surroundings. He was reminded of those stories where the wild orphan or street urchin is adopted by wealthy gentlefolk and brought to the big house for chocolate and lemonade. He suddenly pictured Murf, twenty years on, fat and respectable, a club tie lost in neck bulges, chairman of committees, doing deals over brandy in hotels. No, it couldn't happen. Could it?

"It's not too bad," Murf admitted. "Though it's still a small town. Squinting windows etc. One's exploits monitored hourly and broadcast by Mrs. MacIlwee, the grocer's wife. But it is interesting right now as the noose tightens inexorably around Steppop's brass neck."

"I didn't hear 'Eureka'," Rolo said, leaning back to let the waitress serve two earthenware dishes of steaming steak and kidney pie with side salads. He suddenly wished Maura had joined them for lunch. Murf should have invited her; he could be so inconsiderate at times.

"I have the goods on him, never fear." Murf leant forward. "The scam is this. For six years now he's been supplying a local builder and political hack with lumber and concrete blocks. And the books don't show anything. But I found the inventory records. It all stacks up. He's been siphoning it off all right."

"Could it be pilfering by someone else?" Rolo asked

"No, it's systematic and on a large scale." Murf warmed to his subject. "Fanning is in cahoots with this builder called Furlong. He expects Furlong to nominate him for a safe seat at the next general election. According to the books Furlong never paid us a penny, but I've walked around his sites and, *mirabile dictu,* nearly all the building materials have our trade mark."

"Didn't Crowley say something about Fanning's political ambitions?"

"I think he did. It's a small country."

Rolo washed down some pie with warm Smithwicks beer to which, despite himself, he had been won over. There was an unaccustomed fullness in his concave stomach. Here he was at last in the heartland with his old knock-about. He felt comfortable. What if they both became fat golfers – pillars of the community?

"Sounds like it's open and shut then?"

Murf tapped the side of his nose. Hovering ears. "Hiya Mick?" He called down to a pensioner who had just finished the eighteenth hole. "How did you do?"

The golfer looked up from his score card and rammed the putter into his bag. "A good back nine. But I plumbed the rest. He spoke in the heroic terms of a hunter returning with an elk on a pole. At his age even to finish eighteen holes without having to stop for a leak was quite an achievement.

"Well, keep it up. And do something about that slice." Murf then turned back to Rolo and closed his fist.

"I have him there. Can you believe it, finally after all those years of farting about?" There was something different about Murf. The grim satisfaction in his face and clenched fist held a strain of cynicism that was new. Rolo had imagined that when he came close to the heart of the vendetta he would say, 'what the hell' and move on, or revert to his slaphappy ways, but now he seemed deadly serious about levelling the score with Fanning. It was no longer a fantasy that justified his errant ways; there was a debt to be paid. He had never seen Murf so calculating before.

At dinner that evening, Mr. Fanning sat at the head of the table in the high-ceilinged dining-room. He ladled mulligatawny soup from the tureen set in front of him into bowls which he then passed to the maid for circulation round the table. He certainly did seem to be head of this household; if he had wormed his way into this family there seemed very little sign of it now. Rolo, who had been quietly searching for indications of monstrosity, couldn't find any, although once or twice when he looked up, he disconcertingly found Fanning already watching him. Apart from that, which was probably nothing more than curiosity, Fanning seemed to be downright ordinary, if not indeed boring. Funny things, perceptions, Rolo thought. There was Murf at the other end of the table quiet and brooding like Brando in 'Streetcar', no doubt seeing Fanning as a many-headed hydra.

Fanning served himself last and bent to his soup, filtering it through his reddish moustache which neither drooped with radicalism nor tilted upwards in affirmation of the status quo. Even the moustache was ordinary and lacked symbolic value. His thin hair strategically combed over the balding pate was probably once red. He was unremarkable to a fault.

"So then, Rolo, when you get your degree will you go back to Philadelphia?" Fanning asked, stroking droplets off his moustache.

"It's a difficult decision. I haven't … made up my mind yet."

"You're close to Camelot there, Kennedy country." Fanning followed his own train of thought. "I well remember JFK, God rest him. I met him when he visited us over here. A wonderful man, cut down in his prime. Is your family involved in politics at all?"

"Not really. My Mom knows some people. That's about the size of it."

"Who?" Fanning was interested.

"Oh, the US Ambassador. He used to be in Congress I think…"

Just then Maura came in dressed simply in skirt and sweater. Her hair, freed from the ski-cap, tumbled around her face. She was neat, trim and stunning. Having for years steeled himself against his mother's exhortations to stand when a lady entered the room, Rolo now suddenly understood the meaning of the nicety and would have jumped to attention were it not for the nonchalant and continued soup-slurping of his male hosts.

Maura helped the maid clear away for the main course and carry in, on covered silver platters, the ingredients of the mixed grill: steak, lamb chops, sausage, bacon and eggs. Within the limits set by his neck muscles, Rolo followed her every move, and jumped to hold her chair as she went to sit down.

"How nice," her mother murmured vacantly from across the table, dreaming of the gallantry of days gone by. Maura smiled collusively.

"To get back to the Ambassador," Fanning persisted. "He used to be the House Speaker, if memory serves. Do you think he might visit our little town here? The Council would be delighted to receive him. We could give him the Freedom of the City."

"I ... don't know," Rolo answered with some embarrassment. "I guess my Mom could mention it to him..."

"That would be great," Fanning said. "Let's talk about it again before you leave." He gave a soft implosive burp as the maid removed his soup plate. Rolo hoped, but didn't think it likely, that he would forget.

"We didn't really like ... Onassis." Mrs. Murphy pursed her lips slightly. She smiled then to take the harm out of it, thinking perhaps that she'd gone too far. Her mood was vacant, tinkling in an empty ballroom. Rolo wondered if she might not be on sedatives.

Fanning ignored her and turned again to Rolo. "Maybe we could draft a letter together to the Ambassador..."

Murf cut in. "Rolo is a guest. Stop trying to

use him."

Fanning leant back, seeming hurt rather than angry. "I'm not using anybody, am I, Rolo?"

"Emmm, I don't believe so…" Rolo didn't quite know which way to turn.

Maura, who sat beside him, intervened skilfully. "What do you think of the new potatoes? They're the very first of the year. You can make a wish."

"Oh yes." Her mother smiled. "A wish."

Glad to be rescued, Rolo closed his eyes and crossed his fingers. "I've done it." He looked at the intriguing folds of Maura's woollen sweater. He wondered how she piled her hair up under the ski-cap, probably in soft whirls that he associated with a French bakery. There was something endearing about a girl in her own home, playing hostess, a kind of warm homeliness that set off the more obvious allure, maybe even kept it from being intimidating. One thing was clear: Murf's sister was far more captivating than Murf. Why had he never mentioned her?

"…but then she was always inclined to follow the rich set," Mrs. Murphy said in what was probably another reference to Jackie Onassis. She delicately picked at a bread roll. It was hard to imagine that she held the purse strings, or that she could keep her second husband away from them for very long. Fanning did respond to her on this occasion, though on a more pressing matter.

"Sarah, could you ask the maid to serve the main course?" Was he putting her down or saving her from ridicule? Maybe he was just hungry. Rolo decided to stop trying to analyse him. Murf's opinion of him could not be changed anyway, even if Freud and Jung both deemed him to be a saint.

"She's busy in the kitchen," Maura said, getting up to serve. Her hair briefly touched Rolo's neck as she leant over him heaping up his plate. He threw a look at Murf. This was what they used to dream about on their hard trestle beds in The Cart's, being fed and watered by beautiful young women. Murf's face didn't register anything; sisters presumably were different.

"Have another chop," Maura cajoled him. "I heard about The Cart's cuisine. You're probably running a protein deficiency."

"I'm fine now thank you so much," he said, having graciously accepted another chop. His plate was so full his mother would have taken him to task over his manners. Maybe his system did crave meat. And here it was, a whole trencher full, inch-thick slabs layered upwards in a carnal landscape. Knowing where to start took a full minute; it was like trying to find the door into a pyramid. French mustard was passed around with the horse-radish sauce, and they were off. Fanning clammed up to eat in that snarling reticent way that sometimes betokens a malnourished childhood.

"Do you ... like operating the saw mills?" Rolo asked after the first mouthful of filet mignon had gone down. "Isn't it rather dangerous?"

"Not if you know what you're doing," Maura laughed and curled a loose strand of hair around an ear. "I like working with timber."

"I used to carve once." Rolo was keen to impress. It was more whittling than carving, but it wasn't a lie as such.

"You did? I'd like to do that although I don't think I'd have the patience."

"Oh you would. I'm sure you would," Rolo said. He was conscious of Murf's eyes on him, a deft glance like the pass of a blade, and thought he heard a grunt from that quarter. Refusing to be abashed, he went on, "They do chainsaw sculptures in Canada. They can turn a tree-trunk into a lifelike figure in a few hours."

"We don't respect trees enough in this country," Maura said. "It's awful the way builders just level them when they clear a site. In America people like to have trees around their houses. Do you?"

"Yes. Dogwood and spruce and maple. Every American kid has had the experience of climbing out his bedroom window and down a tree."

"It's part of the culture – and of course listening to the branches rustling against the window panes in a storm."

"That can be scary at first," Rolo laughed. He was enjoying this *tête-à-tête* and didn't feel any responsibility for drawing others into the conversation. If they wanted to munch their way in silence through the meal, that was their problem.

Fanning, however, after the first pangs of hunger had been assuaged, slowed his chewing to observe in practical vein, "House construction in the US is mainly timber-frame."

Rolo nodded, swallowed and agreed. "The building industry over there is not geared to concrete-block construction, which would be very expensive."

Fanning pondered this. "I wonder why we don't do timber-frame here? Maybe we should look into it." He paused as if waiting for an assistant to make a note. "It could be much more profitable. What do you think?"

It was nice to be consulted, Rolo thought, garnering his few facts on building techniques to give a weighty reply, when Murf cut across his bows.

"The reason is simple," Murf said truculently, implying that Fanning, a blow-in, still didn't know the first thing about the building trade and never bothered to learn. "We don't produce hardwoods in this country. And with our rainfall, the softwoods would turn into tissue paper in six months."

Fanning conceded the point willingly with a wave of the hand; it was a mere technicality. It occurred to Rolo that Fanning reserved his energy for bigger issues. It was the only indication, and a rather oblique one, that Fanning was a force to be reckoned with.

"You have those gorgeous tulip trees too…" Mrs. Murphy said fondly.

"Yes, Ma'am." Rolo was determined to acknowledge her. "They are spectacular in full bloom."

Murf then went on a solo run about the need to take the long-run view in business. He was clearly differentiating his Dad from Fanning. Rolo listened in silent amazement to Murf's theories about good business methods and the need to avoid scams and strokes. What psychic transformations were afoot? The leopard's spots had become a dizzying blur of fast-changing hues. At one point he began to choke and Maura had to slap him on the back; he thought her hand might have lingered for a second after his not too unseemly expurgation. But maybe it was his imagination.

Mrs. Murphy went from Camelot to Casablanca and back again, trying to remember Ingrid Bergman's name, which Rolo provided.

When the meal came to an end Rolo still hadn't got a whiff of Fanning's republican views.

That came some days later when they met in the lumber yard. After some preliminary skirmishing, Fanning asked him if he knew anything about Noraid and the American connection. Rolo sang dumb and Fanning didn't pursue it. But Rolo was certain then that there were layers to him.

Murf dragged them off to the rugby club dance on the Saturday. Rolo had a fantasy that Maura was his date but the reality was that they were going as a party. As a guest of the household he wasn't sure of the proprieties of inviting her to a club he wasn't a member of. But as he watched her being repeatedly led on to the dance floor by the local and very fit-looking sportsmen, he realised he should have thrown caution to the winds and asked her to be his date. Instead he had just gone along; that's all he was good for, going along, sidling, and then berating himself.

He sat at a table near the bar, conscious of being a stranger. He felt sure that some of the glances he received were not just appraising but downright hostile. Rugby was all about gaining ground of course, so maybe it was unfair to blame these stout lads for being territorial. There could be a residue of land hunger still lingering in their genes. Unsettling though, those stares. Stomach not so good, probably a reaction to the invasion of protein in the form of red meat. System can't take sudden upgrade of cuisine or the sight of those beefy rugger buggers clodhopping on the dance floor.

Sitting in a bathroom stall, cajoling his stomach to come to a decision, he overheard a group of hearties at the urinals outside boasting of conquests and speculating on form.

" …I'm telling you, she would do a trick. Monica's a real flier…"

"No way."

"Wrong. Hanlon took her home on Tuesday night … accidentally brushed her tits and she was up on him like a cat. She made him put his tool under the cold tap to slow him down. She's a right goer. I'm telling you…"

Rolo cringed in the stall, figuratively covering his ears, hoping against hope that Maura wouldn't have eyes for any of these boors. To his horror the conversation took a dangerous turn. A different voice proclaimed, "I'm going to try Murf's sister."

"Isn't she with that skinny Yank?"

"So what if she is? He's no competition, with that gimpy leg."

"Even so, you'd be wasting your time. She's frigid. Sure, everyone knows that."

Rolo let his breath out slowly; he didn't know whether to feel relieved or not.

"But she's all there. Good bazookas and shafts right up to the arse."

"Yeah, but she doesn't know what she has it for. That's your problem right there."

Rolo couldn't take anymore. He coughed loudly, which wasn't the most gallant way of protecting a lady's honour, but it worked reasonably well. Not knowing who was in the cubicle – for all they knew it could have been Murf – the louts grew quiet and filed out of the bathroom. As Rolo pulled up his pants he decided he would have to be more decisive.

Murf grabbed him when he returned to the dance area and handed him the keys of the house.

"I'm leaving now," he said, nodding towards the door where his latest conquest waited, swinging her handbag.

"I suppose," Rolo said with some sarcasm,

"you've shifted a goer." Murf, he thought, was cut from the same cloth as those creeps in the bathroom. And what about Gobnait? Maybe his Mom was right after all about men being uncouth.

"Sort of." Murf was unaware of the barb. "Just local talent," he added modestly. "With any luck I won't see you until tomorrow."

"Oh God." Rolo clenched his teeth, ashamed of his own gender. "What about Maura?"

"She's a big girl now. Keep an eye on her if you want," Murf threw back as he ploughed his way through the crowds.

From his table Rolo could see Maura dancing with a leering prop forward, removing his hands from her bottom and smiling a rebuke. Which therefore was no rebuke at all! Though was it a come-hither? God between us and all harm, was her partner the foul-mouth he had overheard in the John? Got to do something. A diversion. Shout 'Fire!' Before he fully realised what was happening, he found himself on the dance-floor tapping the prop forward on a massive shoulder in much the same way a bird might peck an ox's back.

"Get lost." He hardly even looked at Rolo, whose tapping presence did not pose the slightest threat.

"Andy, this is a guest." Maura smiled and made introductions, unaware of the hostility between her two suitors. Rolo planted his splay feet and jutted his pointed chin as far as it would jut.

"Might I cut in?"

"I'd be delighted," Maura said. The prop gave him a vengeful look and walked away to prop up the bar.

Rolo's feeling of relief was short-lived. He had exploited his role as a guest and felt like an interloper. His decision to be decisive left an aftertaste. What if she was keen on Andy? Maybe he had interrupted a budding relationship.

"I'm sorry … Maura. I didn't mean to … Shall I get him back?"

"Don't you want to dance with me?"

"Oh yes, I do. But I shouldn't have cut in like that."

She took his right hand and put it on her waist. Her other hand in his had a band-aid on it. He felt a stab of discomfort thinking of her smooth skin being cut, had visions of that screaming circular saw. His thoughts flickered with the strobe lighting, changed colour, moved to the disco rhythms and coiled back on themselves feebly; those thoughts just weren't going anywhere, and merely served to distract him from enjoying the moment with this great girl.

"Andy was getting to be a bore." Maura smiled reassuringly at him. "I can only take so much of what goes on in the front of a scrum. Is that where they all bend down and wrestle?"

"I-I think so." He felt out of it. The rules of rugby suddenly seemed impossibly complex. "I'm probably a bit of a bore too." It was best to put his cards on the table and hope for the best. He felt feverish and lacked the strength to muster the necessary antibodies.

"You shouldn't think that." Her brown eyes held him captive. They were like the eyes of a child contemplating a set of bagpipes for the first time. His desire to be honest was overwhelming and he wanted to add to the litany of his faults. Having been hardened by Murf he was rapidly being turned to putty by Murf's sister.

"Why are you so hard on yourself?" she asked, her head on one side. "I thought Americans were very positive about everything."

Without any rehearsal he seized on this cue and blurted out, "I wish I were positive enough to ask to see you home." His face was deadly earnest, almost tragic. "But I'm afraid you might agree only because I'm a guest."

"I wouldn't."

"Thank you for being straight about it," he answered stricken. The effort to conceal his limp made his leg hurt. His stomach had lost its nerve again and his face was ghastly in the flickering confetti of light. "I hope I didn't offend you by asking."

She squeezed his hand. "I think you misunderstood. I said I wouldn't go home with you *just* because you're a guest."

He stopped shuffling and stared. "You mean…?"

"Yes, of course."

Murf had taken the car so they walked home, over the bridge and up the main street. He liked the sound of her heels on the pavement flags. The only other sound came from a neon sign for beer which sizzled and shorted out. He hardly dared to look sideways at her although he was acutely aware of her presence and had several unnecessary reminders as her skirt occasionally flapped gently against his good leg. It was beyond belief that Murf could have a sister like this. And he never mention her once, the bastard.

"Would you care to come in?" Maura asked when they reached the front-door.

"But, I'm staying…"

"Only joking. Would you like something? I'm going to have a glass of milk but maybe you'd prefer something stronger?"

"Milk would be fine thanks." He sat in a comfortable wing-backed chair in front of the cut-stone fireplace. His head rested against the lace antimacassar whose Celtic design matched the swirling circuits of his mind. But he was a little more content now, reassured; his senses eavesdropped on the hum of his heart.

Maura returned from the kitchen with a tray of milk, biscuits and sponge cake. She sat opposite him, arranged plates on nested tables and poured the milk into frosted tumblers. Indifferently stroking back a tress of hair she said, "That rugby club is such a melee."

"You didn't enjoy yourself?"

"I did. After you rescued me."

"Are you sure I … didn't interrupt something?"

"No, of course not." She reassured him further with a silver-veined laugh that reminded him of the Rathmines town-hall clock that chimed over the rooftops at night, easing the minds of the sleepless. "Andy is all right but he just wants to score. Does that shock you? When you grow up with a brother like Murf you get to understand these things. Most of the boys around here are just trying to prove themselves."

Thank you, God, he thought, for making her so knowing. Knowledge is protection, so she is safe from those primates. Thank you also for not giving me a vocation to the priesthood. I should never have questioned your wisdom. But I'll make it up to you. If you really want me to be a softie then so be it. Amen.

His mind was doing handsprings. Should he make a move and risk rejection? Lord, it's me again. I'm so drawn to this girl. It's not sex. I mean it is in part, but it isn't. Not entirely. You know what I mean. Why didn't you reveal her to me during those wasted years? To think she was here all the time just eighty miles down the road on the same side of the island, and Murf never even mentioned her. Not once. And now she is finishing her milk … and soon may leave…

He began to panic as the level of milk fell in her glass, forcing a decision, action.

"Do you think I might … have a little more milk please?"

"Of course, Rolo. And by the way, make yourself completely at home in this house."

"Thank you." He watched her re-fill his tumbler. But even if he sipped slowly, he knew it was just a reprieve.

"Are you always so polite?"

"I have friends in the Diplomatic Corps." He didn't know what he was saying anymore. Not even the US Consul could save him from this rampage of feeling. So lovely sitting there with her smooth legs tapering down to the sheepskin rug, a trace of milk on her pink tongue, the fullness of the neat gingham blouse. Let not base nature taint this moment. Preserve me from the primates and all things excruciating. Oh, God, napkin on lap beginning to move. Must confess it used to happen as acolyte lighting the Easter candle. When belfries chimed and all affirmed. Look at something else, bubbles in milk, porcelain shepherds on mantelpiece, and, ah yes, the tireless pendulum of that Grandfather clock, over and back, over and back. But she is still there. Damn napkin moves again, so much that crumbs of sponge cake fall off. Fold arms to cover shame. Am no better than those gormless boors.

"I suppose Murf involved you in some of his exploits," she was saying. "I bet you saved his hide more than once."

"Well … maybe…" Not really. Can't elaborate. Mind going now, slipping away like those crumbs off the napkin.

"He's such a featherhead," she sighed. "Why can't he be sensible like you?" She leant forward to pick up the napkin which had also fallen, and replaced it on his exposed lap, without noticing anything, Deo Gratias. Not sure I want to be 'sensible', he thought. Charisma is what I want. Charisma.

"Is he ever going to grow up to be a man like you?"

"I think…" Throat! Words stuck. 'A man like you'…! Larynx seized up. Asthma coming back or crumbs of Marietta biscuit. Try to swallow. Loosen collar.

"Are you all right, Rolo?"

"Think … choking … Urrrghhh…"

"Lean forward!" She jumped up and slapped him on the back. Something gave inside him. The shock drilled through the passages, dislodging something in his head. Breath resumed in fits and starts.

"Better … now … thanks."

"What is it? Can I get you something?" She stood in front of him, flesh and blood in three dimensions. He had to purge by touch, and did so by grabbing her shoulders. Words came tumbling out in a torrent of Pidgin or maybe Tongues. "Must be real thing. Hope more milk. No right to say but must spit it out. I not much. Might get pass in B. Mech Eng. But have bad leg. Can't make decisions. Priest maybe should have been. But now glad not. Hated those louts at club. And Murf never mentioned you. Not once. Never forgive him for that. What saying? Have to be up front. With you. Now it's out, feel a bit better. Sorry I grabbed you. Think I'll sit down now."

He passed a hand over his burning face, drawing it down through the mocking hollows of his cheeks. The catharsis wouldn't last, he knew; already the vacuum was being filled by a wave of embarrassment. He had made a complete ass of himself. In a few minutes he had blown his cover. There was no going back. What was it about her that made him spill his guts all over the carpet?

"Think I'll go to bed now. If you might excuse me."

"Maybe we could go sailing tomorrow?"

Up the stairs, spinning on the landing, he groped his way towards door and bed and lay under the covers alone with his shame. No one to blame but himself. Sleep was out of the question. He would agonise till dawn announced the break of day and found him hollow-eyed and still an asshole. Better to pack his bag and slip away in silent ignominy. How could he have upchucked emotions in such a sorry splurge, him, the associate of a hard chaw of legend, with many Homeric escapades under his belt? He might as well crawl back into the womb for he was still pink, blubbery and inconsequential. The shame would haunt him to the very end. He couldn't even dare contemplate what Maura thought of him now. And she had called him a man. Maybe we could go sailing tomorrow? What was that? To hallucinate now on top of everything else would truly spell disaster. But no, the echo came again of that cloistral voice: Maybe we could go sailing tomorrow?

Rushing downstairs, he found the house asleep. His momentum carried him out through the kitchen into the walled garden. Which window to throw this fist of gravel at? Could wake the sleeping ogre, Fanning, by mistake. God, direct me. A gate squeaking. Christ, I'm caught.

"Rolo, what are you doing hopping around the garden in the middle of the night?"

"Which is Maura's window?"

"That one at the end, you twit. I hope you have better luck than me. There's a ladder in the shed if you want to elope." Murf cast his eyes to heaven and went indoors.

A shadow came on the window and a sash was raised. "Rolo, is that you?"

"Yes … em … did you say anything about sailing…?" Trying to make the whisper reach upwards was like pushing on string.

"Yes. Would you like to come sailing with me tomorrow?"

"I would. Yes, I would like to do that. Thank you very much." The residue of gravel slipped through his fingers.

"Are you feeling all right?"

"Perfectly fine now, thank you."

Back in bed he still couldn't sleep but the reasons were now completely different. He searched the bookcase for something on how to sail. To no avail. He passed the night, hands clasped behind head, grinning at the ceiling.

"I wonder if I really am the narrator?"
—The Present Writer

"He was in a highly malleable condition and full o' Juice de Spree."
—Rudyard Kipling

CHAPTER 7

DRESSED IN JEANS and sneakers, Maura helped the maid clear the breakfast things away. Through the kitchen window she watched the tops of the apple trees respond to the breeze and judged it to be a good day for sailing.

"Mitching?" Murf repeated. "You mean you're not going to work this morning?"

"Right in one," Maura shot back, then turned to Rolo, "Can you believe how responsible and middle-class Murf has become? Talk about the zeal of the convert."

"But will it last?" Rolo nibbled a piece of toast. His stomach was much better but there was no point in pushing his luck with a day's sailing in store. Although he had slept very little he felt renewed.

"Well, I just don't know," Murf muttered, picking up his briefcase at the hall-stand. "Wasters!" he called back just before the door closed behind him.

"He's insufferable when he's good," Maura grinned. "But for God's sake don't tell him that."

Half-way down the small marina she stopped and patted the timbers of a twenty-five foot sloop. "This is 'old green'" she said fondly.

"It's a fine looking boat," Rolo said.

"All aboard that's going aboard." Maura hopped nimbly on to the deck and Rolo repeated the manoeuvre with a little less grace. Murf's sneakers fitted him quite well but the canvas pants were a little baggy in the beam. 'Old green' sank under his weight by more than he expected as if recoiling from a strange touch, and he almost lost his footing. He hoped it wasn't a token of things to come out there on the briny ocean. Murf had once confessed that he had become so sick on the B and I ferry that he almost coughed up a ring. Further questioning established that the ring of which he spoke was in fact his rectum and if that had come through in the wash he would have been turned completely inside out. Rolo decided to banish such thoughts on this balmy day and take the risk of enjoying himself.

Maura opened the hatch and handed him a life preserver which he gratefully donned.

"I'd better come clean. I haven't done much of this before."

"There's nothing to it," she said. "Just a little crewing here and there."

"Aye, Aye. Just so long as you're the skipper … The sea looks a bit choppy further out. I presume we won't be going too far."

"Just as far as Wales," she kidded him. "Could you cast off? No, that line there. Well done, we'll soon be underway. Could you pass me the halyard? Good, that's the mainstay in place."

Rolo watched her fascinated, her sure movements around the little deck. One trim craft rigging another with a fine eye and a gleam of healthy enjoyment. She could have been an advertisement for Cod Liver Oil. He hadn't realized there was so much work involved and had imagined, and half-hoped, they could just lie back and talk about the sea, life, each other.

"Isn't there more I could do? I feel guilty sitting here watching you work."

"Don't worry, I enjoy it. You might take the tiller and keep on course to the lighthouse at the end of the pier." She made fast the shrouds and then tightened the winches. Her sweater rode up showing a crescent of bare back under the yellow life-jacket. Eventually she joined him in the stern and sat between his splayed feet, keeping a watchful eye on the rigging, and reading, from the snapping canvas and ruffles on the sea, the direction and curiosities of the breeze.

"Oh for a life on the ocean wave," Rolo said light-heartedly. He was, however, a little tense trying to learn as quickly as possible how the little craft responded to the tiller. The boat seemed to be alive and he had to get a feel for how it behaved. A fishing trawler passed them to the point heading out to sea. The crew waved and shouted some ribald pleasantries. Good matey sea-salts, Rolo thought as he swerved out of the wash from the trawler and then settled down with growing confidence to the task in hand.

The boat ran well, nosing through the emerald waves, sensing the pull of the wind in its stretched shrouds and creaking sax-board. Some gulls, mistaking them for a fishing vessel, wheeled through the translucent sky to follow them.

"The light is extraordinary," Rolo remarked. "Everything seems magnified. I could be hallucinating … I think I was last night," he added ruefully.

"Oh?" She turned to look at him.

"I mean all that balderdash I came out with." He knew he was trying to make excuses, to prove he was really quite sane.

"You didn't mean what you said?"

"I didn't think I made sense. But I did mean it." The die was cast. He was caught, willingly caught, like this craft in the elements.

"I'm glad."

"You are?"

"Yes."

Looking down at her gleaming hair, he could see highlights of gold among the brown, as she sat hands clasped around her knees. He couldn't quite believe that he didn't have to work really hard to impress a girl like this. And Murf, the bastard, never mentioned her, not once.

"Oh, some crinks in the rig." She scampered forward and tightened the turnbuckle on the mainstay.

"Can't I scupper the deck or something?" he asked. "I feel inadequate."

"You're doing fine. You have a nice light touch on the tiller."

"Maybe that's because I'm a wimp?"

"You know," she said, "I'm beginning to think you're looking for compliments." She re-joined him in the cramped cockpit.

"And I'm still waiting." They laughed in the salty air. The boat was running and heeling well, sails buxom and full, bow waves scrolling gracefully by the prow leaving a tight furrowed wash. The spires and houses of the town behind them dwindled to insignificance as they passed the lighthouse and made out to open sea where stronger breezes blew and the green-faceted water rose and fell in pyramids of jade, glancing blue and dancing green with nuggets of sunlight in the spindrift.

Rolo sat by his tiller wondering, in this dispensation of sea and sky, whether he had ever really worried about mechanics, home, the future – problems which now seemed as tiny as the toy houses back in the harbour. Perspective, that's what he always needed. He was at last out and about, his blood racing with the tide, pulse pounding because of the closeness of his companion. He suddenly knew what harmony meant. What had he done right to deserve this? He who slothed regularly, evaded family ties, ran with the fox and hunted with the hounds, and helped not the peregrine falcon. Someone up there must not dislike him. Don't question it; take it on faith. But still there beat that old Puritan refrain: the piper must be paid.

"Anyway," Maura was saying, "you never told me about playing nursemaid to Murf."

"I didn't do much," he said. "Maybe I should have tried harder to talk him out of some of his escapades. Instead, I went along with some of them. He seems to have quietened down here though." Through his hand on the tiller he could feel the breathing, the inner message of the sea.

"Don't believe it," she snorted. "When he's quiet he's usually planning something. He took Dad's death very badly." A wistful look crossed her face. "He's still hitting back. It's as if he has to blame someone for taking his father away."

Rolo nodded. It all made sense, though Murf would never have admitted it, not in a million years.

"Is Fanning the monster Murf thinks he is?"

"Yes and no. He's exploiting the business all right. But it's not really our concern. Mom knows about it and in a way she allows it. She's not as sharp as she used to be but she is still the majority shareholder … What is Murf going to do for an encore after he confronts him with the embezzling thing."

"Can Fanning get back at him in some way?"

Maura reached back and covered his hand on the tiller to make a slight course correction. "That's a possibility. But even if Murf does win

234

out is he going to feel any better? I wonder if he can cope without an enemy. Will he be able to face himself?"

Rolo watched her shoulders rise and fall. She had clearly thought a lot about her brother. Although three years his junior she was incomparably wiser than Murf.

"He'll be all right, with a sister like you."

"Spare my blushes." She turned smiling. "You have a sister, don't you?"

"Yes, one. But I don't think we're as close as you and Murf. Maybe the sibling thing, I don't know. It's all so complicated…"

The day continued to unfold its quiet enormity. They sat becalmed for a while, throwing out every inch of sheet to snare a passing breath, and then came slowly about. Lying in the cockpit, they watched the world together. He worried no more about making a move; it wasn't that important in the scheme of things. Her presence was what mattered. To the northeast they saw the fishing trawler throw out its lines and move ahead, diesel fumes belching from the wheel-house.

"They seem to be drawing a lot of water," Maura observed. "Look at the plimsoll line… very odd unless," she added with a sidelong grin, "they've caught a whale."

As she spoke the trawler's stern pitched lower than the bow and, to their amazement, they saw the vessel move backwards despite the forward thrust of the engine. Maura sat upright.

"What's going on? They must be in some kind

of trouble." She grabbed the boom and shouted at Rolo to duck. They tacked towards the trawler which was by now going full astern leaving a huge forward wash. The crew members were up on deck running to and fro in bewilderment.

"Something seems to be pulling them backwards." Rolo stated the obvious. "A current?"

The stern sank lower, shipping more water than the bilge pumps could cope with. A few crew members started using buckets.

"My God," Maura cried, "I've heard about this. It's a submarine. The trawl must be caught in a submarine. What else could it be?"

She stood on the hatch and shouted towards the trawler. "It's a submarine. Cut the trawl lines or you'll be pulled under!"

Rolo stood beside her clinging to the mast. "Cut the trawl lines!" he shouted, not really knowing what that meant.

They shouted together. If Maura hadn't been there he'd have shut his eyes and prayed for sanity. He added his voice to hers, "Cut your lines!"

The message got through. The trawler skipper bellowed, "A sub is it? Break out the the axe, Joe. We'll hack the bastards to the last man." The vessel listed badly now. Water, churned by the futile thrust of the prop, cascaded over the stern rail which was almost as low as the surface of the sea.

"The lines. Quick! Give me that hatchet!" The skipper wrestled with his mate, sliding and falling on the deluged deck, but regained his footing, axe in hand. He laid to with a will. Cables frayed and snapped. The trawler listed perilously as the starboard lines still held. The skipper slid down the sloping deck on his back, holding the axe aloft.

"Get those slithery mackerel off me!" The crew had difficulty in reaching their beleaguered captain.

"We can't reach you, Marty, on account of the slope."

"Throw me a rope, for fuck's sake!" Eventually righted, the skipper made two last vicious swings of the axe. "Got it, Bejasus." The trawler, suddenly freed of entanglement, bobbed up and squared off to the horizon. There was jubilation on board even though the catch and the nets had been lost.

"By Christ, I did it. 'Twould take more than a sub to pull Marty McCabe under." He leant over the rail and unburdened himself further into the nebulous depths. "I'll soften your cough anytime. Bugger off out of our territorial waters or I'll gut ye from stem to stern." Mollified, he turned to his loyal crew. "Grog all round, lads. 'Tis a good victory we have to celebrate. The day we beat the Commie navy. They'll talk about this for years to come."

"Good man, Marty, we'll all drink to that."

As an afterthought, Marty directed his gaze to the little sloop that had warned him and stood by during the ordeal.

"Thanks for the warning, lads. Come aboard

for a smathán to wet your whistles."

"Are you all right now?" Rolo shouted

"Begod, a Yank. We must be in the middle of a nuclear hollowcaust. Friend or foe?"

"Oh, friend. Friend."

"Is there a battle raging down below with them subs?" He pointed to the broiling depths. "We could get the other trawlers out…"

"I don't think that will be necessary."

"All right so. We'll be off then. The coast is clear. Here, have a drop."

A bottle of fifteen-year old Jameson came arcing over the water to land a foot away from 'old green'.

Rolo retrieved the bottle and sat nursing it in his lap. "I don't believe it," he repeated over and over. Maura laughed a little nervously. It had not been a bed of roses tacking so near the trawler in that churning sea.

"It was probably a British sub checking on nuclear waste," she said. "I read something about it before."

"Even so," Rolo absent-mindedly unscrewed the whiskey bottle and put it to his lips. "Even so. Marty and his crew thought it was the Russian Navy. The Cold War makes everyone think the worst."

"Not surprisingly," she said.

When they finally entered the harbour from which they'd left four hours earlier, they saw a small boat with an outboard engine chugging towards them. A figure waved and shouted.

"Who's that?" Rolo asked.

"I'll give you three guesses," Maura said.

"I've got him!" the figure yelled. "Got him nailed down at last."

Rolo looked from the waving image to the label on the bottle and wondered if he could take much more. Even the stalwart sea could not remain aloof to the madness of this land. What chance had he? Slim to none, he thought, as he took burning gulps from the bottle.

When he hove to, Murf continued about finally getting the goods on Fanning. He had just put the last piece in the jig-saw and couldn't contain his excitement.

"We had an encounter with a trawler and a submarine," Rolo said and started to hum, "The captain, he took fits, threw away all of the grits…"

"They say the sea can do strange things to a man," Murf said, throwing them a line to tow them into the marina.

"But it's true," Maura said, falling against Rolo who collapsed in the cockpit. They laughed helplessly.

"Don't you want to know how I got the proof I needed?" Murf seemed pained.

"No, not really," Rolo slurred. "We've got bigger fry to fish."

"Not at all … we have to fish for those damned fry." Maura joined him in another raucous bout of laughter as Murf led the pilotless craft into its berth, and warned about the dangers of drinking at sea.

During the remainder of those palmy days, Rolo worked with Maura in the lumber yard. Even though he could see how capable she was, he still flinched every time she operated that snarling saw. Under her tutelage he became adept at cutting glass on the large cloth-covered table, using diamond and T-square, although he never quite matched her confident ability, and sometimes the waste-bin filled up with the broken shards of his mistakes.

Murf sometimes sent them out customers with dockets that made no sense. Maura would remonstrate with him. "There's no such thing as 'a two-by-four one foot thick'" or "Skirting boards don't come in teak." She handled the once-off orders that often required tricky measurements, and dealt mainly with householders rather than builders. It wasn't the most lucrative side of the business but she believed it to be important for goodwill. She charged publicans and butchers a nominal amount for sawdust but there was no charge to the orphanage for off-cuts for their solid fuel heating system.

The DIY customers didn't always do their home-work properly and Maura would often have to help them redesign their projects. To his delight, Rolo found that his knowledge of mechanics sometimes enabled him to make useful suggestions. They had some unusual customers – a priest making flats for a Passion Play, a zany lady who wanted to build a kennel for squirrels, an elderly man who was building a nuclear fall-out shelter in his back garden. But the most unusual by far was the Muslim Slaughterer.

The Iraqi man had virtually no English apart from the name of the object he wished to construct. But even that didn't get them very far along. Murf, who had come out to the yard to interpret, was finding it hard going.

"A Cincinnati Box"? he repeated. "What does it look like? Could you draw a diagram?" He grabbed an imaginary pen and scribbled in the air while the pleasant Arab smiled and nodded. "What's it for, this Cincinnati Box? The purpose … reason?"

"For… beast," the Iraqi said politely.

"I see … a beast … what kind of beast?" Murf nodded in sympathy.

"M-meat…"

"Yes, meat … go on…" Murf beckoned with his hands as in charades, giving positive reinforcement. "Chicken coop? Chicken, wings, flap like so." While Murf impersonated a hyperactive fowl, the Arab shook his head sadly. Maura, who was afraid to catch Rolo's eye, intervened.

" …le but de cet article…?" She went into a huddle with the customer who had a smattering of French and, after a while, pronounced that the mystery was solved. A Cincinnati Box was a wooden structure designed for the slaughtering of animals according to the rites of Islam.

"I knew that," Murf said, returning to the safety of his office while Rolo assembled the timber and Maura set up the electric saw.

Sometimes they went for lunch to the golf club; at other times they joined the workmen in the main warehouse where they sat cross-legged on planks of white deal and swapped sandwiches and stories. The workmen knew that Maura and Rolo were becoming an item and sometimes ribbed them about it.

One afternoon Murf came running out of the office and jumped up on a pile of concrete blocks to make an announcement. He waited for his audience to assemble and cleared his throat.

"I just got word from the big smoke that Rolo here, our own poet, scholar and dogsbody, has been awarded a degree in mechanical engineering, second-class honours, grade one." A cheer went up. Maura hugged the benumbed Rolo and the men gathered around to slap him on the back. As if performing a conjuring trick, Murf whipped a tarpaulin off a wheelbarrow full of beer which he dispensed with gusto.

Rolo was surprisingly close to tears. The news and the hearty response were too much to take in. Manhandled on to the concrete-block podium, he made a speech which Murf described as 'totally incoherent as usual'. It was like living in Aladdin's cave, Rolo thought, there was no end to the treasure trove. But could it last; was it real?

"Murf, are you sure about the results? I mean…"

"I triple-checked." Murf laughed at his uncertainty which was so typical of him. "I had two good men stand by the bulletin board for the last week. You'll get official word tomorrow. Accept it, you twerp. You're home free. Just as well I got canned. Gave you some time to work."

A slight grin formed on Rolo's face. He was an engineer, a professional. A minute ago he wasn't and now he was. Good God. He looked to Maura for confirmation. Her warm smile encouraged him to accept the good news.

In a quiet moment of reflection Rolo would probably have admitted that there was a design in his apparently misplaced presence on the landing of the stairs late that night. Maura crossed the landing a couple of times in her dressing gown and Rolo dithered and lurked, murmuring something about a glass of water. Giving up the ghost, he returned to his own room, read ten pages of a thriller without taking in a word, and prowled back out on to the landing again, where he watched soulfully the strip of light under Maura's door.

He caught his breath as she appeared again, gliding in slippers, ostensibly to get an aspirin.

"Are you all right?" she asked softly although she was the one in search of aspirin.

"Yes … thank you … I'm just standing here, for the moment. I can't really … get to sleep."

"Me neither."

"I was … em … wondering…" He coughed to

disguise the shake in his voice.

"Yes?"

His nerve began to go. He reached for the wall to steady himself. "This wallpaper is ... very nice..."

Murf flung his door open and stuck his head out. "Bugger the wallpaper! Cut out this French farce and get your act together. Some of us have to sleep because we have to work in the morning." He withdrew, slamming the door. In the wake of tension and with great relief Maura and Rolo moved closer smiling, and held each other. It was, they agreed later, funny what a laugh could do.

The next morning they worked furiously in the yard, exchanging grim nervous glances, trying to distract themselves from what was happening in the office. The big show-down was on between Murf and Fanning.

"...I had the help of an independent auditor," Murf said after he'd made the charge of embezzlement. "There's no question about it." This was the moment he had dreamed about and feared at the same time. Now that it was upon him he couldn't deny that fear had the upper hand, even though for him there was little to be afraid of. At least he didn't think so, but then again he knew that Fanning was as slippery as an eel. The tension may have been irrational but it was still real.

"Commendable thoroughness," Fanning said. "It's a pity you didn't pursue your studies with such diligence."

"The fact remains," Murf said doggedly, "you have to make restitution of one hundred and seventy-five thousand pounds to the company."

Fanning laughed drily but his eyes bulged like boiled sweets, suggesting he wasn't quite as suave as he wanted to appear.

"I know you hate my guts but don't do this to yourself. Stay in the junior league where you belong."

They faced each other across a table on which the incriminating ledgers lay. Despite the stress of confrontation, Murf was conscious of the irony of the situation. This was the first time he was not on the receiving end. Lacking experience, he found the role of prosecutor to be awkward and unnatural. Even now he couldn't quite deny a modicum of sympathy for the underdog. He had to remind himself of how Fanning had preyed on the family and business after his father died.

"You don't give a damn about the business, do you? It's just a means to a political end for you."

"That's rich coming from you, a waster of the first order. Take my advice and drop the whole thing. You haven't a shred of evidence. You would have to prove that whoever the culprit was actually received payment." Fanning walked towards the door.

Murf said to his departing back. "I've got the proof. You became careless in the last year, didn't you?" He reached inside his jacket and pulled out a letter. "This is a memo from your political friend, Furlong, There are several references to building supplies he received from you at no charge. It's there in black and white. If you want to avoid legal action you will have to make full restitution and resign from the board." That was it, the bottom line. He'd said it. There were no more cards to play.

"Do you by any chance see yourself as the new chief executive officer?" Fanning inquired.

Murf's reply was simple but it showed he'd thought about it. "No, I'm not experienced enough. I think Jim Sinnott should take over."

"You've got it all figured out, haven't you?" The undisguised sneer gave Murf the assurance he needed. The dénouement wasn't as he'd expected; there was little relish in it.

"It is what it is."

"Let me ask you something," Fanning spoke slowly. "Do you think I didn't know what you were up to these last few months?"

"Maybe you did know." Murf shrugged. "But it makes no difference. I have the proof that you embezzled building materials and gave them to your crony, Furlong, no doubt for political favours."

Fanning stood up. "Ah, but it does make a difference. I'm a great believer in insurance." He drew a manila folder from his briefcase and laid typed sheets on his desk. "This is an exchange of affidavits between Mr. Furlong and myself. You can see that he acknowledges on behalf of his Party the donations we made. In other words the donations were to the Party, not to him personally…"

"But they *were* personal," Murf blurted out. "Furlong is a builder."

"That's not what is stated here," Fanning said smoothly. "And it's notarised by the Party solicitor."

"It's all backdated. It's a con…"

"A minor detail. The fact is that Party contributions are not illegal. So, I'm afraid all your little efforts to trip me up have come to nought."

Murf felt his stomach heave. "You didn't have the agreement of the Board…"

"Oh but I did." Fanning laid another document on the table – the relevant Board minute. "I only needed a majority, and there it is, including your Mother."

"She doesn't understand what you're up to."

"You should have more respect…"

"You won't get away…" Murf felt sick. He had underestimated Fanning, a fatal error.

"I told you you were out of your depth. There's something else you should know. I heard about your attempt at impersonating the IRA at the border. It had little significance. *We* know that. But some of my colleagues up North are not sure what to make of it and would be keen to know your whereabouts. The situation up there is becoming very tense. Sophisticated weapons are being provided to the UVF."

"Is that some kind of threat?"

"I leave you to figure it out." Fanning returned the documents to his briefcase and left. Murf leant against a filing cabinet feeling drained. His eyes were hooded with fatigue. He felt sure that Fanning was also contributing directly to the IRA, and he would of course be able to do far more if he were elected to office.

Passing through the yard to his car, Fanning waved pleasantly to Maura and Rolo and drove away in a cloud of exhaust and sawdust. They exchanged questioning looks; he didn't appear to be a beaten man.

Without a word Murf stalked past them and went to the end of the yard. Throwing off his coat, he picked up an axe and started to chop wood with a fury unmatched even by the skipper of the fishing trawler. Rolo made to intervene but Maura restrained him. They stood and watched from their little corral by the electric saw, like some kind of Greek chorus. Murf chopped and split everything in sight until steam rose off him. Then he threw the axe aside and marched back to the office. From the yard they could see his profile bent over the drawing board. He appeared to be writing.

When Rolo joined him he saw what he had been writing: Fanning, Fanning, Fanning, Fanning … Sheets of drawing paper were filled with the reviled name. Rolo wondered if he wasn't unravelling. Murf eventually stood up.

"I have one more card to play. Come on, we're

going to the bank."

"Banks can't divulge information," Rolo protested. "Let it go."

"Cat … skinning … different ways."

Murf didn't seem too badly out of sorts as they walked along the main street towards the bank. Rolo was really humouring him by going along; there was little to be gained by the trip.

"Hiya, Murf," the teller greeted them. "How's she cuttin'?"

"Fine Charlie. How's the world of high finance? Take my advice. Always withdraw before leaving a deposit."

Charlie raised the teller's window and craned forward. "Now that you bring up the subject, could you see me all right for the week-end? I've run out of Seáníní."

Murf silenced him with a raised hand. "Say no more, Charlie. For you anything".

It was the first indication Rolo had that Murf's distribution network extended into the provinces. Maybe, after all, Charlie would provide some information on Fanning's finances.

"Well, what can I do for you?" Charlie beamed.

Murf handed him a cheque. "We've a big payment to meet in cash," he explained. "I want to stall, but Bob Fanning feels his reputation might be hurt. That's why he signed this cheque on his own account." Rolo caught a glimpse of the cheque which was made out for sixty-five thousand pounds. He retreated from the counter and sat on a highly polished mahogany chair normally reserved for aging dowagers. Even his good leg had gone rubbery. It was Fanning's signature Murf had been practising on the drawing board.

Charlie sucked in his breath. "It's a bit irregular…"

"I told him that," Murf heartily agreed, shaking his head at Fanning's disregard for red tape. "I said, 'let the damn creditors wait'. But would he agree? No." He tossed his head, despairing of the man. "'Cash on the nail, he said'. You know how stubborn he is."

Charlie still hesitated, turning the cheque over in his hands, yet trying to appear not to be scrutinising it too closely.

"Don't tell me he's not good for it," Murf said with a sardonic laugh.

"It's not that," Charlie said. "The account is well in funds." This confirmed Murf's suspicions that Fanning made regular payments of large amounts. And he already knew who the recipients were. He was taking a big risk but he didn't care any more.

"You've got it made here, Charlie, being able to make your own decisions. So many bureaucrats nowadays have to go running to their bosses if a paper clip is out of place…"

Rolo looked out the stencilled window that boasted the assets of the bank in gold-leaf numbers with a proliferation of zeros. He tried not to hear what was going on at the counter, though innocence could not be bought so easily. Murf had reverted to type and was back at the precipice. Gone was the daily routine, work ethic, the golf club. He had suddenly cut his lines to the middle-class sub that was about to drag him under. He had bobbed up again. Rolo's knotted stomach began to gurgle. An elderly woman stood beside him coughing pointedly, but he could not trust his spaghetti legs to offer her the seat.

"Well," Charlie said, "we do have to be careful these days. You'd be amazed at the bare-faced cons people try to pull."

"I can imagine," Murf replied with a world-weary grimace of sympathy. "Although I'd say you could spot a con a mile off."

"We do our best," Charlie said. "How would you like it? In hundreds I suppose."

"That would be fine."

Rolo sat rigid as the huge notes smelling of manure – for only farmers at cattle fairs dealt in these denominations – were placed in a large manila envelope. He dimly heard Charlie's offer of the bank's security van, and Murf accept.

"Don't spend it all at once," Charlie quipped.

"No, not at once. 'Bye Charlie. I haven't forgotten the Seáníní."

"Good man."

Riding down the main street in the security van, Rolo looked wistfully through the steel grille as if he were already a prisoner. A refrain from 'The Ballad of Reading Gaol' haunted his mind: 'I never saw a man who looked with such a wistful eye upon that little tent of blue which prisoners call the sky.'

"Bridge Street," Murf told the helmeted driver.

"Charlie said you were going to the yard."

"No," Murf said. "You can drop us at the house in Bridge Street."

As soon as they got inside the house Rolo grabbed him by the lapels and forced him back against the hall-stand.

"You've done it now! This is felony..."

"No, it isn't..."

"Yes it is, you dumb fucking nutjob." Rolo forced him back against the coats and umbrellas and might have throttled him if he hadn't caught a glimpse of his own murderous face in the mirror, and froze at the vision of insanity.

"Calm yourself, old son," Murf said with maddening composure. The bastard even smiled. "It's not a felony. It's just a down payment on the old birth-right. Anyway the money is more mine than Fanning's. And it's definitely not the IRA's."

The last comment didn't register with Rolo, whose head still rested among the scarves and mackintoshes. "Fanning could be ... upstairs right now," he croaked.

"So what? The cheque won't clear for a day or two."

"What about ... tomorrow and tomorrow and tomorrow ... ?"

"I won't be here," Murf said simply.

"You're going to Leave? Leave?" It hadn't occurred to Rolo, but now as his head began to clear, he realized there was no alternative.

"Yes, and now I must visit Mother in her boudoir to say 'adieu'. You know, the sad thing is that the yard will go to rack and ruin." He was up to his old tricks again: worrying about the business or any damn thing that came to mind to distract himself from the real pain of leaving. He ran upstairs, thus insulated, to say farewell.

Rolo sat on the stairs gripping the newel post as if his life depended on it, and maybe it did for he had to touch something solid. If he phoned Maura at the yard what could he say? If he told her about the theft he would be making her an accomplice. He couldn't contact her until the news broke. He needed time to figure out what to do but there was none. Dragging himself up from the steps, he wrote a note: 'Will explain later. I love you. Rolo'. He limped upstairs and shoved it under her bedroom door. She would get it that evening. Tears streamed down his face.

They kept to the side streets as they left town. Murf was in his element setting out on another adventure; he swung the duffle bag that contained more money than clothes. Mrs. McIlwee, the town gossip, was feeling her cauliflowers in the shop window while surveying the street. Arched like a preying mantis among the vegetables, her white curly hair camouflaged against the cauliflower, she could tell by their walk that they were leaving town. She had seen men head for the harbour with that same loping stride, join the crew of a Dutch merchant ship, and never be heard from again.

On the outskirts, Murf turned to look back at the town where he once had lived and dwelt in innocence. It was years after his father died that he discovered the significance of the boiled blackberry leaves. An old farmer told him they were thought to be a cure for throat cancer. Some months before he died, his Dad, then in the County Hospital, asked to see him. He said goodbye, put his hand on his head and asked him not to visit again. Those last weeks were spent at home wondering, trying to read his mother's face as she returned from the hospital. He would stand in the hall and watch her face as she hung up her coat, and study her expression. Wondering, and never knowing until it was all over. His Dad's attempt to protect him had not even deferred the pain.

Even in those last weeks, Fanning had been a frequent visitor to the house. His chatter was a mockery of his Dad's gentle reticence. It was Fanning who made the funeral arrangements. Murf hated him for that and hated himself for being so young and helpless.

And here he was walking away having accomplished nothing except for that sixty-five grand which probably wouldn't even put a crimp in Fanning's life-style – unless of course he had already promised it to the IRA.

"What the hell are we doing?" he asked aloud, jerking himself back to the present.

"Hitching a ride, I guess."

"And me with sixty-five big ones. My God, old habits die hard."

They got a hackney car and were driven in comfort to Arklow for twelve pounds fifty. As planned, they got out at a used car lot.

"Something with flair and panache," Murf said to the salesman, eventually plumping for a near-vintage Standard Vanguard, complete with running boards.

"One doesn't drive a car like this," Murf said, sitting behind the large wheel. "One motors."

After money changed hands – and there was a discount for cash – Murf nursed the huge black heap along the narrow leafy roads.

"We should have goggles and scarves. And a flag on the front wing. Family crest. Crossed Gold Flakes athwart a chevron, gules argent, a bottle of stout rampant. Motto: Ever upwards, inwards and outwards." One might have said he was his old self again, but more properly he was his old act again.

Rolo watched the trees and hedges turn dark olive as the evening closed in. Having a degree under his belt gave him a certain confidence and maybe even a glimmer of a future. But he was plagued by thoughts of Maura. Would she understand what was going on and forgive him for his complicity?

What of Murf? The money wouldn't last all that long. He had burnt his boats behind and would, if he ran true to form, burn his bridges in front. Having appeared to be on the verge of settling down he was now back on the brink, working without a net.

A couple of hours later they stopped off at Northbrook Square for Rolo to collect his things.

"You're leaving?" The Cart expressed surprise. She was sorry to see him go. Rolo wasn't a character in her book but he was a gentleman and that was the next best thing. It was a strange feeling sitting with her in her private quarters downstairs. They weren't lodgers any more and by some weird alchemy had acquired the status of visitor.

"Heard you did well in your exams. Congratulations," she said grudgingly, then turned on Murf, "More than can be said for you."

"Ah well, Mrs. McC, we can't all be geniuses like Rolo here." On the way out he thanked her for all the quids she lent him. He left a hundred-pound note on the little flower-filled shelf under the picture of the Sacred Heart.

After Rolo had packed – fortunately the malodorous radio officer was out – they looked into the front room where the inmates still whiled away the hours. It could not have been otherwise; there was a constancy about that room. Tim smoked and stared, and hardly noticed when Murf slipped a couple of big notes into the top pocket of his jacket.

Murf had a quiet chat with Crowley which reinforced his belief the Fanning was contributing to the IRA via Noraid which, if true, meant that Murf may have just bitten off a lot more than he could chew. He gave Crowley the log-book for the Standard Vanguard and promised to send the car around to him for keeps when he was finished with it.

"It'll keep you warmer in the winter," he said. "You won't have to spend so much time airing those damn long johns."

"Thanks," Crowley mumbled to his old adversary. Take care of yourselves now." He turned to Rolo and whispered, "I'm having great success with the coots. This time it will be different."

Standing on the front steps, the brass knocker clunking down for the last time, Rolo stated the obvious, "Leaving is not so easy."

They drove down the square and glimpsed for the last time, through ivied railings, the Loreto girls cracking a hockey ball along the green sward, their pink thighs nipped by strong knicker-elastic. They booked into the Wellington Hotel where once they used to sneak for baths when The Cart's geyser was out of order or Tim's bowels were working overtime, before they were rumbled and deposited dripping on the side of the street. Discomfited by sudden legitimacy, they rose in the wrought-iron lift of Parisian *art nouveau* style to their elegant room which looked on to St. Stephen's Green and the purple mountains beyond.

Shaved and tonsured by the hotel barber, they sat down to dinner in the main dining room among the tweedy set and polyester parvenu. Chandeliers struck sparkles from the silver and crystal tableware as they perused the leather-bound menu. They dined on Dublin Bay prawns as pink and fat as chicken-pluckers' fingers, tranches of beef resting on beds of cress like lily-ponds. They had their brandies in the horseshoe-shaped bar, famous for high-profile trysts. Rolo laid down his glass suddenly on the marble-topped counter and snapped his head around, "What did you say about the IRA?"

"When?"

"In the bank. Something about the money not being theirs…" His voice went higher as his recall improved.

"The money may have been destined for the IRA. OK, it's a problem. But who cares? It's a problem for Steppop too, remember…"

"I don't care about Steppop. But I do care about my survival…"

" Don't worry. We'll be leaving the country tomorrow. I've always wanted to visit the US of A."

"The US…?"

"You know very well," Murf said smoothly, "that it's high time you visited the Fatherland. Don't deny it."

"Maura…" Rolo blurted. "Maura…" He went on as best he could to explain what she meant to him.

"I feel the same way about Gobnait," Murf said. "But we can't involve them right now. When things settle down we can come back … or maybe they could join us in the US?" He went on to say how they could keep the girls in the picture in the meantime – there were ample means of long-distance communication.

As Rolo reflected on this he was edged aside by members of a wedding party anxious to get to the bar. The bride, they said, was upstairs getting dressed for the honeymoon; they needed to charge their glasses to toast the happy couple as they left.

Feeling a little left out, and unable, because of over-eating, to feel the effects of the brandy – the *bonviveur*'s dilemma – they retired to their room. Rolo wanted to call Maura but the danger was that Fanning might answer and he would want to know why they had left so suddenly. Murf tried to raise Gobnait but she was out, presumably on the tiles with her Vet.

"You'd think," Murf said peevishly, "She'd have made an effort to be in."

"You didn't tell her you were coming,"

"What about intuition?"

Most of their old knock-abouts were out of town for the holidays, canning peas in England or running amok in the provinces. They just couldn't raise anyone. Murf threw himself on the bed disconsolately. A last night in dear old Dublin with a bag of cash, a need for diversion, and they couldn't get in on any shenanigans.

"Christ," he grumbled. "I feel like Ossian returning to the old sod to find his cronies eating the feet off the statues and the big-arsed Finn pushing up daisies." He tried to reconcile himself to an early night.

Rolo looked out the window, thinking that tomorrow they would fly over the Atlantic and see this pernickety little island dwindle and fade into mist, holding close its secrets, which always slipped through his fingers whenever he tried to grasp them. His reverie was broken by sounds of giggling, interspersed with shouts, coming from the room next door. There was also the enchanting music of glasses and popping corks. Murf sat bolt upright with eyes that seemed less sad.

"Maybe we should investigate."

A slinky bridesmaid opened the door to him and said, "We're not ready yet." Like most people at a wedding she assumed that everyone was part of the celebration. Weddings exuded that sort of inclusiveness.

"I see," Murf said, stalling. He needed time to figure this out. "Can we do anything?" His offer of help was vague enough to prevent discovery.

"Aren't you on the groom's side?"

"Yes, of course." The pieces were beginning to fall into place. "Well, are you ready yet?" He could see the other bridesmaid putting the finishing touches to the bride who was seated at the dressing table. Except it wasn't the bride. He wanted to be in on this skulduggery whatever it was.

"Tell 'em we're going as fast as we can." The bridesmaid giggled and sipped her champagne.

"Maybe we could come in and help?"

"Into the bride's room? Are you crazy?"

"That's not the bride in front of the dressing table," Murf said. "It's a bloke."

"Oh damn. Get in here fast. Promise not to say

anything."

"We promise." Murf gave Rolo a nudge. His eyes had that glazed yet concentrated look of a sow farrowing. He carefully read the room. The real bride, he noticed immediately, was bombed out of her skull, prostrated on the bed in her satin undies. Her place, it appeared, was to be taken by her cousin, Tom, who had already slipped into her going-away outfit and was having his face made up by the two bridesmaids, Doreen and Therma.

"I don't know about this," Tom said, having second thoughts about the prank.

"It's a great idea," Murf entered into the spirit of it. "They'll talk about this for years to come."

"Wait till Sammy gets you into bed tonight. Rita's kept him at bay for two years. He's mad for it." The two bridesmaids laughed helplessly, fluttering in their pink finery, looking like a double scoop of strawberry ice-cream.

"That's it!" Tom bridled. "I'm not going through with it."

"Oh, come on. It's just a bit of craic."

"Anyway," Murf began reassuringly, "they'll be wise to you before you even get in the car. In the meantime Rita will have sobered up. So don't worry."

Therma stood back to examine the effect of the rouge she had just applied.

Murf decided to help. "Might I suggest a touch more mascara there on the left eyelid? Good, that's it. And perhaps," he looked from the slumbering bride to Tom, "a little more padding in the upper area."

"You can't make a silk purse out of a sow's ear," Doreen tittered.

"We can but try," Murf said. "Oh, Damn, we left our drinks downstairs."

"Help yourselves. We've got plenty."

He toasted everyone in the room including the prone bride in her new going-away underwear. He picked up a fallen carnation and stuck it in his button-hole to look the part he had been so suddenly cast in.

When they finished, Tom looked surprisingly bride-like. Indeed, the final addition of a veiled pill-box hat gave him a compelling air of mystery. Murf was enjoying himself no end. Crashing a wedding reception was good but being part of an impersonation had a special piquancy for him. He wasn't of course in the front line himself, so there was no risk, but that was a small price to pay. Besides, one never knew how a caper like this might turn out; there could be a scattering of flak in unpredictable directions. It was all shaping up to be a good last night.

While going towards the elevators, Tom wobbled a bit in his heels and received some last-minute coaching from his acolytes. Rolo tugged Murf by the sleeve.

"We can't do this," he hissed.

"Yes we can. These bridesmaids are going to need some cheering up after the climax of this stunt. Don't you want them to have an enjoyable wedding?"

The band stopped abruptly as the group entered the ballroom and the large steamy crowd gathered unsteadily around them. Sammy, the groom, took his shrinking bride, Tom, into the middle of the circle and bellowed out his gratitude to Mom and Dad on both sides, his best man, Uncle Joe and Father William. The crowd cheered and hooted, gave a few raucous bars of 'For they are Jolly Good Fellows', and generally made enough noise to prove to the departing couple and the bride's father that it was a wedding to remember.

Sammy led his bride through the foyer to the waiting car. Elderly ladies kissed her tangentially, murmured last bits of wedding-night advice and straightened the cute little going-away pill-box hat. On the distaff side there were tears among the cheers in the final outpouring of felicitation.

"Good luck now and call the first one 'Benjamin' after your Granddad."

"Drop us a card from Majorca if you have time. Har. Har."

"Don't come back with a suntan."

"Now we can get on with some serious drinking."

Tom's eyes stared helplessly out the window as the car took off at speed heading for the airport. The disguise had worked too well relative to the perception of the guests which, it had to be admitted, was a good deal less acute than normal.

"You've done it now." Murf poked Doreen in her ribs.

"What'll we do?" She covered her mouth and gurgled through her fingers. "I need a drink."

"Why not get Therma and meet our side of the family?" Women at weddings, he knew, responded well to the notion of family.

Rolo was against the idea but tried not to be a wet blanket when the intimate little party got underway in their room. Both bridesmaids sat on the floor throwing back champagne, their pink dresses so flimsy they could have been blown off like petals.

"What a terrific wedding," Murf intoned, walking in his bare feet over beds and chairs seeing to civilities, charging glasses and passing cigarettes around. 'Wedding' and 'family', these were the two key words to implant in their minds. In his experience there was only one other thing that had the same melting effect on women and that was the image of lying on a sun-drenched beach in a bikini. He wasn't sure how that one worked exactly but thought it had something to do with the effect of rubbing suntan lotion into, and contemplating, one's own glistening skin while the sea kept up that old hypnotic rhythm. Maybe preparing Tom for the nuptial bed had the same mesmerising effect on the girls. It was all a question of thought-implantation.

"Come Ladies, a little more aerated plonk to set the seal on this *wedding* and to celebrate *family* life." He might as well cover all bets. "As well as believing in *weddings* and *family*, I think sun worship has much to recommend it. Imagine lying on a *beach*, oiled and tanned, the *waves* flopping in and out…"

"What are you on about?" Therma inquired. The little top-knot of forget-me-nots that sat askew on her hair was wilting fast. "Oh God," she moaned, "And Rita next door sleeping it off. What have we done? My head is spinning."

"No." Rolo said.

"No what?" Murf queried. "I haven't done anything."

"The thought is father to the deed."

"Oh, gimme a break." Murf noted that Doreen had slumped against the legs of an armchair and was snoring gently. "Now look what you've done," he said accusingly to Rolo. "At least Therma is awake."

"It would be taking advantage," Rolo said. He knew that Murf had slipped into the part of seducer; it wasn't really him, but the problem was how to extricate him from that role.

"We need whatever edge we can get to counter nunnish propaganda. This is the *feeling* decade, for Goodness sake. We're supposed to feel and frolic. Make love not war."

"And what about Gobnait?" Rolo brought up the heavy artillery, and it stopped Murf in his tracks.

"Why did you have to mention her?"

"Because you need to get off the stage, and join the rest of us in reality-land." The shells found their target and Murf fell into a brown study of sorts.

Relocating the two girls in the room next door where the real bride still snored peacefully through her wedding night, Murf expostulated. "I can't believe I'm doing this." He looked at the untouchable roseate maids, both of whom they deposited on the spare bed – slumbering lambikins in sequestered loveliness, bosoms undulating in hushed pentameter.

"Out!" Rolo said firmly. "Back to our room. Now."

Murf tossed on his bed for a while wrestling with the thought of what might and should have been, and bounded into the bathroom for a cold shower that did no good.

"They're still in there, you know," he said, wildly, wrapped in towels. "We only have to walk in. Think, man. I didn't get 'em drunk. They did it themselves. It's not my fault. They'll wake up tomorrow wondering what's wrong with them, whether they're unattractive in some way. My God, we could give them a complex for life."

"It would be taking advantage," Rolo insisted. "Just zip it."

Murf paced the room, fists gouging the sockets of his bleary eyes. This was not how such a scenario was meant to end.

"Settle yourself," Rolo advised unhelpfully.

Murf continued to pace, leaving wet footprints

on the carpet. He looked out the tall Georgian window at the city sleeping with its night lights on, the dark mountains brooding in the background. Nature, poor Stepdame, couldn't slake his drought. "I'm going back in," he said in a broken voice.

"No, you're not."

"Why not?"

"Gobnait."

Murf ground his teeth; he had no answer, no come-back. He got into his bed; the show was over.

"I knew you'd see sense," Rolo said smugly. He grinned under the sheets. It was good, he thought, to be in control of oneself with the memory and promise of Maura.

"Go to sleep, you kill-joy Philadelphia Puritan." Murf punched out the pillows and wrestled himself under the blankets.

They must have slept for a while because the return of consciousness was abrupt and wrenching. There was a row going on next door occasioned by the return of the unamused groom.

"…some fucking joke. We had to cancel the honeymoon because of you … get those bitches out of here." A loud crash suggested that Sammy had knocked over a table lamp in an effort to separate his bride from the bridesmaids.

"Sammy Darling, I knew you'd come for me…" The bride didn't sound fully sober yet.

"Shut up. We could have been in Majorca by now. Dammit, woman, couldn't you stay sober on your wedding day? I did, and look what it got me. A black eye from your crazy cousin, Tom, and a kick in the nuts from a bunch of gay-bashers at the airport."

Murf sat up hollow-eyed, his hair standing in spikes. "This is the last straw." He banged the wall. "Shut up in there. After all I did for you, this is the thanks I get." The hush he expected didn't materialise so he put the clincher in. "Tiocfaidh ar lá!" That brought better results, much better. The ensuing silence was so perfect that Rolo couldn't help worrying about it.

"Shit, I can't sleep anymore." Murf reached over and turned on the radio. It happened to be the Civil Defence Force broadcasting a simulated nuclear alert. After some strange bleeps and electronic hums the announcer continued, "There is heavy fall-out in North-East Donegal. Keep under the stairs or if you have a cellar, better still. Don't milk the cows for three days and then strain the milk through muslin if you have it. A bit of nylon stocking will do, if you haven't. Be sure to tell the children that the white stuff on the ground is not snow…"

A crazed look appeared in Murf's eyes. He burrowed under the bedclothes holding his head.

A kind of normality returned at breakfast in the Saddle Room. Murf was lighting up his first Gold Flake of the day when he was summoned by the PA system to take a telephone call. In his absence Rolo slathered his last croissant with butter and red-current jam and sipped his *café au lait*. He glanced at the headlines of a newspaper held aloft by a man at a neighbouring table and had a feeling of *déjà vu*.

"Who was that on the phone?" he inquired when Murf returned.

"The Cart." Murf seemed withdrawn. He had a gift of concentration when faced by a contingency. The distant look in his eye this time suggested something more pressing.

"What about?"

"She said some roughnecks called to the digs looking for us. She wasn't sure if they were Special Branch men or not. But they forced their way in and turned over our old room. It seems that they caught some radio officer and for some reason stuffed his socks in his mouth. Maybe," he conceded, "it's all getting a little out of hand. I think perhaps we should head for the airport sooner rather than later."

Rolo's anxiety started to build. Murf's concession to fear was in itself terrifying. It was like being in a wood at night when the leader of the gang stops suddenly and asks if anyone else has heard a weird noise. He suddenly knew why the headlines of the newspaper looked familiar. It was yesterday's paper. They were probably being watched right now, right there. God alone knew who was after their hides, the IRA, Noraid, the Ulster Volunteer Force, Special Branch, perhaps all four. Once they were pursued by Vets; now it was guerrillas and secret police. He was half-way across the foyer when Murf caught up with him.

"Take it easy. Walk normally."

"We're dead," Rolo said simply.

From the bedroom Murf called Ashur, who launched into a tirade of abuse, not over the damage to his car, but because several 'mouth-breathers' had been following him around since the border incident. "I can't minister to the sick," he complained, "with those turds hanging around the surgery."

Murf hung up and said in a strained voice, "Yes, I think we should head for the airport." He hadn't finished speaking when there was a loud knock on the door. They stood frozen in the middle of the room.

"Not a sound," Murf whispered. He looked towards the window. No good. They were six floors up. The doorknob started to turn. He might just have time to reach the bolt. Except that Rolo held him in a bear hug.

"Are ye ready to have the room done out yet?" The chambermaid looked in to see two grown men embracing each other, and she withdrew silently.

"Get off me." Murf shook himself free. "We've got to get to the car. I'll slip across the hall. I think there's a fire escape at the back. You finish packing."

"You'll be coming back?" It was a cry from the heart of a child asking not to be deserted. He gathered up their few bits and pieces, packing Murf's bag as well as his own. In the bathroom he held one of the bags under the glass shelf and swept the contents into it. Must keep occupied, he thought, must keep doing things. While Murf does the thinking to get us both out of this. It's only ten miles to the airport. We can be safe over the Atlantic in an hour. Home. I want to go home. Come back for Maura when things blow over. Settle down then. Six children maybe. Preside over table. Sunday lunch. All will be fine. Have B. Mech. Eng. now. They can't take that away. He caught sight of his ashen face in the mirror and turned away. To see two huge uniformed guards in the doorway, pointing guns at him. His heart stopped.

"Take it easy," the Sergeant said, "and you won't get hurt. Move back against the wall and squat down. Good. Nice and easy now."

"It's … it's … a mistake…" Why did they all look like Paudge?

"Shut up. Lower. Take off your jacket and slide it over here."

His Mom used to correct him for pulling sweaters off over his head in a way that widened the neck. Once, as an altar boy he had burnt his surplice with charcoal from the thurible. Sorry, Mom for all those trials. Yes, he would live his life differently if he had it to live over again … If only the lights would stop flashing.

While the rookie went through his jacket, the Sergeant, who trained the revolver on him, said, "So, we've finally caught up with you."

"I'm … it's all … the US Consul…" He leant against the toilet bowl; the plumbing gurgled in his ears. Not the most edifying place to meet his end.

"Glad you brought that up," the Sergeant said. "We've been wondering about the American connection." He was still crouched in the doorway both hands on the revolver.

"He's clean, Sir," the younger guard said. "There's no sign of a weapon or the money."

"Where have you hidden the money?" They inched towards him. He curled up beside the toilet bowl; at least the porcelain felt cool to the skin. Just before he abandoned himself to his fate, he saw Murf sneaking up behind the guards.

"Don't turn around," Murf grated in his best Northern accent, jamming a wooden coat-hanger into the Sergeant's back. "On the floor. Fast! Slide those weapons back. Slowly."

Rolo opened his eyes. There was just a chance his meagre brains would not be splattered all over the tiles of this bathroom.

"It's McGlinchey," the young guard breathed. He started to unbutton and remove his tunic.

"What are you doing?" Murf asked bewildered.

"We know your trade-mark, McGlinchey," the Sergeant answered thickly. "You'll want us to look stupid in our underwear when we're found."

"Oh right. Hand over the uniforms then and be quick about it." Murf had some qualms about being mistaken for McGlinchy who, by regularly disrobing the police, had become public enemy number one. But, the guards could hardly give chase in their somewhat off-white underwear. He beckoned to Rolo who picked his way in a daze over the large, string-vested bodies and joined him at the bathroom door. He wanted to go to the toilet but it was impossible now with two half-naked guards stretched in an attitude of prayer at the base of the bowl.

"We're going to be outside the door for ten minutes," Murf said. "If there's a sound out of you we're coming back in." He closed the door and grabbed the bags. They rushed across the hall and clattered down the fire escape. The Standard Vanguard started on the first kick. They merged into the traffic, drove up Kildare Street and around the Green.

"I think there's a car following us," Rolo said. It came to him that he had uttered these words before, perhaps in a previous existence.

"Christ, who is it this time?" Murf peered into the mirror. It was an unmarked Datsun but that meant nothing. They had their choice of enemies. He drove around the Green a second time. The Datsun was still behind, staying in the middle lane ready for any sudden turn to left or right. As far as he could tell there were four men in the car. The windows had that dark congested look suggesting that the passengers were not lacking in brawn.

Passing by the College of Surgeons, Murf stayed in the inside lane, then suddenly turned right, crossed three lanes of squealing traffic, mounted the kerb and drove right into St Stephen's Green through the Roman arch.

"Let them try that," he gloated as Rolo stared

dumbly ahead. They drove over the little humped-back bridge and around the flower-edged fountains in the middle of the park. The hundreds of sun-worshippers lounging in deckchairs did not take kindly to this intrusion and yelled for officialdom.

"I don't believe it." Murf saw the Datsun sailing over the bridge in hot pursuit. The Vanguard, he knew, wasn't fast or manoeuvrable enough to outrun them. Already he was having trouble negotiating the flower beds, and snap-dragons and tulips bedecked the front grille of the car. He barked out orders to Rolo who, without demur, reached into the duffle bag and threw fistfuls of currency out the window. Nothing happened at first but then some uninhibited children started to pick up the notes and stuff them in their pockets. They were followed by adults who pushed them aside in a mad scramble for cash. It was a recession after all and the bills had to be paid. The largesse did not seem to come as much of a surprise since there was a general election in the offing.

The Datsun was forced to stop dead in its tracks. The driver honked and hollered at the crowd which, perceiving that some large bills had fluttered under the wheels, lifted the car bodily and deposited it in the lake.

The Three Fates were still spinning man's destiny when Murf gunned the car out the Leeson Street gate, shot past Earlsfort Terrace and down Harcourt Street. He crossed the Liffey at Butt

Bridge and drove through Drumcondra and Santry without incident. Murf's optimism over the money ploy was short-lived, however, for the airport was crawling with police who made little attempt to disguise their presence. There were squad cars everywhere. Murf drove past the departure area and on down the ramp towards the exit. Catching sight of the tail wing of the New York bound plane on the tarmac, he felt cheated and depressed.

"We can't even get out of the Goddamn country." He swung the car on to the main road back to Dublin.

"I want to leave," Rolo said like a child wishing for the moon. He sat in the front seat with the same kind of hurt resignation as a mother-in-law on a Sunday drive.

"We'll have to lie low for a while," Murf thought aloud. "Wait for the heat to die down. What we need is a safe house."

"Nowhere is safe for us anymore," Rolo murmured pathetically, shaking his sad, fair head.

Murf had an idea. "Lightning doesn't strike the same place twice."

They parked the Vanguard in the alleyway at the end of the back garden. The Cart, who had been looking out the window, knew immediately what was up.

"Get in quick," she hissed through a chink in

the back door. "Why didn't you say you were working for the cause?" She bolted the door after them. Her face shone with admiration and excitement.

"We're not." Rolo felt obliged to put the record straight.

"Ah sure I understand. I'm with you." She tapped the side of her nose; their secret was safe with her. "You must be famished." Men on the run were always famished. "I have a nice shepherd's pie in the oven. Just make yourselves at home and I'll slip out for some beer and take the lie of the land." After all the years of frying sausages for unappreciative lodgers and mopping urine off the bathroom floor, she finally had a cause. The Corporation would probably put a plaque over her front door one day in the future.

In the front room Crowley was jubilant and yet humble. His character had also slipped its leash and gone astray.

"I'm sorry we got off on the wrong foot. I read you wrong, lads. But that's all in the past. At least I hope you can forgive an old Fenian like me. I'll make out a list of safe houses for you around the country."

Murf parted the curtains and looked out the window. He knew that the chase was on, the city spinning on a ha'penny, shaking its reddish fur like a dog jumping out of a bog-hole. He thought of all the tight spots he had survived before, but recognised that this was different.

Crowley looked up from his list of safe houses

and told them he had a ham radio upstairs.

"It's yours if you want to contact the lads up north."

"Thanks. We'll bear that in mind. What we need now is sleep."

"Go right ahead. Tim and I will keep watch."

They stretched out on the black leatherette chairs and nodded off. When The Cart returned, Tim was afraid she'd complain about resting their feet on the furniture. But nothing was further from her mind. She looked at the sleeping heroes with pride and asked Tim to get some blankets from the hot press. In the meantime she put a cushion under Rolo's bad leg which rested awkwardly on a hard chair, and joined Crowley at his look-out post by the window.

"They were probably hiding out in the Wicklow hills," she murmured.

"You know, Mrs. McCarthy," Crowley said, watching the street lights pierce the dusk, "I was wrong about students. These lads are all right."

"We were all wrong," she sighed, thinking of how her husband would have taken a shine to these brave youngsters. "Mr Crowley, would you like to join us in some shepherd's pie when they awake?"

He looked at her in happy disbelief. Blissfully, and with a slight tremble in his voice, he replied,

"Why, Mrs. McCarthy, I'd be honoured."

Loud knocking on the door woke Rolo up. Suddenly, Crowley was beside him whispering into his ear, "Get downstairs to the cellar fast.

There are three men at the door."

Rolo shook Murf violently, and half-dragged him down the stairs. He heard The Cart open the door and say in her normal menacing voice, "Yeah, what do youse want?"

A shrill northern voice indicated that they were from the gas board and had come to read the meter.

"Three of youse?" She asked for identification while she barred the way.

"Look Missus, stand aside."

"Bugger off. I don't use gas. You're UVF bastards. If my husband were alive today you wouldn't be standing there I can tell you."

Sensing that something was afoot, Tim joined her at the door, scratched himself and asked the UVF how much they earned.

"Get out of our way." One of the men pulled a gun which didn't impress The Cart. It took the other two all their strength to push her aside. Tim grinned, having the time of his life. He only hoped The Cart wouldn't take it out on him afterwards. The gunmen grabbed Crowley who was sidling back into the front room.

"Where are they?"

"Who?" Crowley panted.

"You know who." The gun was put to his temple and cocked. Crowley, Treasurer of the Irish-German Society, amateur ornithologist, staunch republican and renowned Anglophobe, spilt the beans without further ado.

"In the cellar." Although he would hate

himself afterwards he would not come even close to The Cart's loathing for him. Having been on the brink of hanging his hat up in the house, he had now blown it. The Dean of Digs would henceforth be treated as a leper, much worse, an informer.

"They're not in the cellar!" The Cart shouted to give them warning.

Murf and Rolo bolted from cover in the coal-hole, raced through the garden and vaulted over the wall. The Vanguard screeched away out of Northbrook Square and turned into Ranelagh village. Rolo sat clutching the dashboard. There was no point in fastening the seat belt; they were as good as dead.

"Disguises," Murf said. "That's what we need." He took the corner into Appian Way on two wheels and headed towards Donnybrook. The car was too identifiable and would have to be abandoned. At Belfield he did a sudden U-turn and raced back towards town. He overtook a double-decker bus, screamed to a halt at the next bus-stop and ditched the car.

The oncoming bus honked loudly. The conductor leant out the door and shouted at them for parking a car at the bus stop.

Murf jumped on board. "We're being chased by the UVF. Get going!"

"Got it," the conductor said. "Full throttle, Mikie." The driver took off in top gear. It was the easiest hijacking in history.

"And don't stop until I say." Murf stood behind the driver who tipped his cap in compliance and put his boot to the floor. Rolo sat weakly on the bench seat normally reserved for foot-weary shoppers. He saw the gunmen run across the street to the abandoned Vanguard, stop and stare in bewilderment at each other.

A lady with a shopping bag tugged the bell-pull and shrieked, "Driver, you've passed my stop. Halt immediately or I'll report you to CIE." A line of irate passengers began to form behind Murf, trying to get at the driver. The conductor tried to placate them.

"Ladies, this is an emergency. Bear with us now like the decent women ye are."

Turning at amazing speed into Waterloo Road, the bus leant over at a crazy angle that engineers like Rolo, would have thought impossible; it was saved only by the human ballast downstairs which lurched violently to the left then back again. There was yelling on the upper deck where the roll was even greater.

In sight of Herbert Park, Murf said, "OK, this'll do."

The driver slewed the juddering bus into the kerb and the conductor made a path for them to the exit.

"Good luck lads. Éire go bráth."

"Our day will come." Murf raised his fist and stepped off the bus, giving Rolo a hand down. The driver took off at speed, not letting any of the other passengers off.

Gobnait tightened her robe about her and listened incredulously to the story. At regular intervals she looked to Rolo for confirmation.

"So that's why we need disguises," Murf explained, "to get to the airport and out of this spot of bother."

She ran a hand through her hair. "If you want to run out on me just say so. You don't have to invent this ridiculous…"

"But it's true," Rolo confirmed. "Call Ashur if you don't believe us … or The Cart." His pallor and trembling limbs lent credence to the story. He tried to roll a cigarette but his hands weren't steady enough. Murf gave him a Gold Flake.

"Where were you last night when we needed you?" Murf asked.

"Where did you expect me to be? In a rocking chair waiting for you? I was out." She looked at him with the glare of a liberated woman.

"With your Vet, I suppose." Murf sniffed the air with the haughty demeanour of a giraffe nibbling a tree-top.

"Yes, but he's not *my* Vet." Her expression indicated that she was not on trial and didn't have to explain herself to him." Behind the relative composure of the exchange there were psychic sparks flying.

Murf prodded his chest with a forefinger. "I made sacrifices for you last night … I gave up golden opportunities…"

"What does that mean?"

"Could we cut this out?" Rolo interrupted nervously. Their lives hung by a thread and these two were beginning to flirt. He was scared of hearing another knock on the door. Every second of silence was in itself nerve-racking.

"All right," Gobnait sighed. "Come into the bedroom and let's see what we can do." She led the way. Murf looked longingly at the crumpled inviting sheets she had so recently left, and lingered a while with the thought of burrowing there in snug safety while the world outside boiled over and blew its gaskets. He looked wistfully from the bed to Gobnait who seemed to understand.

"It'll have to be drag, of course," she said, going through the wardrobe.

"No way," Rolo said. He thought she was joking.

"What else do you expect me to have here? Three-piece suits and overcoats? Anyway, this is your best chance, maybe the only one. Now go and shave … legs, chest, everywhere. Go." She shooed them towards the bathroom across the hall. Murf shared Rolo's reluctance but shrugged, to indicate that there was no other way.

A little while later they returned raw and pink from the bathroom and tried on the strange vestments she had laid out. Because of his height and bad leg, Rolo would have to wear brogues rather than heels. So, for consistency, Gobnait argued, he would have to be the dowdy one. Roughly translated, this meant an old twin-set with a string of costume pearls, a tweed skirt, a pink plastic mac and matching beret. Murf's rig-out proved to be more Bohemian – dark stockings, Cuban heels, a bolero set off by a Victorian choker, a nurse's skirt and a shaggy Afghan-type embroidered overcoat. Thus clothed, he seemed buzzard-like, his head too small for the fuller plumage below. A wig and floppy hat made all the difference.

Murf groaned as the lipstick was being applied. His discomfiture, however, was nothing compared to that of Rolo, who had spent the last fifteen years trying to slough off the trappings of femininity and was now padding his own bra.

Gobnait stood back from the mirror and ran a critical eye over them. "It might just work at that." The laughter muscles in her face were straining and twitching. "You are rather attractive, Rolo, in spite of those old duds. You have a good figure."

"Thank you."

"What about me?" Murf asked.

"Could do better." She walked around both of them. "You should swing your hips a bit more. Strut your stuff." She was having fun with her protégés. "Murf, don't stand like that. Turn one knee into the other for modesty's sake. And if you sit down remember to keep your knees together. Practice for a while and I'll get you something to eat."

"No thanks, Gobnait. We'd better make tracks.

There's a flight at seven."

Just then their attention was drawn to the little black and white television screen which showed an unruly scene in the vicinity of Donnybrook. An announcer described the controlled explosion which was about to take place. Murf's heart sank when he recognised the Standard Vanguard in the middle of a cordon of sandbags.

"Oh no," he groaned. "They must think it's booby-trapped. And I promised it to Crowley."

Gobnait went to tune it in better and to adjust the cat's whiskers. The reception improved a little. She also turned up the volume

A deafening blast scattered sandbags in all directions. Shock waves shattered windows in houses for miles around. The beloved Vanguard rose up in a million pieces, seemed to hang a while in the grainy air, then fell slowly piecemeal to the ground with the gentle patter of an April shower. The stained-glass windows of Donnybrook church cracked and slid down the granite buttresses. The shock reached into the belfry and rocked the clappers. Thinking it might be the Angelus, many by-standers blessed themselves. Murf stared at the pile of rubble and twisted metal that was once the proud Standard Vanguard on which he might have flown the family crest.

"I'm sorry." Gobnait sensed what the car had meant to him.

"We'd better go," Rolo said. The not-so-controlled explosion had lit a fuse under him.

She stood in front of Murf. "Do you really

have to go?"

He bit his lip. "'Fraid so. You're a brick, Gobnait. Many thanks. I'll call you."

"Do you need money?"

"No thanks. We knocked over a bank."

"Oh go on." She kissed him. "Mmmm, that lipstick tastes good. Rolo, keep an eye on him."

"Will do. Thanks for everything."

As darkness fell they began to feel a little more secure. The first big test was getting on a bus and although Rolo, constrained by his skirt, had some difficulty in mounting the step, they passed muster quite well. The conductor didn't turn a hair when Rolo croaked out, "Two one-and-sixes please."

Murf was a bit uneasy, however. "What age do I look? It's hard to play this role without knowing your age."

"I guess you'd pass for thirty. How about me?"

"Shit," Murf said. "You don't look so good. Fortyish."

"Thanks a lot."

Appraising himself in the darkening window, Murf adjusted the tilt of the floppy hat. He felt sure he was a lot smarter than Rolo and quite with it. A casual observer might have thought that Murf was a slightly zany do-gooder and cat-owner, probably from a Ballsbridge mews, who had taken a bag-lady (Rolo) under her wing.

When they reached the bus station they decided to change to a cab and were relieved that the driver wasn't too talkative or indeed interested in them. When they reached the airport they noticed that there was still a heavy police presence. The question was whether their disguises would do the trick.

The cab-driver opined that the notorious McGlinchey was trying to leave the country and added, "The guards are mad to get even with him for leaving them in their underwear."

As his passengers straightened their skirts after alighting from the cab, he said, obviously concerned about two spinsters travelling alone to foreign parts, "Mind yereselves now."

They got through airport security without a hitch and sat in the terminal building within sight of the Aer Lingus reservations counter. Murf used the mirror of his powder compact to read the area to his rear. He was reasonably satisfied that none of the uniformed and plainclothes men in the building had given them more than a passing glance. Success was at hand. All they had to do was wait for the queues to dissolve then saunter over to reservations, buy their tickets and check in.

Rolo was quite agitated, however, and had an irresistible urge to go to the bathroom which he did, but exited quickly as the gents at the neighbouring urinals zipped up rapidly in astonishment.

"OK," Murf said when he returned. "There's no queue now. Let's give it a try." There was a man at the reservations desk flicking through some brochures. Murf guessed he was special branch, but felt the disguises would pass muster.

"I have to go to the bathroom," Rolo said

miserably.

"You've just been. What's the matter with you?" Murf looked straight ahead, speaking out of the side of his mouth.

"I went in the wrong one."

"Well, go in the Ladies then…"

"I can't do … that…" Being shy of bladder was bad enough, but he had not fully anticipated the additional difficulties of the transvestite life style.

"You can go on the plane. It's boarding in twenty minutes. Now come on up to the ticket counter. And for God's sake don't limp."

Crossing the fluorescent-lit, echoing floor was the longest and most painful walk Rolo had ever taken. His brogues clattered on the simulated marble, he sweated inside the plastic mac and the padding started to slip out from under the C-cups. He grabbed the edge of the counter like a drowning man.

The pert ground hostess punched up the flight on the computer and announced that there were still seats available. "Will it be cash or cheque?"

"Cash, Miss," Murf simpered, reaching into his large handbag which contained the bulging swag. He made sure to turn his back on the special branch man who was reading a colourful brochure on package tours to Benidorm.

"Have I seen you somewhere before?" The hostess eyed them closely between smudges of matching green mascara.

"I don't believe so, Miss." Murf produced a

wad of notes while Rolo tightened his grip on the counter.

"Perhaps not. It's just that something strange happened last night. There was a man disguised as a bride, believe it or not." She shook her head mystified. "I don't know what reminded me of that."

"Life is strange," Murf said. "I'm told that there are men who like to dress up as women. Can you imagine that?"

Rolo tried to loosen his collar and in the process ripped his necklace, scattering pearls all over the floor. Legs apart, he went to retrieve them, frantically scooping them into one hand only to spill them out again.

"May I have a word with you, Madam?" The special branch man clapped a hand on Murf's shaggy Afghan shoulder. "Could you and your friend come with me?" The jig was up. Murf swung his handbag and screamed.

"Help! Get this maniac off me."

Waiting passengers jumped to their feet. A lady's honour had to be protected even if she did look like a tart. Murf grabbed Rolo who was now on his knees, trying to gather up the elusive pearls, and yanked him away from the counter. They dashed towards the exit only to find it blocked by a group of heavy-set men. They turned, sliding on the polished floor, and raced towards the elevators. But there, two uniformed guards stood, holding their arms low to tackle. More branch men materialised from unlikely places, some dressed in

Bermuda shorts and Calypso shirts, and closed in. It was the ring of steel all over again. Without slowing, Murf pulled Rolo to the left. They ran through a cosmetics boutique and into the Ladies at the back.

Murf tried all the stalls until he found the one with that glorious window above the cistern. He pushed Rolo through the window; he went easily like a pipe-cleaner. Murf stood on the toilet bowl. A lady in the neighbouring stall hunkered up and screamed. He launched himself through the window, ripping his embroidered bolero on the metal nipple. He landed well on the grass verge, took the brunt of the fall on his arms and tumbled over.

"Quick, the car park."

All the cars they tried were locked. They had to settle for the first motor bike that responded to their desperate kicks. Rolo hiked up his skirt and mac to sit on the pillion, clutching both handbags. They took off with the front wheel clear off the ground. A former biker, Murf soon got control of the machine as he read its feisty personality.

A line of cars gave chase around the coiling ramps and loops of the airport. Murf took the curves well, leaning into them. His Afghan coat skimmed the ground and the Cuban heels gradually wore down as he took the hairpin bends at speed. The floppy hat blew off and went sailing into the night like a lost soul. He should have used a hat-pin, Rolo thought.

At the main road Murf had to decide. Dublin

or Belfast, the rock or the hard place? Nowhere was safe anymore. He revved the bike south to Dublin. The convoy of unmarked cars stuck to his tail. Maybe it would prove to be their funeral. The bike knifed through the heavy traffic on this potholed congested road, and they gained an edge. Dodging and feinting on this spirited machine, Murf extended his lead. To clinch it, he turned sharply at a zebra crossing, doubled back to Clondalkin and zoomed into the dark immensity of Phoenix Park. He pulled over to take stock while courting couples, like startled fawns, bolted into the deeper undergrowth of subconscious desire.

"I think we've shaken them off. Oh Christ, commentator's jinx. Here they come."

A trail of menacing headlights illumined the misty darkness, coiling like some Chinese dragon seeking vengeance. Murf kicked the bike to life again and careered into the pitch blackness of the Hollow Glen. Then past the chain-link fence of the Zoo where, sensing a hunt, exotic animals awoke and growled and roared in sympathy with the fleeing prey. The bike sped on through the Polo Ground, its knobbed tyres gouging svelte grass. And still the convoy came with unperturbed pace.

"Bugger you all!" Murf roared at the stars. He shot through wilder moto-cross country, scattering red deer startled awake. In the distance lay the US Ambassador's residence where Rolo had once taken tea with watercress sandwiches. Closer still the Papal Nunciature shimmered with piety. Gripping the pillion with blistered hands Rolo looked longingly at the graceful portico and sighed for holy orders and sanctuary. And still they came.

"Shit, I don't have the speed." Murf turned suddenly and raced back towards the Zoo. The convoy also turned but with less facility. Sounds of squealing tyres and stifled curses brought rooks, like screaming shrapnel, from the trees. But soon the chase was on again.

Traffic was safer, Murf thought, zooming into Parkgate Street and down the quays where people stopped to see two spinsterish bikers in a flying escapade. Through Bachelor's Walk they sped, weaving and twisting, the promise of freedom growing with every car they passed. Until they reached O'Connell Bridge where, thrown across the intersection, three squad cars lay in wait.

The bike skidded sideways to a halt but Murf kicked it to life again, mounted the pavement, wove through queues of cinema-goers and shot up d'Olier Street. Crashing the lights at College Green he spun right at The Foggy Dew into the safer labyrinth of narrow cobbled lanes. Bumping over the cobblestones was agony enough, but there was worse in store. Rolo uttered a feeble, "No!" as Murf throttled the bike up the steps to Merchant's Arch. Buskers jumped aside as the bike shot through the narrow passage-way and descended stepwise to the quays again. Rolo wanted to shake his head clear but felt that one more jolt might stun him into oblivion. For we are born, he thought, in others' pain, and perish in our own. Now at the end of his life he was sad but not bitter.

He'd had a reasonable innings, though hoped for longer. A loving God might at this point have said, 'They've paid their dues. So be it. Let my people go'. But it was not to be. Murf had been too clever by half doubling back to the quays. The brave bike could not outrun the air-waves. And that was why the convoy now waited for them, had even formed a sort of funnel for Murf to enter.

He revved the bike angrily in the centre of the cordon. It was the futile growl of a trapped animal. Chattering from the jolt of steps and cobbles, feeling his groin for signs of rupture, Rolo had had enough. He welcomed capture, the safety of a cell, words of comfort from a kindly chaplain.

"They've got us." He held up his arms still clutching the handbags.

"Like hell they have!" Murf gave a savage twist to the throttle, mounted the steps to the Liffey and rear-wheeled the snarling bike across the Ha'penny Bridge, for pedestrians only. Startled lovers ungrappled and threw themselves against the railings. The bike sailed over the apex of the delicately curved bridge, flew for a while and came to rest on the far side of the river under the shelter of the Woollen Mills. Murf looked back at his foiled pursuers, revving their balked vehicles like marauding animals scraping helplessly at the foot of a tree.

"Ha!" He snorted. "We showed those bastards." He slipped the bike into neutral. It was almost out of petrol. Rolo tried to get off the pillion which was ignominiously wet, and failed.

"We'd be… better off in jail."

"Oh ye of little faith. We're still ahead of the game." Murf's face shone. "We'll just lie low for tonight and try the ferry to Holyhead tomorrow. Where can we go tonight, you might well ask?" The quays were almost deserted, and it was getting late. Murf stood resting one leg on the saddle. "We can't involve Gobnait or The Cart any further," he reasoned. "And we've got to get out of these clothes." He thought for a while over a Gold Flake. If he looked anything like Rolo with his sweat-soaked wig and smeared make-up, hotels would be out of the question. Besides, the word was out on them. There were clubs of course, and discos with names like 'Truffles' and 'Snaffles', but they wouldn't exactly blend in. Where was that place Ashur's friend used to patronise? "I think I've got it."

Standing at a Georgian door in Henrietta Street, Murf pulled the old-fashioned bell which said, 'Please Fondle', and waited for a response. A little wicket opened in a panel of the door, an eye peered out and looked them up and down. A handsome woman in a ball gown welcomed them inside.

"My dears, new members are always welcome. Please follow me." She rustled down a dimly lit corridor and bade them sign a visitor's book.

"There's a show in progress right now," she crooned. "But we will have an opportunity to introduce you to the other members afterwards. How does that sound?"

"That sounds fine." Murf didn't make any attempt to raise the pitch of his voice. The lady looked them up and down one more time and smiled in a sympathetic way. She ushered them into what seemed to be a small theatre with a ramp leading down from the makeshift stage.

There was a sort of fashion show in progress. The emcee, who was dressed in a formal gown, was in full flow. "Our next offering is shown by Seamus, our civil servant from the Department of Agriculture and Fisheries. A large, thick-set model started down the ramp doing bumps and grinds to the acclaim of the audience. "Seamus is wearing a brocade evening dress cut low with a cute detachable bodice and full flare. Note the matching accessories and the way the earrings pick out the highlights of the sequins. For underwear, Seamus has chosen a shot-silk bra and…"

Rolo was aghast. This was a nightmare. He had tried to preserve his manhood; God, how he'd tried. Yet here he was in his twin-set and peed-on skirt in a den of transvestites. He gripped Murf's arm. "I want to leave."

"Shut up," Murf whispered back. "They're harmless. We'll be able to get some proper clothes if we play our cards right. Besides, we're safe here."

"But it's awful," Rolo protested. "Some of them are masturbating under their skirts."

"So what? Did you never play pocket billiards in the cinema? Just relax and enjoy the show."

More models paraded down the ramp. The emphasis seemed to be on evening wear, rich and full and womanly. A spun-silk flouncy number brought groans from the audience, and a knowing, teasing smile from the model, Brian, an investment analyst with the Phoenix Life Insurance Company.

"That was our last item, folks," the emcee announced to murmurs of disappointment. When the house lights came on Murf and Rolo were taken in hand by the club secretary, who wore a devastating little black number and smoked a pipe. "Hi, Turlough's the name. I'm in Wavin Crane-Hire. This here is Peadar and Mark. They're in computers."

"And we're in deep shit," Rolo thought.

"Rolo and I are with the security forces," Murf said cordially. "But we wouldn't like word to get back to the barracks if you know what I mean…"

"Of course not," Turlough replied. "Confidentiality is the strictest rule of the club." He handed them some brochures of club rules and activities. "May I be personal?"

"Please." Murf spread his hands. He had no hang-ups. What you see is what you get.

"I mean to say," Turlough began diffidently. "Surely, you don't get off on that Afghan coat? It's not exactly… state of the art couture." He was dreadfully apologetic but it had to be said. The club had standards to maintain.

"I know," Murf confessed sadly. "We're novices … I was going for a sort of Janis Joplin stroke hippie look, but it's obviously not working."

Turlough traced the contours of Rolo's pink mac, biting his lip. "I don't mean to presume, old man, but surely something with a bit more flair is called for. As we say here, 'frills are thrills, lacy is racy'."

"I know exactly what you mean," Murf agreed. "But it's all so sudden. We've just recently stepped out of the closet. We're not quite ready for the heavy stuff yet."

Turlough nodded in sympathy, recalling his own early days when a headscarf flapping against his neck was enough to send him into a transport. "Well, we're here to help each other. To compare notes and raise standards. But we don't believe that one size fits all. We're none of us the same. I personally go for fishnet but it does nothing for Peadar here. He prefers cotton, believe it or not."

"That's Gospel," Peadar chipped in. "Even the mention of the word 'cotton' is enough to give me goose bumps. Would you perhaps say it? It's always good to hear it in a new voice. It's a sort of verbal promiscuity, if you follow me."

Murf looked right and left. It was no skin off his nose. "Sure." He shrugged. "Cotton, cott-on…"

"Mmmnnn. Very nice. You have a good timbre. Can I return the favour?"

"Tweed," Murf said, rolling his eyes.

"Tweed? Are you sure?" Turlough asked. "This is most unusual. But it proves my point.

Chacun à son goût. Fabrics for courses as it were."

"Tweed, tweed," Peadar and Mark chorused.

"Oh that's good." Murf closed his eyes in ecstasy.

Rolo sat cringing, hoping that no one would ask him what his favourite fabric was. To be on the safe side, though, he had thought of one, cheesecloth, especially freshly laundered cheesecloth, dried in the sun. Good God, it was getting to him...

There followed a talk by a veteran in a blue jump-suit who had discovered his true nature in a launderette, how he had learnt to cope with the derision of shop assistants in drapery stores and how he kept his secret from his colleagues in the Land Commission. Girlfriends, he said, adjusted to the situation and even liked to borrow his clothes from time to time. Above all, he argued, one should not feel guilt. He walked off to loud applause.

It was one way to spend the night, Rolo supposed, marginally better than flying across bridges on the pillion of a gut-wrenching bike with half the city in hot pursuit. He wasn't sure what this nocturnal conference reminded him of, a crypt-full of Dracula's brides or a witches' coven. But he did unwind a bit and even managed to roll himself a cigarette.

After a talk on dress design and some practical demonstrations on a sewing machine with special emphasis on shirring and box pleats, Turlough returned to them and brought them into another room.

"I'd like you to see our new wardrobe. We've just got some Elsa Schiaparelli in, beautiful summer lines. It's not just a question of fabric, you see. There's an aesthetic side to it. Classical simplicity really does it for me. You've got to find your own style." He seemed very keen to improve their education and seemed to feel they had a lot of potential.

"I understand," Murf said solemnly, nodding in appreciation as Turlough held dress after dress up to his chest, fluffing out a hem here, a pleat there, pointing out subtleties of design.

"I think we've seen enough," Murf said finally. "There's no point in getting over-excited."

"I know what you mean," Turlough answered. "It can be overpowering for newcomers."

"Actually," Murf said, looking at his watch. "We have a bit of a problem. We had our regular duds in a suitcase but Rolo left it on a bus. I wonder if perhaps we could borrow…"

"Say no more." Turlough laughed heartily. "We've plenty of straight stuff here for emergencies." These fellows were nothing if not obliging. If only the Superpowers could follow their example, Rolo thought, the cold war would soon be over. Turlough opened a second closet and said with a generous wave of his arm, "Help yourselves."

"This is very kind of you. We'll pay of course."

"Wouldn't hear of it. The club is in funds.

Brian won a prize on Ladies Day at the Horseshow this year."

"Well then, we'll leave you our kinky stuff."

Turlough looked them over again with a slight twitch of the nose. "There's no need."

"We insist. Don't we Rolo?"

"Well, all right then. Thank you." The Afghan coat, Turlough thought, might provide a useful lesson for neophytes in what to avoid. Thank Goodness the Carnaby Street era had passed.

They picked out the most basic slacks and jackets they could find. With quiet amusement Turlough watched them dressing.

"You don't have to shave your body hair, you know," he pointed out gently, shaking his head, recalling his own naïveté in his early days.

After exchanging phone numbers with several members they were given a warm send-off into the straight world, in which the sun was now beginning to rise. They promised to return for Wednesday's meeting which would feature Prionnsias, an estate agent, in his Ascot regalia. Turlough kindly insisted that they call him at home if ever the pressure got too much and the urge to transvest too strong.

"We can talk you down," he said sympathetically, "or failing that you can come here and indulge yourselves. Remember, your friends are only a phone call away. But don't," he advised kindly, "transvest among straights. They just don't understand."

"Thank you," Murf said sincerely. "Maybe our

day will come some time."

"We can but hope."

"We'll be off then. See you all on Wednesday. Thanks again for everything."

"Tweed," Turlough said with a twinkle in his eye. "Tweed."

"Oh don't," Murf sighed, "We've got to get down."

"Cotton," Peadar said.

"MMnnuuuf…"

"Gaberdine."

"Cheesecloth."

"Wow…"

"Tweed," Turlough repeated reflectively. "You know you might have something there."

Murf looked up and down the street. They had broken the back of the night, and morning, with any luck, would see them off the premises for good.

"I wonder if I'd said 'polyester'?" he mused aloud. "Who said 'cheesecloth' by the way? Was it you?"

"Absolutely not," Rolo lied. "I don't even know what that is."

They wandered over to the markets and had a breakfast of tea and buns in a pub that opened early for the fruit and veg traders.

"Do you know what day it is?" Murf had been watching a group of porters playing darts and noticed the sprigs of shamrock on caps and lapels.

"I don't know what month it is."

"It's St. Patrick's Day. I hope the parade won't

interfere too much with the traffic. We have to be at Dún Laoghaire pier by around mid-day to catch the ferry. Ironic isn't it? Emigrating to Blighty on our national day. From there we can get a flight to the US. How about Philly?"

"Let me think about that," Rolo replied. "No point in rushing our fences." The sound of the word, 'Philly', had brought him up short and he knew he would have to make a decision soon.

As they passed down the gullet of Grafton Street into the maw of College Green, they saw the crowds already forming to watch the parade. Soon every vantage point, wall, tree, office window and statue was occupied by spectators. A brave gurrier straddled the neck of Thomas Moore while others sat on O'Connell's plinth and on the surrounding angels.

The floats, when they emerged from South Great Georges Street, owed more to improvisation than design. Apart from the Gael Linn cottages and Croagh Patricks mounted on the backs of trucks, there were a number of commercial offerings, Chubb Locks, Wavin Pipes, Peat Briquettes, Albatross Fertilizers, of which the cultural and spiritual links to St. Patrick were not immediately obvious. There were marching confraternity and pipe bands, cohorts of the Local Defence Force, Scouts, Legion of Mary dressed in their blue burial shrouds, Knights of Columbanus, and this year, for the first time, The Concerned Criminal Action Group with a banner that read 'Give the Ordinary Criminal a Break'. Then the

US marching bands came with high-stepping razzamatazz, leggy baton-twirlers and earnest, blue-eyed drummers. The review stand at the General Post Office was bereft of notables since all politicians were away on junkets.

But the crowds seemed to be enjoying it. Even the guards who tried to control the spectators were tapping their size-twelve shoes. Rolo studied a guard who stood with his back to him, and nudged Murf.

"I'd recognise that thick neck anywhere," Murf whispered. "Let's slip away."

Perhaps the hairs on the bacon-rind of Paudge's neck bristled, for he turned around at that moment and copped them. They worked their way through the crowds but it was slow going. Thinking they were trying to improve their view of the parade, several people deliberately barred their way. Because of the authority of his uniform, Paudge made better progress and was gaining on them. With no option but to join the parade, they fell into step with a charter group of Irish Americans, The Friendly Sons of St. Patrick, Philadelphia Branch, who took them warmly into their midst, in the same way a herd of buffalo protect their young from marauding wolves. They supplied them with green boaters and sashes.

The parade swung proudly left at Trinity College and meandered down Westmoreland Street to the skirl of pipes and the rattle of kettle drums. Along the edges of both pavements there was a coalescing of navy uniforms; the guards were flanking them in a move known as 'the parallelogram of forces'.

"What now?" Rolo pleaded, skipping to keep in step.

"They can't touch us in the middle of the parade."

"But it's going to end at the top of O'Connell Street."

"Let us cross O'Connell Bridge when we come to it," Murf quipped. He strutted and waved to the crowds, smiling hugely, and occasionally went over to the barricades to shake hands with the kiddies held out to him by proud parents.

There was growing activity in the side-lines as the guards huddled with their Supers and took instruction. Worse still, a group of men in anoraks broke through the crowds and mingled with the marchers, studying faces and asking questions. For the IRA it was business as usual, even on the national day.

"They just have no respect," Murf complained. He and Rolo left the Irish-American contingent and hid behind a float bearing a monster hamburger. From there they joined a troupe of Irish dancers which unhappily provided little cover. They ran crouching to the Guinness float but this was one of the better exhibits and attracted too much attention. They skipped from float to float, resting a while in the slip-stream of the Bishop Kearney High School Marching Band.

The guards must have received new orders because they now infiltrated the parade, which was rapidly losing its rhythm. Parade marshals bawled at the drivers of floats and at drum majors to close up and keep the pace. Twirlers lost their batons and dignity, pipers lost the run of their wind, and their tempestuous instruments went caterwauling out of control. Floats rear-ended each other and the Knights of Columbanus ran right into the Legion of Mary.

Dignitaries on the reviewing stand at the GPO bravely took the salute as if nothing had happened, but a harried marshal shouted into the PA system, "Cut the cameras. It's a total fucking disaster." The crowds went wild. This at last was real entertainment. The few guards who were left in charge of crowd control couldn't cope, and the great unwashed surged on to the street to join the bogged-down chaotic remains of the parade. In the general mayhem, Murf and Rolo made good their escape, slipped down Henry Street and jumped into a cab. The driver, who wanted to stay and watch the shambles, accepted a fiver in compensation and set off.

At Dún Laoghaire, they hung around the seafront for a while mingling with the crowds taking the air on this national holiday. The huge funnelled ship strained at its moorings, its great gob open to receive cargo. The sea which stretched out beyond the bay promised ineffable freedom. They had simply to board this bark to make their escape. Murf wandered around the ticket office doing reconnaissance.

"It looks OK," he said uncertainly, "but I just

don't know." It bothered him that there was no police presence, for this was the very spot where most arrests were made, as diverse felons tried to skip across the channel. What if the guards had assembled *inside* the embarkation area? Could they be that devious, especially on the day that was in it?

He studied the crowds until he found a suitable candidate in the queue for tickets. The youth had a green Mohawk haircut which looked like a caterpillar lying dead on his otherwise bald head, a three-day old fuzz of adolescent beard and a number of metal objects dangling from his anatomy. He wasn't particularly interested in the proposition until Murf produced a tenner. Then he listened with interest and repeated the instructions.

"That's it," Murf confirmed. "When you get inside, stand by that window and raise your arm if there are any cops in there. Then show how many by raising your fingers."

"I'd like to give 'em all the fucking finger," the youth replied, demonstrating his perfect credentials for the task at hand.

"Good man," Murf said. "I'll be waiting over there for your signals. Good luck now. Have a good break."

"I'm fuckin' emigratin'," the youth replied. "This kip is fucked." He ground out a reefer with one of his large boots.

Murf joined Rolo at street level, where there was a good view of the window, and waited. The youth gradually got to the head of the queue, bought his ticket and went inside. Murf began to wonder whether he had misjudged his man, when the Mohawk head appeared at the window. A little later an arm went up, then ten fingers, and another ten.

"My God," Murf croaked, "it's alive with them. Those lousy bastards waiting inside. We can't get out of this Goddam country even on St. Patrick's Day." On that sour note he turned away in disgust and headed for the bar of the Marine Hotel to sit and think. Through the bay window of the bar they saw the ferry cast off and reverse slowly from the pier. A last minute drunk jumped on the rising gang-plank only to remember his suitcase still standing on the jetty. A kind porter threw the case on board after its owner. The voyage was underway, across the pond to Britain. People who had said farewell turned slowly for home to houses that would seem strangely empty, and wonder at the inability of the old sod to hold its young. The land was a sort of ridge that people tried to balance on. Many fell east or west; those who stayed grew scaly with prehensile toes and minds.

Several pints later Murf was still mad, and couldn't forgive the guards for their sneaky behaviour. Being beaten up in the station by Paudge and his grinning colleagues was bad enough, but at least it was direct. Lying in wait for the unwary on St. Patrick's Day was unacceptable, too clever by half. At the core of his grievance was the thought that if the guards ever became smart there would be no hope at all for the free play of anarchy. He also believed that case history had established the right for malfeasors to go to England.

"You might get out on your own," Rolo suggested. "It's this leg that gives us away."

"Don't get noble on me." In a way he needed Rolo's caution to dilute his own reckless instincts. His screwed-up concentrated expression gradually melted into the gentle smile of a martyr who was being assumed into Heaven.

Rolo should have known immediately why Murf bought a can of petrol and a Swiss army knife but it didn't dawn on him until, under cover of darkness, they descended a flight of moss-covered stone steps from the West pier and climbed aboard a small motorboat.

"No. Oh no. No!"

"Shut up for Christ's sake, and get in." He poured petrol into the tank, fired up the engine and set the tiller to points east. Clearing the harbour, he opened the throttle and left it open. Chugging by the end of the pier, Murf imagined a pleasant sight: the forces of law and order, Vets and budding politicians, guerrillas and the Fannings of this world, all of his relentless pursuers, racing down the pier after them, fists waving vengefully, to fall into the drink like lemmings, one after the other. He lay on his front in the bow like a hunting dog with a wet nose, and smiled in the darkness.

They went by the stars as St. Brendan had done, though not to spread the gospel light. Nor did they trust in the Lord to move the tiller. Dalkey Island and the coastline receded into mist, old ways dying easily, without a murmur of protest. How time passed was as mysterious as the gently heaving ocean. The search helicopter came and went. Rolo wanted to send up a distress flare but Murf wouldn't hear of it. And so the wild goslings spread the grey wing upon the tide.

EPILOGUE

A ROGUE WAVE nearly pitched Rolo out of the boat but the freezing brine helped bring him to his senses.

"Destroy yourself … but not me. Fanning's an old man. Be dead in a few years … What'll you do then?" Maura had asked that, wise, lovely Maura.

"I'll find something." Murf tried to give more throttle to the labouring craft as if motion were the answer, perpetual mindless motion.

Rolo launched another attack on the locker to get the flare gun, the pain in his leg now singing aloud through his whole body. "You have time on your side. Use it…"

Murf pushed him away from the locker. "He can't get off that easily…"

"He isn't getting off, you shithead." Rolo lost his temper for the first time, elbowed him in the ribs but he slumped against the locker door, blocking it. "Does your Dad want you to ruin your life? Does anyone? Be yourself…" Rolo tried to drag him backwards but could not get a purchase on the sodden jacket.

"Get off me. You've lost your marbles…" Murf shouted. What the hell was happening? Even Rolo changing now. Mutiny all round.

"Get real," Rolo shouted back. "You're not fucking Hamlet … Wise up. Think of Gobnait … You don't deserve her." To lend point to his words he drew back and punched him to the side of the jaw. Maybe Paudge was right. A few belts to drive home the message. Sort of muscle memory.

Rolo ripped open the door of the locker and snatched the flare gun. Murf wrestled him for it as the boat rocked violently, completely at the mercy of the waves.

"No flares…"

An elbow to the throat sent Murf sprawling into the bilge water where he choked and spluttered. To emerge drenched and with a sobriety of sorts, though he made one last half-hearted effort to regain control.

"Since when did you…? Never mind…"

"Maura, if you must know."

Murf's hands slid from Rolo's throat and he stretched them out to the elements in mute appeal. Slumping back into the watery hold, they watched the first flare soar into the dark sky, an orange comet-tailed seed of possibility.

"I hope I've satisfied Rolo's request and narrated this story fairly. Needless to say, fairness does not necessarily rule out a sequel. I don't think he, or Murf, would mind that I gave myself a small part in the story. Did anyone recognise me?"
—The Present Writer